I0723328

Wild
IN A KILT

Other Books by Anna Durand

Dangerous in a Kilt (Hot Scots, Book One)
Wicked in a Kilt (Hot Scots, Book Two)
Scandalous in a Kilt (Hot Scots, Book Three)
The MacTaggart Brothers Trilogy (Hot Scots, Books 1-3)
Gift-Wrapped in a Kilt (Hot Scots, Book Four)
Notorious in a Kilt (Hot Scots, Book Five)
Insatiable in a Kilt (Hot Scots, Book Six)
Lethal in a Kilt (Hot Scots, Book Seven)
Irresistible in a Kilt (Hot Scots, Book Eight)
Devastating in a Kilt (Hot Scots, Book Nine)
Spellbound in a Kilt (Hot Scots, Book Ten)
Relentless in a Kilt (Hot Scots, Book Eleven)
Incendiary in a Kilt (Hot Scots, Book Twelve)
Unstoppable in a Kilt (Hot Scots, Book Fourteen)
Lachlan in a Kilt (The Ballachulish Trilogy, Book One)
Aidan in a Kilt (The Ballachulish Trilogy, Book Two)
Rory in a Kilt (The Ballachulish Trilogy, Book Three)
The American Wives Club (A Hot Brits/Hot Scots/Au Naturel Crossover Book)
Brit vs. Scot (A Hot Brits/Hot Scots/Au Naturel Crossover Book)
A Novel Secret (A Hot Brits/Hot Scots/Au Naturel Crossover, Book Three)
The Dixon Brothers Trilogy (Hot Brits, Books 1-3)
One Hot Escape (Hot Brits, Book Four)
One Hot Rumor (Hot Brits, Book Five)
One Hot Christmas (Hot Brits, Book Six)
One Hot Scandal (Hot Brits, Book Seven)
One Hot Deal (Hot Brits, Book Eight)
One Hot Favor (Hot Brits, Book Nine)
Natural Obsession (Au Naturel Nights, Book One)
Natural Passion (Au Naturel Trilogy, Book One)
Natural Impulse (Au Naturel Trilogy, Book Two)
Natural Satisfaction (Au Naturel Trilogy, Book Three)
Fired Up (standalone romance)
Echo Power (Echo Power Trilogy, Book One)
Echo Dominion (Echo Power Trilogy, Book Two)
Echo Unbound (Echo Power Trilogy, Book Three)
The Janusite Trilogy (Undercover Elementals, Books 1-3)
Obsidian Hunger (Undercover Elementals, Book Four)
Unbidden Hunger (Undercover Elementals, Book Five)
The Thirteenth Fae (Undercover Elementals, Book Six)
Cyneric (Undercover Elementals, Book Seven)

Hot Scots, Book Thirteen

ANNA DURAND

JACOBSVILLE BOOKS JB MARIETTA, OHIO

WILD IN A KILT

Copyright © 2023 by Lisa A. Shiel
All rights reserved.

The characters and events in this book are fictional. No portion of this book may be copied, reproduced, or transmitted in any form or by any means, electronic or otherwise, including recording, photocopying, or inclusion in any information storage and retrieval system, without the express written permission of the publisher and author, except for brief excerpts quoted in published reviews.

ISBN: 978-1-958144-17-6 (paperback)
ISBN: 978-1-958144-18-3 (ebook)
ISBN:978-1-958144-19-0 (audiobook)

Manufactured in the United States.

Jacobsville Books
www.JacobsvilleBooks.com

Publisher's Cataloging-in-Publication Data
provided by Five Rainbows Cataloging Services

Names: Durand, Anna, author.
Title: Wild in a kilt / Anna Durand.
Description: Marietta, OH : Jacobsville Books, 2023. | Series: Hot Scots, bk. 13.
Identifiers: ISBN 978-1-958144-17-6 (paperback) | ISBN 978-1-958144-18-3 (ebook) | ISBN 978-1-958144-19-0 (audiobook)
Subjects: LCSH: Highlands (Scotland)--Fiction. | Wyoming--Fiction. | Man-woman relationships--Ficvtion. | Scots--Fiction. | Americans--Fiction. | Romance fiction. | BISAC: FICTION / Romance / Contemporary. | FICTION / Romance / Romantic Comedy. | FICTION / Romance / Action & Adventure. | GSAFD: Love stories.
Classification: LCC PS3604.U724 W55 2023 (print) | LCC PS3604.U724 (ebook) | DDC 813/.6--dc23.

Chapter One

Natalie

I never used to believe that a vacation could change a person's entire life, but now I'm thinking it might be true after all. As I paddle down a river in Wyoming, gazing at the bluest blue sky and the lushest forest I have ever seen, I can't help smiling. This is freedom. My life back home in Indiana? Nope, I will not think about that. I have two weeks to rinse the grime out of my soul.

Can I wash the memories out of my mind, though?

I feel a slight chill that slithers over my skin. No, I refuse to think about the reasons why I needed to escape to Wyoming. So I focus on paddling my kayak and enjoying the scenery. I've never before seen snowcapped mountains this tall or a landscape as beautiful as in this region. Birds chirp in the trees and fly past me way above my head. The air even smells better here. Maybe I'll never leave this place.

An oddly shaped rock catches my attention. The large slab lies in the river but with its surface above the water. It's kind of lumpy. Weird. Then the lumpiness moves. Okay, that's not just a rock. I grab my binoculars to focus in on the mystery creature. And I blink several times, sure I must be hallucinating. That can't be…a naked man. I look again, and yep, it's definitely a big muscular man with long, wild hair and a thick, bushy beard.

Uh, what? A naked man? Am I dreaming?

No, I don't think so. What if he's some kind of psycho? My safest option seems to be to avoid that man. I could use a break, anyway, so I might as well find a good place to pull over onto the shore and wait for the stranger to leave.

Up ahead, the river curves gently. The shore there offers a nice spot where I could beach my kayak and enjoy the lunch I brought with me. Hopefully, the nudist will have left by the time I'm done eating. So I steer myself toward the shore and manage to climb out of the kayak, then tug it up onto the relatively flat ground here. I close my eyes and inhale a deep breath full of sweet, clean air.

My nose wrinkles. Is that poop I smell? *Yech.*

I tiptoe around this little flat area, searching for the source of that stinky odor so I won't accidentally sit down on it. But I don't find anything. When I bend over to pick up a fallen twig, just to make sure it's not hiding the poop, I lose my balance and careen into a tree.

A crack reverberates overhead.

Tipping my head back, I hold a hand above my eyes to shield them from the sunlight and try to figure out what made that noise. At first, I see nothing. Then I spot the culprit. A thick tree branch dangles high above me, seeming to be held up only by another branch. I back away slowly, like I'm worried my footsteps might dislodge that thing. *Oh, please.* What are the odds that will happen? I've gotten so paranoid, though for good reason.

When I try to turn around, I trip and fall to the ground flat on my back. A grunt bursts out of me.

And that branch suddenly breaks free.

I lie here frozen in place as I watch the branch tumble down, down, down. The thing smacks onto my thighs. Pain ricochets through my legs.

And I scream.

Once the initial burst of pain subsides, I try to catch my breath and reassemble my wits. I can't get myself free no matter how much I wriggle and try to push the branch off me. Oh shit, is this how I'll die? Alone in the woods where no one will ever find me? Bears will probably come along and crush my skull with their gigantic jaws just so they can eat me.

Like hell.

I pull in a big breath and scream, "Help! Please help, I'm trapped!"

What are the odds anyone else is within earshot? For my wilderness adventure, I'd chosen a remote river, the name of which I don't even know. My cell phone doesn't work out here. I'd already determined that while paddling down the river. Oh God, I am going to die. Slowly. Painfully. Dehydration will hit me before starvation, or so I read in a book once, years ago. Unless the wildlife gets me. Bears? Cougars? Not sure which will devour me first.

"I'm coming!" someone hollers.

I hear a loud splash that originates from further down the river. Then I hear smaller splashes, as if someone is swimming this way.

Do bears know how to swim? But those animals don't talk and definitely can't shout "I'm coming." My pulse pounds in my ears, and my heart thuds in my chest. I can see the river from here, sort of, but I can't tell what type of wild beast might be heading this way. *Please, please, don't let me die this way.* Then I amend my plea. *Whoever is up there watching, please don't let me die, period, okay?*

A figure erupts out of the river. Water sluices off the naked man's body as he stalks up to me.

The muscular guy who just halted a few feet away stares down at me with water pouring down from his long, dark hair and bushy beard. His chest heaves. But those aren't the things about him that capture my focus. No, I only glance at the rest of him because I can't stop gaping at his dick. This must be the man I saw lying on a large rock slab.

My savior hoists the branch off me and tosses it away like it's nothing but a toy.

"Oh God, thank you," I say. "You saved my life."

"Are you injured?"

"Don't think so." When I start to sit up, he crouches to offer me his hands to pull me into a sitting position. That means I get a close-up view of his blue eyes. When I run my hands over myself, I'm relieved to find no broken bones. "Everything feels okay."

"Good. What were ye doing here?"

"Kayaking. This looked like a pretty spot to take a break."

He speaks with some kind of accent, but I can't quite place it.

My scruffy savior rises from his crouch, unfurling his body to its full height. "Since you're all right, I'll be on my way."

I can't stop myself from staring at him. I mean, the guy is completely naked—in the woods. What if he's a pervert? Some kind of sicko who wants to sneak up on me while I'm trying to get back into my kayak, then kidnap me to his underground bunker where he tortures women. Maybe I should stop ogling his dick if I don't want him to abduct and murder me. But I can't help it. I've never been saved by a naked man before. Though I keep averting my eyes, they keep forcing me to look at his manly parts. Yeah, that's right. It is totally not my fault.

Finally, I scramble to my feet and dust myself off. Then I avoid looking at the man while I speak to him. "Um, why are you...naked?"

"Does it matter?" he growls. "My lifestyle choices are my business."

"Uh-huh." I bite my lip as if that will stop me from gaping at his groin. "Well, thank you. For helping me. Think I'd better get going."

I try to make a suave exit from this bizarre situation, but I stumble over a small rock. Luckily, I don't fall down. As I hiss "damn" under my breath, I shuffle over to the kayak and attempt to climb in. But I slip again. Jeez, when did I become a klutz? I blame the naked guy hovering behind me. I can't keep a calm demeanor with a muscular bear-man mere feet away.

Then I notice I've kicked my kayak away and it's now sliding off the riverbank into the water. Before I can even try to grab it, the kayak gets swept away in the current.

"No, no, no!" I cry out while I helplessly watch my only means of transportation float away.

I flail my arms in a desperate attempt to snag the kayak. But I slip again, teetering on the edge of the riverbank. My heart pounds hard enough to make me woozy.

Thick arms lash around me, and suddenly, I find myself pinned to the naked stranger. Face to face. Unable to break free. Did I try to get free? Not really. I'm staring at his pecs, though not because I want to do that. He's so freaking tall, compared to me, that I can't stare at anything else but his chest.

At last, I summon enough wherewithal to wriggle and try to escape his hold. It doesn't work. "You can let me go now."

He takes a single step away from me and points over his shoulder. "Follow the game trail until you reach the hollowed-out tree. Then turn east—"

"I don't know which way is east. Can't you take me where I need to go?"

"Which is where?"

"The campground." I really, really hope there's only one of those around here since I can't remember the name of that place.

"It's too far to walk."

"Don't you have a car?"

"The transmission is shot. I'm waiting for a friend to bring me a new one."

I feel my forehead tightening. "You're way out here alone with no car? What about a phone? Can you take me to one of those?"

"The only phone anywhere nearby is at my house."

"Okay. Please take me there so I can call someone to pick me up."

The man growls low in his throat, like a freaking wild beast. "Come with me. But you will wait outside after you make your call."

"Where are you from? You sound Irish or something."

He clenches his fists, and his jaw too, I think. "I am Scottish, not Irish. Now haud yer wheesht and follow me."

"Um, what does that mean? Hide my wish?"

"Haud yer wheesht. It means—Never mind. Just be quiet."

"Do you live out here alone?"

"Stop talking," he snarls through gritted teeth.

I hustle to catch up with him, but I only do that because I have no choice. This man has a phone, which I can use to call for help. Uh, who will I call? I don't know anybody in Wyoming.

A solo wilderness vacation? What a fantastic idea, Natalie. You are a fucking idiot.

"Where exactly are we?" I ask. "I mean, I know what river that was. But the mountains must have a name too. Are there grizzly bears here? Maybe that's only in Alaska. No, wait, that's Kodiak bears. Right? Probably are grizzlies in Wyoming."

Shut up, you moron. And why did I say I know what river that was? I haven't got a frigging clue. I guess I was subconsciously trying to present the impression that I'm not a yokel who has never visited the wilderness before except on short Girl Scout trips when I was a kid.

God, I hope this guy isn't a psycho.

Because I so do not want to die alone in the woods and get eaten by a cannibal.

Chapter Two

Munro

I refuse to glance at the bloody annoying woman while we trudge down ever narrower trails, headed toward my cabin. This hike will take longer than it should because I never go this way unless I've been hunting or fishing somewhere further upriver. Now I'm stuck with this irritating, beautiful lass for who knows how long.

Not that her looks matter. I will never shag this woman. She would probably tell me that I'm doing it wrong. Aye, she seems like the sort who would complain about that.

"Wait! You're walking too fast."

The woman's voice makes me stop and glance around to find her. She's not beside me anymore. What has that lass done now? I spin around, expecting to see her hanging from a tree branch or lying in a pile of bear shit. But she isn't doing any of those things. She's rushing to catch up to me, breathing so hard that her breasts rise and fall swiftly.

Bod an Donais. The lass might be annoying, but she has a body that makes me want to fuck her right here in the woods.

"Slow down," she gasps. "Please, I can't walk that fast. My legs are shorter than yours."

I flap my hand, a clear sign she should hurry up.

But the lass just squints at me with her mouth gaping.

So I flap my hand again. "Get your erse moving, woman. I want to be home before sundown."

"It's barely afternoon, right?"

Aye, it is. But I won't give her the satisfaction of knowing for certain that she's right. I live in the middle of nowhere in Wyoming because I want my peace and quiet.

"*A Dhia*," I hiss. "*Greas ort, Ruaidh.*"

She stares at me blankly. "What did you just say? Are you having a stroke or something?"

"No, I'm speaking Scots Gaelic." I stalk up to her and grab the lass's wrist to drag her along with me down the trail.

"What did those words mean?"

I grunt instead of explaining. No, I won't tell her that I said "oh God, hurry up, Red." It sounds bloody stupid in English. But she does have bonnie red hair that complements her bonnie amber eyes. What I can see of her figure, cloaked in her hiking gear, is enough to make my mouth water. But no, I will not have a poke with the lass. She would probably haver the entire time. I wouldn't mind if she wanted to shout about how good I am while we fuck, but she would most likely complain instead. Aye, she seems like that sort.

She stabs a finger into my upper arm. "Tell me what you just said. Was it an insult?"

Instead of answering her question, I grunt again. Then I resume trudging through the woods.

"Do you even know where you're going?" she asks as she comes up beside me.

"Aye." I flash her a dark look. "That means 'yes.' I know every inch of this landscape."

"You still haven't explained why you're naked."

"Because I disrobed."

She huffs. "That is not an answer."

"It's all the answer I plan on giving."

When she opens her mouth again, I shoot her an even darker look. "Haud yer wheesht, woman."

"My name is not 'woman.' It's Natalie Saari." She lifts her chin even while she struggles to keep up with my swift pace. "It's rude to use weird Scottish terms that I don't understand. Maybe you're doing that so I won't realize you plan on holding me hostage in your basement so you can torture me."

"Dinnae have a basement."

"Okay. But I told you my name, and you haven't told me yours."

I blow out a sigh. The lass will not leave me be, which means I have no choice. "I'm Munro MacTaggart."

"That's a cool name."

"So glad you approve of the name given to me by my parents." All right, my tone might have dripped with sarcasm. I make no excuses for that. But when she seems about to speak again, I decide to make a preemptive statement in the desperate hope she'll shut up if I give her a wee bit of information. "I'm naked because I was bathing in the river. This is a remote area, and I dinnae like wearing a swimsuit."

"Thank you for explaining. See? Conversation isn't as difficult as you made it."

I might have just growled at her. "I like my privacy, so dinnae expect me to blether with you."

"Does 'blether, mean to have a conversation?"

"No, it means ye talk incessantly. Blethering is right next to havering, but that mainly refers to talking nonsense."

She seems confused, but fortunately, she doesn't press me for a longer explanation. We proceed in relative silence, which means she makes wee huffing noises occasionally but doesn't actually speak. Since I never use a watch or carry a mobile phone with me, I have no concrete idea of how long we've been walking, though I'm sure it's been more than twenty minutes.

Natalie begins to slow her pace.

"Keep up," I say. "You'll get lost if you lose sight of me."

She's breathing hard and bends over to set her hands on her thighs. "Need— a break. Please."

I grumble out a sigh. "Have your break—for a few minutes. But we need to get moving again soon."

"What's the rush?"

"Getting you out of my hair, that's what." I sit down on the bare earth. "Rest your erse, Natalie."

"I guess that means 'sit down', huh?" She drops onto the ground and slumps against a small tree. With a pitiful moan, she closes her eyes. "Could I have ten minutes to rest?"

She's clearly exhausted. *Bloody hell.* We still have a ways to go to reach my cabin, but she seems unlikely to make it there without an extended period of rest.

"When did you last eat?" I ask. "Or drink something other than water."

"I had a protein bar an hour ago."

"And before that?"

She peeks at me through her half-closed eyes. "I ate a couple oat bars and drank some coffee."

I shake my head. "No wonder you're running out of energy. All that silly health food rubbish won't keep you going in the wild." I study her for a moment. "Have you ever kayaked before?"

She bites her lip and wriggles her erse. "I read all about it."

"Reading is not the same as knowing. An inexperienced person should never go into the wilds alone."

"Are you an expert on that stuff?"

"I used to be a river guide in the Grand Canyon. So aye, I know a wee bit about survival skills." I suddenly realize something. "Why don't you have a backpack?"

She winces. "I left it in my kayak."

The lass is exhausted and ill-equipped for the wilds. What am I meant to do with her? She can't hike the rest of the way to my cabin, not when she's eaten only light, so-called healthy snacks. I need to get her to my home quickly. And that leaves me with only one option.

I rise and pick her up, cradling the lass in my arms.

Her eyes go wide. "What are you doing?"

"Providing transportation."

I jog down the trail, dodging minor obstacles and making the necessary turns to reach our destination. Though I begin to sweat, that doesn't bother me. I've hiked the Grand Canyon, after all, while being pursued by villains. Finally, we emerge from the woods into a small clearing. My cabin lies in the center of it.

At the porch steps, I stop and set the lass down.

Her eyes are almost bulging. "That was amazing. You ran through the woods while carrying me."

I shrug.

She stares at me, incredulous.

Though I can handle carrying someone that way—I've done it before as a river guide—I'll need a few moments to recover. So instead of speaking, I wave for Natalie to follow me into the house. Then I gesture for her to sit on the small sofa. The most miraculous part of this experience is that she finally has stopped asking me questions.

I grab a towel from the bathroom and wipe off the sweat, then hunt through a pile of clothes I'd left on the floor until I find what I need. Now that I'm dressed, I return to the sofa and drop onto the end opposite Natalie.

She turns toward me slightly. "What's the name of that river out there?"

"You know the name. That's what you told me."

"Um, I kind of fibbed." She winces. "Didn't want to seem like a complete moron."

I bite back a caustic retort, though I can't fathom why I care if she feels insulted. "It's called Anonymous River."

"Seriously?" she says with a wee laugh. "Whoever named it was too lazy to come up with a real name, huh?"

I clench my jaw. "Anonymous River is the real name."

"Oh, I get it."

"So glad you finally grasped the concept." I narrow my gaze on her. "Dinnae have trendy food. If you're a vegan or prefer some other type of silly rubbish, you'll need to adapt."

"To what?"

"Real, protein-rich food."

"What does that mean?"

Maybe I shouldn't do it, but I can't resist playing a wee trick on her. So I lean forward, nailing my gaze to hers. "Insects provide the best protein. I can go outside and gather some crickets, maybe a few worms. If we're lucky, I'll catch a frog that I can cook over the fireplace spit."

She stares at me.

I lean toward her even more. "How do ye feel about maggots?"

Her lips pucker. Her gaze narrows. Then she slants toward me and...slaps me in the face. "Are all Scottish people total jackasses?"

"No insects, eh? I thought you were an outdoors enthusiast."

"I don't believe for one second that you eat bugs. Not unless you're lying injured in the woods and maggots are the only available food option." She jabs her finger into my chest. "Your hospitality needs a lot of work."

"Hospitality? Never had any of that. There's a reason everyone who knows me calls me 'Wild Man.' Dinnae give a fuck about social graces."

She snorts. "No shit."

"Do ye want food or not? I have red meat and butter, among other politically incorrect dietary selections."

"Whatever you've got, I'll eat." She wrinkles her nose. "As long as it's not bugs."

"All right." I leap off the sofa and race into the open kitchen.

"Um, where is the TV?"

"Dinnae have one."

"What do you do for entertainment?"

I give her a devilish smile. "I was naked when we met. What do you think I like to do for fun?"

"We are not having sex."

"I meant skinny dipping." I wag a finger at her while clucking my tongue. "Ye have a filthy mind, Natalie."

But aye, I would love to shag her.

Chapter Three

Natalie

The kitchen has an open design, but so does the entire cabin. It seems to consist of one big living area plus a bathroom, though I can't see the bed. He must have one, right? Well, maybe he sleeps on the floor because he's just that tough. With his long, unkempt hair and his big scruffy beard, Munro reminds me of the mountain men I'd seen in movies, though he seems much more buff than those guys.

How did this happen to me? I'm stranded in a strange man's home with no way out. I even lost my belongings. The river took them away.

I scan the room again, growing more and more confused. "Um, where is your bedroom?"

Munro has his head in the refrigerator while bent over from the waist. He mutters something I can't understand.

"What was that? I couldn't hear you."

The scruffy Scot lifts his head to glare at me. "I said you're sitting on it."

"Huh? What am I sitting on?"

"My bed."

I look down at the sofa cushions, but I'm still confused. "I'm sitting on your what?"

Munro growls and stalks over here, halting right in front of me. Then he shoves his hand under the cushion I'm sitting on and leans in so his face is inches from mine. He wriggles his hand, making the cushion and me jiggle. "It's a sofa bed, ye daft woman. It folds out. You're sitting on the mattress right now."

"Oh, right. I get it." I suddenly notice what that word he said must mean. "Daft? Are you calling me crazy?"

"No, I called you a fool."

"Gee, that sounds much better."

He whisks his hand out from under the cushion, making me almost fall over sideways. "Ye want food or not?"

"No, I enjoy starving to death."

"All right. I'll eat the steak, then, and you can feast on your self-righteousness."

He stomps back to the kitchen.

"I was being sarcastic," I shout. "Please give me food, Munro."

The man smirks at me, then crawls halfway into the fridge again. After a moment, he starts flinging packages onto the island. They slide here, there, and everywhere. Finally, he straightens and smacks a jug of milk down on the island too. Then he slams the refrigerator shut and studies the items he has assembled. With a satisfied smile and a nod, he picks up the largest package and rips it open.

I can't help it. My curiosity gets the better of me, and I walk up to the island to hop onto a stool. Munro glances at me but then goes back to whatever he's doing. Cooking something, that's all I can tell. "What are you making?"

"Food."

"What kind?"

"Steak."

"And what else?"

He slaps his palms down on the island and glares at me. "Food."

"You already said that. You must be cooking something to go with the steak."

"Potatoes."

Jeez, it's like talking to a caveman. *Me make food. Me give woman food. Woman eat food.*

Since he clearly won't engage in conversation right now, I observe while he whips up a meal for us. I don't eat steak often, but I'm so hungry that I could devour a whole cow. Paddling my kayak turned out to be harder work than I expected, and I not only got wiped out but also became ravenously hungry. The sight of savory food makes my tummy rumble.

Munro has just turned on the stove and placed a big frying pan on the burner. Now he twists around to squint at me. "Gas?"

"Excuse me? Like I know what kind of stove you have."

He rolls his eyes. "I meant do you have gas? Your stomach is making noises loud enough that I can hear it. You should eat more than granola bars. Kayaking uses a lot of calories."

"Yeah, I didn't realize how much energy it would take. I've never been kayaking before."

Munro squints at me harder. Then he tears open a package of butter, hacks a huge chunk off the stick with a dull knife, and tosses it into the frying pan. The butter sizzles and slowly melts. "Why the bloody hell would you go kayaking alone if you had never done that before? You are daft, for sure."

"I had my reasons."

"Aye. Ye wanted to drown in the river."

"No." I rest my arms on the island and rub them. "Not sure I want to bare my soul to a complete stranger."

He slaps one huge steak onto the counter and uses a sharp knife to stab the meat repeatedly. Is he imagining that steak is me? No, I think he's generally irritable. After rubbing seasonings into the meat, he tosses it into the frying pan with the pool of butter. It snaps and sizzles.

Just the smell of the butter makes my tummy rumble again. My mouth has started to water too. Damn, I really want that steak.

Munro stops squinting at me. He stares at my mouth instead and rubs his hairy chin.

"What's wrong with you?" I ask. "You're acting weird again."

"Me?"

"Could you stop speaking in caveman-ese? I don't understand grunted, monosyllabic words."

He slants toward me across the island, and his voice turns deeper and gruffer. "You are licking your lips while staring at my dokey."

"Your what? Honestly, I don't think you know the English language at all."

"My dokey is my cock."

I freeze. Was I staring at his dick? I can't really see it, not since he put clothes on, but I think my gaze might have accidentally landed on his groin. I swear I didn't mean to do that. "I was thinking about steak, not your body."

"Were you?"

"Yes."

He grabs a spatula and flips the steak over to cook the other side. That makes the meat and butter sizzle again. And for some stupid reason, I glance at his groin again. Munro chuckles. "Admit it, lass, ye want this."

Munro palms the bulge of his dick.

"Oh, please." I roll my eyes. "I'm not that hard up for sex."

"When did ye last have a poke?"

"Like I had time to poke the steak before you threw it into the frying pan."

"That's not what having a poke means."

I throw my hands up. "I give. What does it mean?"

His mouth slides into a mischievous smile. "Fucking, that's what it means."

"Oh." Heat rushes through me, but I have no idea why. I can't be attracted to Munro. He's rude and grumpy. "I will not have 'a poke' with you. Not ever."

"We'll see."

"No, we won't." I sit up straighter and fold my arms over my chest. "I will never have sex with you. I mean, we just met, and I don't even like you."

"Lust is a powerful thing." He glances at my breasts and licks his lips. "I predict we'll be naked and fucking inside of two hours."

I huff. "You aren't that hot. Besides, I don't like men who have rat's-nest hair and lice in their big, scruffy beards."

Munro's lips flatten. His nostrils flare. Through clenched teeth, he snarls, "I do not have lice."

He turns away and prods the steak with his spatula.

"Oh, look," I say. "You're having a poke with your steak. Some kind of perv, aren't you?"

Munro growls. "*Pit air iteig.*"

"What on earth are you saying now? Maybe you just had a mini stroke."

"That was Gaelic."

"And it meant…what?"

He winces and almost seems sheepish. "Never mind."

Munro grabs a handful of potatoes and keeps his head down, focused on peeling them.

Maybe I shouldn't harass him so much, but he hasn't been super nice to me. Why should I cut him any slack? Of course, I'm at his mercy, with no way out of the wilderness unless he helps me.

Okay, time for reconciliation.

I clear my throat. "I'm sorry, Munro. We clearly speak different languages, in more ways than one, and I shouldn't have gotten snippy with you. I'm grateful for all your help."

He glances at me with his head still bowed, but he doesn't speak.

I bite my lip. "Do you forgive me?"

"Aye." He goes back to peeling potatoes.

No reciprocal apology. Well, I hadn't really expected one. Maybe I'd hoped for that, but I never thought the crabby, disheveled Scot would offer a mea culpa.

"Can I help?" I ask. "I know how to peel potatoes too."

"I finished that." He twists his mouth into a slightly less irritable slant. "But I suppose you could prepare the green beans."

"Don't want me to cut up the potatoes?"

"No need." He grabs a huge carving knife and whacks the potatoes with it, cutting them up so fast that I think I must be hallucinating. "It's done. Do the beans, please."

Munro MacTaggart just used the word please. Wow, I didn't think he knew what it meant.

I hop off my stool. "Sure, I can do that."

While Munro dumps the potatoes into a big bowl and adds a bit of salt and water to it, I gather the beans and start slicing. He lays a dinner plate on top of his bowl, then shoves it into the microwave. And he punches a button to start the potatoes cooking. When he catches me watching him, he squints at me yet again.

"What is it now?" he demands. "Staring is impolite."

A laugh I couldn't quite suppress splutters out of me. "*You* think staring is rude?"

He drums his fingers on the microwave's top. "What have I done now to upset Her Highness?"

"I'm not upset. But I thought it was funny that you—Oh, never mind. Why did you put a plate on top of the bowl?"

"To steam the potatoes. My ma taught me that trick."

"Good idea. Your mom sounds like a smart lady."

"Aye, she is. That's why she's upset with me for moving to America."

I freeze in the middle of slicing the ends off the fresh green beans. Munro shared a sliver of personal information with me. I have no idea how to respond to that. I bite my lip to stop myself from blurting out a question that will probably annoy him. Besides, I don't care to talk about my life back home, so I won't ask him questions that might encourage him to do the same to me. I'd rather he growled at me and called me a "daft" again.

Maybe I am a fool. I believed my ex-husband's lies, after all.

Chapter Four

Munro

Why did I tell Natalie that mother disapproved of my choice to move to America? It's none of her concern. To avoid thinking about what I did, I focus on getting our meal ready since Natalie is clearly undernourished. After we finish preparing the food, I set our plates on opposite sides of the island and pat her erse. "Back on the stool, lass. Cannae have you dropping food bits all over my sofa. I sleep on it too, ye know."

"You sleep on the stool?"

"No, ye cheeky lass. The sofa is my bed."

"I know. I was teasing you." She climbs onto the stool. "Thank you for making me a delicious, nutritious meal."

"You haven't tasted it yet. Maybe it isn't delicious at all."

She leans over her plate and inhales deeply. Her eyes fall partly closed. "Mm, nothing that smells this yummy could taste bad."

The hunger in her voice almost sounds erotic, and I dinnae want my *slat* to wake up right now. After we eat, maybe. But not now. So I rest my erse on a stool and focus on my food. "Eat, lass. You need nourishment."

Natalie consumes a big bite of steak and moans. "Oh, this is soooo good."

One side of my mouth kicks up. "You seem like a woman who hasn't eaten for days, the way you're turning a simple meal into a culinary fuck."

Her head pops up. She blinks rapidly, then curls her lips into a teasing smile. "Culinary what? That must be another Scottish-ism, huh?"

"No. I invented the phrase a moment ago." I spear a green bean and point it at her. "When you eat, you sound like you're about to climax. That's a culinary fuck."

"You're obsessed with sex. Has it been a long time since you had a girlfriend?"

"Aye. But I dinnae need to date a woman to have a poke with her."

She wrinkles her nose. "Casual sex? That's not my thing."

It's not mine either, but I refuse to admit that to Natalie. Maybe I haven't been with a woman in a bloody long time, but she does not need to know that.

"I need to make that phone call now," Natalie says. "So I can get a taxi to pick me up."

"Taxi? Do you think this is New York City?" I spread my arms. "You are in the wilderness. Unless you're wanting to swim back to the campground, you won't be leaving this house until my mate arrives with the new transmission."

"Do you know how to install one of those?"

I shove a big forkful of potatoes into my mouth and chew instead of answering her question.

She puckers her lips. And drums her fingers on the island. Then she leaps off her stool and scrutinizes the interior of the house. "Where's your phone? You said you have one that I could use."

"Willnae do you any good."

Natalie whirls around to look at me. "Why not? Did you lie about having a telephone?"

"No. It's because you won't find anyone who will drive all the way out here to pick you up. It's remote. That's why I like living here."

"But your friend—"

"Might not come for a day or two, at least. Ahmno in a hurry."

She flaps her arms. "Well, I am. May I please have the phone?"

Despite using the word please, she spoke that question in an annoyed tone.

I sigh and wave toward the far corner of the cabin. "The landline phone is on the desk."

She marches over there and reaches for the phone but stops before she can pick it up. Then she swivels her head to gawp at me. "You have a computer."

"Aye. Have you never seen a laptop before?"

"Of course I have. But you don't seem like the type who uses the internet."

I strap my arms over my chest. "Ye think I'm a savage, don't you?"

"No, I—" She makes a sheepish face. "Okay, maybe I did think that. Sorry."

"Just make your bloody call."

"Do you have a phone book?"

"Aye. It's in the drawer right in front of you."

While she gingerly pulls out the desk chair and sits down on it, I continue enjoying my meal. The word enjoying might not be the most appropriate way to phrase it. I do not like having "company" in my home, and I especially do not like sharing my sanctuary with a havering woman who thinks I'm a savage because I live in the wilderness.

Natalie brings out the phone book and dials a number. "Hello? Yes, I need someone to pick me up and take me to the campground." She bites her bottom lip while listening to whoever is on the other end of the call. "Mm-hm. What? Oh, of course. Give me a minute."

Natalie turns toward me and holds the phone to her chest.

I raise my brows.

She waves at me as if we're good mates and she just noticed me sitting on the sofa. "What's the address here?"

Cannae help smirking. "Number One Summer Trail, Yestermont."

Natalie recites the address to whoever is on the phone with her. She jerks and holds the phone away from her ear. She blinks once rather slowly. "What a rude man."

"Who, lass?"

"The guy at the taxi company. When I told him the address, he laughed and hung up on me. Why would he do that?"

I rub my chin, pretending to consider her question. "Hmm, I wonder."

She flashes me an irritated look, then taps her finger on the page in the phone book. She dials another number. "Yes, hello? I need a taxi, please. What? Oh, it's Number One Summer Trail, Yestermont."

Tinny laughter erupts from the phone, and she jerks it away from her ear. The lass claps the phone down. "What is wrong with the people around here? I thought you were the only jackass in the area. But no, it's an epidemic of incredibly rude men."

"Aye, every one of us is a *cacan*. Go on, try a woman. Missy Reynolds runs a taxi service in Yestermont, and I'm sure her number is in the book."

Natalie picks up the phone but doesn't dial. Instead, she wrinkles her brow at me. "What is a kekin?"

"*Cacan*. It means 'wee shit,' which is what you're claiming all men are."

"Not all men. Just the ones who live in this area." She dials the phone, and after a few seconds, she perks up. "Yes, hello, I need a taxi, please." Natalie slouches in the chair. "Oh, thank goodness. You are a lifesaver. What? The address…"

I try not to smirk. All right, I don't try *that* hard.

Natalie winces. "It's Number One Summer Trail, Yestermont." She slumps lower in her chair and covers her eyes with one hand. "Uh-huh. I understand. Thank you."

She hangs up the phone—and glowers at me.

"Is there something wrong?" I ask. "Ye look a wee bit deflated."

"Why didn't you warn me?"

"About what?"

She shoves the phone book into the drawer and slams it shut. "You didn't warn me that no one will come out here to pick me up because your driveway is a mile long and full of potholes."

"It's also surrounded by federal land, which makes my driveway closer to ten miles long if you include the connecting roads."

Her eyes go wide. "I'm never getting out of here, am I?"

"Dinnae be ridiculous. My friend will take you into town."

"Someday. When he gets around to it."

I thrust a chunk of steak into my mouth and use chewing as an excuse not to respond to her statement. Maybe she does have good reason for feeling stranded, but I'm not a wilderness taxi service. My car is broken. So even if I wanted to help her, I can't—not until I have the new transmission.

"May I make another call?" Natalie asks.

"Go on."

She eyes me with skepticism but then dials another number. It apparently rings and rings, because she leans forward and begins to chew on her bottom lip. Suddenly, she snaps up straight, and her face lights up. "It's Natalie. I could really use your help. Uh-huh. I need a lift. Well...I'm in Wyoming."

Aye, she sounds like she wished she didn't have to tell the other person where she is. Maybe I had set her up for a fall when she wanted to call for a taxi. I shouldn't have done that, but her attitude toward me—saying I'm a savage—rubbed me the wrong way. I don't want the lass to be stranded here. I don't like having a guest, but mostly, I don't like seeing her anguish.

Natalie drops her head into her hand and moans. "Yeah, I knew it was a long shot. I mean, you're a former client, not my best friend. Never mind, I'm sure I'll find a way. Goodbye."

She sets the phone down and covers her face with both hands. Her shoulders begin to shake. She sniffles.

Bod an Donais. I cannae abide seeing women cry. I might be a grumpy bastard, but I'm not callous. What else can I do? I walk over there, kneel beside her chair, and pat her shoulder. "What's the bother, lass? We'll get you home sooner or later."

A sob explodes out of her, and she throws her arms around me.

I stifle a groan and cautiously pat her back. "It's not that bad. I have plenty of food, and I'll sleep outside if that would make you feel more comfortable."

Her head pops up. "You would really do that?"

"Aye. I'll even call my friend and see if he can bring the new transmission sooner. And I'll try to find out if anyone has found your kayak and your backpack."

No bloody idea if I can do that, but I will keep to my word and try.

"Wow. Thank you, Munro."

Her face hovers so close to mine that I can feel her breaths tickling my skin. Just as I'm about to pull away, she mashes her mouth to mine. I freeze. We gaze into each other's eyes, our lips fused, neither of us moving a muscle, not even our eyelids.

I pull away first.

Natalie licks her lips.

A daft impulse overtakes me, and I pull her snugly into my body. Then I crush my mouth to hers and thrust my tongue inside.

Chapter Five

Natalie

I kissed a stranger and let him kiss me back—with tongue. Have I gone completely insane? No time to think about the answer to that question. Munro keeps coiling his tongue around mine, and my eyes have drifted shut all on their own. I might have moaned too, a teeny bit. Damn, he knows how to kiss. I never would've guessed that a scruffy mountain man would have top-notch make-out skills. When he slides his hands down to my ass, the logical part of my brain realizes I should knee him in the balls or slug him in the gut and then run away. But I don't want to do that. I love the way he's exploring my mouth, and I can't stop myself from savoring his mouth too.

Munro pulls away, though only enough that we can look each other in the eye. We're both breathing harder. I stare into his blue eyes, and he stares right back at me. When he drags his tongue across his bottom lip, my gaze flicks down to his mouth. Did he do that on purpose? If he thinks I'm going to kiss him again, he's dead wrong.

My body disagrees. *Shut up, hormones.*

I try to roll my chair back but realize too late this isn't a wheeled office chair. It's the regular old wooden kind. The chair starts to topple over backward.

Munro leaps up and ,with one hand, grabs hold of the chair's back to stop it from falling. He tips it upright again. "Are you feeling unwell?"

"No."

"I thought you might have lost your balance."

"The chair lost its balance, not me."

He grunts and snatches the handset away from me. Then he stalks over to the front door.

Does this cabin even have a back entrance?

Munro flings the door open and steps outside, slamming it shut.

I know I shouldn't do it, but my nosiness has gotten the better of me. I tiptoe over to the front door and plaster my ear to it. I don't hear anything yet. He's probably dialing. I lay a hand on the wood, leaning my shoulder against it.

"It's me," he says. "Munro MacTaggart."

Wow, I can hear him better than I expected.

"Of course I know ye remember my name, Owen. I was being polite." Munro growls under his breath. "Caller ID? I don't want or need that. I have something else that I need your help with. Any chance you can bring the transmission today?"

Silence follows. I hear birds twittering outside.

"Please, Owen," Munro says. "I will beg if that will help, and you know I never do that. I rescued a lass from nearly drowning in the river, and she needs to get back to her campground or hotel or whatever it is."

I did not almost drown in the river. I got caught under a tree branch on the shore. Is he trying to make himself sound more heroic? What a jerk. Can't believe I kissed him.

Munro sighs heavily. "I understand. Thank you, Owen."

A beep tells me he must have hung up the phone. So I rush over to the sofa and sit down, trying to look casual and not as if I'd been spying on him.

When Munro stalks into the cabin, he seems even grumpier than before. He flops onto the opposite end of the sofa. It thunks and scrapes across the floor. "My friend can't bring the transmission today. He said he'll try to bring it tomorrow."

I'm not surprised to hear that, but I do feel like throwing my head back and moaning pathetically. But I restrain that impulse. "Thank you for trying, Munro."

He grunts. Maybe the man time-traveled from the Stone Age where everyone grunts because language hadn't been invented yet, and he only learned how to speak a few months ago.

Munro scrubs a hand over his mouth. "You can have the bed, and I will sleep outside."

"What if it rains?"

"Did you check the weather report before you took off on your barmy kayaking expedition?"

"Yes, I did. But the forecast can change."

Guess what he does? Munro grunts. Big surprise.

He rises and stretches, groaning deeply. "I'm away."

"Away from what?"

"This cabin." He leans over me and plants his hands on the sofa's back at either side of me. "I meant I'm leaving."

"Where are you going?"

"Are you my keeper now? I dinnae need a woman harassing me about everything. If I want to go somewhere, that's my business."

"Do what you want." I cross my arms over my chest. "I can take care of myself."

"Like ye did earlier along the shore." He straightens. "I'm going down the river to see if I can find your belongings."

"I'll go with you."

He screws up his mouth. "No thank you."

Munro stomps out the door.

I race after him and seize his arm just as he's about to step off the porch. "You don't have any shoes."

He smirks. "I'm aware of that."

Munro jogs to the riverbank, strips off his clothes, and leaps into the water. As he swims downriver, I gape at him. That's how he plans to search for my stuff? By swimming? What if he runs into a grizzly bear? It might think he's a very large salmon and eat him. No, that wouldn't happen. He's so scruffy that a girl bear would mistake him for a boy bear and drag him back to her den so they can mate.

I don't care what Munro does. Really, I don't.

To prove that to myself, I march back into the house and slam the door. Then I march over to Munro's desk and flip up the lid on his laptop. Maybe I can find someone online who will come rescue me from the Scottish savage.

His laptop has a password.

Jeez, the guy seems like a Luddite. But he knows how to create a computer password? I bet he can't remember it without help, though. That means he would have written it down somewhere. I lift up the laptop and flip it around to look for clues on its backside. Nothing there. Then I flip it upside down.

Eureka.

I found Munro's ultra-secret password, and it is…password. Why did he bother writing that down? I turn the laptop over and wake it from sleep mode, then type in the password. Invalid, the computer says. What? I try again, carefully pressing each key to spell out the word. Invalid, it says again.

My chair suddenly falls backward. I yelp.

And Munro gazes down at me while I hang suspended halfway to the floor. Only his hands prevent me from falling. Water drizzles from his soaked hair and his naked body. "What are you doing?"

"Um..." I wince. "Trying to hack into your computer so I can check my email."

"Try again."

"Hacking into your computer so I can find somebody else to drive me back to the campground."

Munro sets my chair upright. "Couldn't break my secret code, eh?"

"Your password is 'password,' but your laptop is clearly broken. It wouldn't accept the code."

He slants over my shoulder, his wet beard rasping against my cheek. "That's because I'm using the Gaelic version of 'password.' No one will ever hack my computer."

"What is the Gaelic version of that term?"

"*Facal-faire.*"

"How is that spelled?"

Munro rubs his stubble against my cheek on purpose this time. "If you're wanting to know my secret code, all you have to do is fuck me."

"Sure, I'll do that." I push a hand between our cheeks and shove him away. "When the African continent becomes one giant glacier and lions turn into penguins."

Munro reaches for something behind me, bending over to get it. He drops the package onto my lap. "You're welcome."

"It's my backpack," I almost shout. Seeing my stuff again makes me so happy that I feel like whooping. But I tamp down my enthusiasm. "Thank you, Munro. Where did you find my stuff? It must've washed ashore, huh?"

"No." He leans his hip against the desk beside me. "I swam down the river until I saw three laddies sitting by their campfire. They were having a good time rifling through your unmentionables."

"What? Those good-for-nothing slimeballs."

"I liberated your belongings and returned them to the backpack. Then I jogged back to the cabin."

He really is a strange man. Very fit too, considering that he carried me for who knows how far and then swam down the river only to jog back here. Holy shit, he's amazing. Physically, that is. I don't appreciate his abrasive personality, no matter how good he is at kissing.

"What about my kayak?" I ask. "Did those guys wreck it?"

"Not sure what they did with it. I hunted about but couldn't find the kayak."

"I don't know what to say, Munro."

He taps the laptop with one finger. "Don't need this. You'll never find anyone who wants to drive out here for you."

"But the scumbags who took my stuff must have a car."

"They were on a week-long hike through the wilderness. And besides, they took off like wee laddies being chased by a moose."

I probably don't want to know the answer, but I ask anyway. "Why did those guys really run off?"

"Because they think I'm an alien Sasquatch from another dimension. No idea where they got that idea." He shakes his head. "A bunch of dafties. The second I jumped out of the river and started running toward them, they screamed and took off."

Uh, yeah, it's a mystery why three young twerps would flee when they saw a big, naked, hairy Scot heading straight for them. I bet Munro was growling or snarling or both. I would've skedaddled too. I almost did when I met Munro, but my fear vanished quickly. I somehow knew he meant me no harm.

Other than annoying the hell out of me, that is.

"Maybe people wouldn't think you're scary," I say, "if you cut your hair and shaved your beard, or at least trimmed it."

"I don't give a toss if I scare a spineless *cacan* or two."

His nakedness is starting to bother me, though not in a "will this guy go serial killer on me" way. No, I'm starting to get turned on. Only a smidge. It hardly counts. Besides, it's his fault for standing there naked and soaked.

"Why are you still dripping wet?" I ask. "You jogged here from how far away?"

"About half a mile. I took a dip in the river to wash off the sweat before I came in here."

He can't possibly have done that because he wanted to be clean for me. No, that's crazy.

"I have work to do," he says. "And I need peace and quiet to do that."

"Okay." I unzip the front pocket of my backpack—and whoop with joy. "My phone is still in here!"

"Won't do you any good in the wilderness. No service."

"Yeah, I found that out while I was paddling down the river. But at least I can play games or something on it to pass the time. Unless you have a radio or…might let me use your computer?"

He points at the laptop. "My work is on the computer."

"Oh. Well, I'll find some way to entertain myself." I accidentally glance at his dick, and a wave of warmth rushes through me. "Think I'll go outside to sit on the porch."

"Aye, do that."

I'm sure he wants me out of his hair. So while he opens up a hidden door that turns out to be his closet, I amble out onto the porch and sit on the swing. Since Munro's house is the most utilitarian cabin I've ever seen, with zero luxuries, I think it's weird that he has a porch swing. But I'm glad he does. I can sit here and gently sway, listening to the birds and the calming sound of the river rushing past. An eagle flies by, swooping down as if it wants to check me out.

This is a beautiful place. Maybe this can be the hideaway I've needed—for a little while at least.

Chapter Six

Munro

Today, I've done many things I never imagined I would do. First, I took in a strange lass who was clearly unprepared for life in the wilderness. Then, I told her about myself. Not all of it. Not even half of it. But I dinnae blether with anyone. Is it still gossiping if I only talk about myself? *Mhac na galla*, who cares.

I take my laptop to the sofa and start working.

After half an hour, I need a wee break from staring at the screen. So I go into the kitchen strictly for the exercise. Something outside the window catches my eye, and I lean forward to get a better view.

Natalie is walking in a circle around my truck.

I shove the window open. "What are you doing, woman? Do not touch my truck."

She halts with her hands on her hips. "I was only looking at it."

"Dinnae be doing that either."

"What, I can't touch or look at the sacred pickup truck?"

"Aye, that's right. No one touches it without my permission—which I do not grant to you."

She lays a hand on the hood, tapping her fingers. "Are you a drug mule? Is that why you live way out in the hinterlands?"

"Haud yer wheesht, woman. Take yourself and your questions away from my truck or I'll lock you in the closet."

"Your beat-up vehicle isn't worth arguing over."

She walks away, out of my sight.

That bloody woman.

I grab a snack and a drink, then return to the sofa to do more work. A wee while later, my phone rings. I hiss a Gaelic curse under my breath and trot over to the desk to snatch up the handset. "Who the fuck is this?"

A man chuckles. "No wonder nobody wants to visit your place if that's the way you greet everybody. Did your houseguest run away yet? She's probably shacked up with a grizzly bear by now, hey? Oh, wait, that would mean she's still with you."

"Did you want something, Owen?"

"Yeah. I decided to change Chapter Eight. I'm sending you new pages. Just replace the old ones, okay? I know it's a pain since you've probably worked on that chapter already, but I'll pay extra for your trouble."

"Don't worry about it."

"My fault, anyway." He sighs heavily. "Still can't write as fast as I used to."

"Aye, divorce will fash anyone. Give it time, Owen. I know what I'm talking about."

He pauses, and all I hear is a faint hissing on the line. "Do you think this new book sounds different? Like the divorce has wrecked my signature style?"

"I'll let you know the answer once I've read the whole manuscript. It's good, though, so dinnae fash."

"But is it…you know."

"No, I don't. What are you getting at?" The truth occurs to me, and I can't help chuckling. "How can you write those sort of books and still be shy about discussing the subject?"

"I don't know. Might have something to do with my ex-wife."

Naomi is bonnie, but I've only ever seen a photograph of her. Never met the woman. Still, it didn't take a genius to realize Owen's wife did not approve of his career or the sorts of stories he writes. He's better off without her, but I'm sure it will take time for Owen to recover from his marriage and the divorce.

"I'll email you if I see anything that doesn't sound right," I say. "But so far, it all looks good. I need to get back to work right now."

"Sure, yeah. Thanks for putting up with my neurotic attacks."

"Go for a walk or something, Owen. Clear your head."

"I will. See you tomorrow."

We say goodbye, and I go back to the sofa to do what Owen is paying me to do.

A flash of movement makes me glance at the porch window.

Natalie is peering through the glass with her hands cupped around her face so she can see inside.

What is that woman doing now? I leap up and race to the door, yanking it open. "Why are ye staring through the window like a burglar casing the house?"

"I wondered if I could come inside, but I didn't want to bother you while you're working."

"And spying sounded like an appropriate alternative."

"No." She approaches the doorway, tipping her head back to look at me. "May I please come inside, Munro?"

"Did you tamper with my truck?"

"Like I would know how to do that. You're awfully suspicious, aren't you?"

"Aye. But so are you."

She stuffs her hands into her trouser pockets and hunches her shoulders. "Yeah, I know. I've got good reason for that. I guess you must too."

I do not care to have a conversation with her. Women want to share feelings or discuss relationships or some such bollocks.

"So, may I come in, Munro?"

"Aye, come in." I step aside. "But don't touch my computer."

She salutes. "Yes, sir, General MacTaggart."

"Just get your erse in here, Natalie."

The barmy woman heads for the sofa, and I sprint over there to grab my open laptop before she can glimpse what's on the screen.

She settles her erse on the sofa. "Were you watching internet porn?"

"No."

"You grabbed your laptop so fast that I figured you must be doing something naughty."

"My clients require complete confidentiality. That means no bonnie redheads poking their noses into my files."

Natalie tucks her legs under her. "Guess your red-haired clients are out of luck, then."

I drop onto the sofa, staying at the opposite end from her, and turn sideways just enough that she won't be able to see the screen. "Take a nap. I need silence to work."

"Not tired. But I have my phone now, so I can listen to music."

"There's no cellular signal here."

"You already told me that. But I have music stored on my phone." She roots about in her backpack, bringing out two items. She inserts a pair of earbuds into her ears and straps what looks like a sleep mask over her eyes. "I'll be quiet. You have my word."

"Since I don't know you, I have no idea if I can trust your word."

Natalie sighs. "It must exhausting to be you, always suspecting everyone of something."

She lifts her mask just enough to look at her phone and taps the screen several times. Seeming satisfied, she relaxes into the sofa.

I focus on my work. Well, I try to do that. But having a sexy lass at the other end of the sofa distracts me. I can't help noticing the sweet wee smile that curves her mouth or the way her breasts rise and fall with every breath she takes. Even fully clothed, she has a body that any man would love to explore. Naked, she would be stunning, I'm fair certain. When she shifts position slightly, the movement draws my focus to her shapely thighs.

Stop admiring her body, ye cacan.

Maybe it's been too long since I had a poke. Living in the back of beyond means I don't meet women except when I make my once a month trip to the grocery store, and then I meet only one lass, the same cashier every time. She has a beard almost as long as mine. And she's married.

I suddenly realize I've wasted ten minutes on thinking about how much I'd love to fuck Natalie. *Bod an Donais.* I've never before become obsessed with the idea of shagging a woman, but I cannae stop thinking about it today. I need her to be gone. She seems like the sort who would want to do more than have a poke. She'd want to…date me.

With more effort than seems rational, I force myself to get back to work. No more glancing at Natalie's body. No more picturing her naked. And absolutely no more thinking about dating her. I do not want that.

The lass begins to snore softly.

Even that gets me randy.

Grumbling under my breath, I take my laptop over to the desk. Now that I have my back to the sexy lass, I will not be distracted anymore. Aye, that belief lasts about ten minutes. How can I not be distracted? Reading Owen's book only serves to ensure I keep thinking about Natalie and I keep picturing her naked and writhing beneath me.

An Diabhal fhéin. Aye, the devil himself must have crawled into my brain and implanted those lustful thoughts.

Natalie snorts loudly once and then yawns. "Did you hear a weird noise?"

"That was your own snoring."

"You sure? Maybe I was dreaming."

"Listen to your music and stop bothering me."

I might be almost snarling at her. It's Owen's fault. So I write a quick email telling him that I won't be able to work on his books anymore, but then I delete the message without sending it. Natalie is driving me off my head.

When I glance back at her, I'm relieved to see she's listening to her music again. I notice the clock on my computer and realize it's dinner time. No wonder I'm feeling off. I need food. But when I leap out of my chair, it tumbles over backward. I hiss a Gaelic curse and right the chair, then stomp into the kitchen.

Natalie removes her earbuds. "What are you doing?"

"Making dinner. Unless you want to fast for the rest of the day."

"I'm starving." She hops to her feet and pads over to the island. "I don't usually have dinner at four o'clock, but I'm so hungry I could eat a pine tree."

"That won't be necessary." I make a shooing motion with my hand. "Go back to the sofa. I prefer to cook alone."

"You do everything alone, don't you?" She climbs onto a stool, resting her arms on the island's countertop. "That must be a lonely existence."

"Not for me."

A loud electronic noise erupts, and Natalie shrieks. She slaps her hands over her ears, wincing. "What the hell is that racket?"

I lean over the island to peel her hands away from her ears. "That's my weather radio. It receives emergency broadcasts from NOAA. There must be some sort of storm coming."

"Jeez, do they have to explode my eardrums to get the point across?"

The noise ends, and a man's voice begins to recite the weather warning.

Natalie jumps off her stool and almost tumbles over in the process. I rush around the island to wrap my arms around her, strictly to stop her from falling and cracking her head open. Now that I have her body pressed against mine, I cannae remember what I'd meant to do next.

She stops wincing. Her eyes have become glossy.

Even while the radio laddie recites the details of a severe thunderstorm watch, I can't focus on what he's saying. Natalie's body feels so fucking good crushed against me.

"Did he say severe thunderstorm?" she asks, her voice huskier and softer.

"Aye, he did." I sound the same way.

The radio transmission repeats, then ends.

I'm still clasping Natalie to my body. Her tits have mounded against my chest, and my *slat* is rousing.

"Will there be tornadoes?" she asks.

"Not sure. Strong storms, that's all I heard."

"Thunderstorms make me horny."

"Me too."

We stare into each other's eyes while her hands drift up my chest and my palms glide down to her erse. She rises onto her toes, bringing her lips to within a few inches of mine. Her breaths tickle my mouth, and I can feel her nipples hardening. My cock is doing the same thing.

I push her away. "Need to start dinner."

"Uh-huh." She sashays toward the sofa. "Since you don't want help, I'll listen to my music some more."

"Aye, do that."

I cut my fingers twice while making dinner, though neither wound is anything more than a minor annoyance. Despite employing all my willpower not to look at Natalie, I keep doing that anyway. Trying to cook slowly so I won't need to sit on the sofa with her does not help. Still, I manage to create a decent meal and not blow up the cabin by accidentally snuffing out the propane flames while running the microwave. It was a close thing, though.

My reactions to Natalie make no sense. Shagging her is out of the question.

I accidentally glance at her.

The lass is stretching her arms above her head while smiling, and the action hoists her tits.

Bod an Donais. She's going to drive me insane.

Chapter Seven

Natalie

I've lost count of how many times Munro snarled words that I don't understand while making dinner. I assume those were Gaelic phrases. Based on his tone of voice, I'm pretty sure he was cursing like a drunken sailor. What is his problem now? I've just been sitting here on the sofa listening to music, not even glancing in his direction, and certainly not talking to him. I've tried to give him space.

When he curses again, I crank up the volume on my music. At least now I won't hear every grumpy thing he barks at me. Normally, I don't like to play music at high volume, but Munro leaves me with no other options. I sink into the sofa and let the tunes blast away. My lids gradually slide shut, and I melt even deeper into the plush cushions.

Suddenly, the earbuds are torn from my ears.

I flinch and jerk upright.

Munro is leaning over me, his face no more than a foot from mine, scowling like the Scottish grump he is. "Dinner is served, milady, if you'll deign to eat it."

"Why are you in such a bad mood? I haven't spoken to you since you announced you prefer to cook alone."

"I shouted your name five times, and you didn't respond."

"Oh. Sorry. But that's no excuse for your rudeness." I plant one foot on his chest and shove him away. "Don't ever sneak up on me like that again."

He stumbles into the coffee table but catches himself before he hits it. "I made dinner, if you're wanting to eat."

"Yes, please, I'd love to dine with such a charming gentleman."

My acerbic tone surprises me because I rarely get snarky with anyone. Not sure what it is about Munro, other than his obvious grumpiness, that makes me behave that way. Well, maybe I have an idea of why. But no, it can't be…sexual tension. Of course not, it's crazy. Maybe he did save me from slowly dying of dehydration while trapped under a tree limb, and maybe he did hunt down my backpack and liberate it from obnoxious twerps. Okay, that means what I'm feeling is nothing more than gratitude, which annoys me because *he* annoys me. I can live with that.

Munro picks me up and slings me over his shoulder. His brawny arms lash my legs to his chest. He stomps over to the island, setting me down on a stool. "No one eats on my sofa. Dinnae want to be picking crumbs out of the fabric for the next week."

A smart retort wants to come out of my mouth, but I squelch it. If I harass him too much, he might take my food away.

He stalks around to the other side of the island and perches on a stool. Two plates of food sit in front of him. He hands one to me.

Well, at least his scowl has eased up, seeming more like a slight frown now. I avoid looking at him while I dig into my meal. Sausage and hash browns have never tasted so good in my entire life. I even gobble up the sauerkraut, though I've never been crazy about that dish. If Munro had tossed a dead squirrel onto my plate, I probably would've eaten it raw. No idea why I'm so hungry. I had a good meal at lunch.

Annoyance burns a lot of calories, I guess.

My gaze flicks to Munro. I watch in rapt fascination while he saws off a hunk of sausage, opens his mouth wide, and slides that meat onto his tongue. He chews the food slowly, almost sensually, and groans with satisfaction. For reasons I refuse to analyze, watching him devour his meal makes my nipples tighten and sets off a tingly sensation between my thighs. I don't like cavemen. I cannot be attracted to him. But I kissed him earlier, then let him thrust his tongue into my mouth.

He notices me observing him and narrows his gaze on me. "Eat, ye daft woman."

I decide the prudent response is to ignore his testy command and start eating. Not because he told me to do it. I'm hungry, that's all.

Munro focuses on hacking off another piece of sausage. "While you were ruining your eardrums, NOAA radio announced that the National Weather Service issued a severe thunderstorm watch and a tornado watch, as well as a special weather statement about the potential for powerful cloud-to-ground lightning. There might be severe thunderstorm and tornado warnings later this evening."

"What? Tornadoes?" My pulse has sped up, and I drop my fork. "We're stuck in a rickety cabin, and there might be severe storms. That doesn't sound like a good combination."

Naturally, he scowls at me. "My home is not rickety. It's well-built and sturdy, and it's survived many storms in the past."

"I didn't mean to insult your cabin. Severe weather scares me, though. I like normal thunderstorms, but I get anxious whenever anyone uses the word tornado. I'm panicking, and that's why I called your house rickety. I'm sorry."

No, I won't mention to him that the sound of rain makes me horny, especially if there's mild thunder too.

While we enjoy our meal in silence, I keep glancing out the window behind him. Is the sky getting darker? It could just be the sun going down, but I don't see any sunset glow. Bluish gray clouds keep expanding across the horizon, gradually spreading across the sky.

Munro reaches across the island to hook his thumb under my chin and lift to close my jaw. "You're gawping at the sky like you've never seen a raincloud before."

"That's not just a raincloud. It's a big bruise in the sky. What if that's a severe thunderstorm?"

"The weather radio would have gone off by now." He picks up our empty plates and sets them in the sink. Then he leans toward the window, peering out at the darkening sky. "Let me check the NWS website."

"What is the NWS? And what is NOAA? You never explained that either."

"Those are the National Weather Service and the National Oceanic and Atmospheric Administration."

At least he didn't snarl those words.

I tag along behind Munro while he strides over to the desk and lays a palm on it, then flips up the laptop's lid. He types in his password with one finger yet manages to do that so fast that I couldn't tell which letters he typed. Since he told me his password is the term password in Gaelic, I have zero chance of deciphering his secret code.

The home screen appears.

While Munro navigates to the NWS website, I hug myself and try not to glance out the windows.

Rain ticks on the glass. It's nothing more than sprinkles so far.

My eyes decide now is the right time for me to stare at Munro's ass. His jeans fit snugly, highlighting the powerful muscles hidden beneath the fabric. Every time he shifts his weight from one foot to the other, I flash back to the moment I'd first seen him, while he was buck naked and dripping wet. I couldn't stop myself from staring at his naked ass and that dick. At the time,

I'd been too scared to get aroused. But now, the memory and the present reality of his body instigate a slickness between my thighs.

I blame the rain.

"We have a severe thunderstorm warning," Munro says. "And the special weather statement has been updated. It now says frequent, powerful cloud-to-ground lightning is occurring."

"Oh, shit. What do we do? I mean, there are windows everywhere and lightning can go through glass."

He shuts the laptop and faces me. "Relax, lass. My house will not crash down around us. And if we stay away from the windows, we'll be fine. At any rate, lightning would be attracted to the highest objects, which means trees, not this cabin."

"Okay, sure, that makes sense." My voice came out shaky. *Damn.* Then I realize something. "Why didn't your weather radio go off?"

Munro's brows draw together. He puckers his lips. "Maybe I should have replaced the batteries."

He yanks open a desk drawer and roots around until he finds a package of C batteries. I peek around his big body to see what he's doing. Munro replaces the batteries, and within two seconds, the radio starts blaring its emergency tone.

I jump and yelp.

While the weather person recites the warnings, Munro slings an arm around my shoulders and guides me to the sofa. We both sit down, though at opposite ends.

Thunder rumbles.

I lash my arms around myself again.

Munro slants toward me to pat my hand. "Take it easy, Natalie. Why dinnae ye listen to your music?"

"Um…"

The rain abruptly turns heavy, pounding on the metal roof.

"Is that hail?" I ask. "Are you sure the roof can handle that?"

"Aye, I'm sure." He peers out the windows. "Don't see any hail. It's only a downpour."

Thunder detonates overhead, so loud that the house trembles.

I scoot closer to Munro and huddle against him. Why the hell did I do that? But I don't want to move away—only because I'm scared, not because I want him.

But he does smell good.

Another crack of thunder rattles the cabin, and blinding bolts of lightning lance the sky, one after another after another.

I huddle even closer to Munro.

He slips an arm around me, gliding his hand up and down in a soothing gesture. But instead of comforting me, his touch turns me on. My sex grows wetter and tinglier while my breasts become so sensitized that the slightest movement sets off a chain reaction of lust, from my nipples down to my clitoris. Maybe rain turns me on, but I've never gotten this aroused from a thunderstorm, especially not a severe one.

Munro wriggles his hips, like he's trying to get more comfortable. His movements make me glance down at his lap.

I swallow hard because the bulge of his dick has enlarged. And that makes my clit throb.

"Natalie," Munro growls, in a sexy way this time. "Stop looking at my cock, lass. I can see your nipples, how stiff they've gotten, and it makes me want to devour those rosy peaks."

The raw hunger in his voice shoots another electric charge down my nerves, from my nipples to my clit. But when I look up at him, the lust on his face takes my breath away. I've never slept with a man I just met. Never. But I don't know how much longer I can restrain my lust for Munro MacTaggart. I don't even like him, but I need to feel his cock inside me.

Another round of thunder shakes the cabin, and its rumble goes on and on and on. Combined with the rain pelting the roof and the windows, the thunder intensifies my desire until it becomes a thick, molten pool inside me and my cream soaks my panties.

"Last chance," Munro growls, his voice even hotter now. "Ahm seconds away from fucking ye. So walk away if ye dinnae want that."

Despite my every effort to stop it, my eyes roll down to stare at the bulge of his dick. It's even thicker now—and much harder, for sure.

"Five seconds," he says. "Then I'm kissing you, and it willnae end there. Five, four—"

I should back away, but I can't. Don't want to either. Oh God, all I want right now is to experience the sensation of his cock filling me up and his hips pumping, in and out, in and out.

"Three, two, one."

We both freeze, our gazes bound, while the storm rages outside. The blustering wind forces the rain to buffet the windows. The storm sounds like a roaring beast, just like the man who's about to fuck me.

Munro wraps his arms around me and hoists me onto his lap. Our lips collide, and we waste no time on foreplay. We devour each other's mouths while groping and grunting, moaning and writhing. I can feel his hard cock every time I rock my hips into him. Soon, we're tearing each other's clothes off.

And there's no turning back now.

Chapter Eight

Munro

Our mouths stay fused while we desperately struggle to get naked. I lose track of whose shirt got ripped away first, and I have no idea where any of our garments landed. My eyes are closed. Natalie's must be too, considering the way she's thrusting her tongue into my mouth and clawing at my back. Her nails scrape my skin, but I dinnae care.

Buttons pop and fly away as I tear my shirt open, and I hear the sound of fabric rending apart. Natalie's tits rub against me, but she's still wearing her bra. Fortunately, the clasps are in front, so I grasp the halves and yank, destroying the wee hooks.

She grunts while we're still kissing.

I fling her bra away. She gropes around until she finds my fly and undoes the button, then thrusts her wee hands inside the jeans in an attempt to remove them. I try to help her by bucking my hips, but that makes her fall off my lap. Somehow, we keep consuming each other's mouths even while I get rid of my jeans.

Aye, I'm glad I didn't wear undergarments today.

Natalie pounces on me, but she's so overexcited that I cannae manage to get my cock inside her. *Bod an Donais*, I could *caith* just from the way she wriggles on my lap. I want to come inside her body, not on her belly.

When she clutches my *slat*, I take hold of her wrists to stop her from ending this before we've gotten started. I try to shift her hands behind her back, shackling them with my hands again, and move to flip us over on the sofa so one of us will be on top. But her frenzied passion will not be contained. We end up sideways on the sofa with her erse hanging off the edge. I can feel that, though I still can't open my eyes enough to see anything.

Natalie nips my bottom lip.

I grunt and lose my balance. That means we tumble to the floor and land between the sofa and the coffee table, trapped in the narrow space. I kick the table away. It sounds like the thing tumbled over and probably landed upside down. But when I open my eyes, I realize the table never tipped over. It slid across the floor, or more likely, scraped across it. Now that we have more room, I shove a hand between her thighs and run into a barrier—her knickers. A swift tug of my hand gets rid of that obstacle, and now I can feel how hot and wet she is.

And I need to feast on her.

"Oh, God, Munro," she cries out. "Don't stop, don't stop, I need you inside me."

"Dinnae worry. I'll be fucking ye very soon."

Thunder explodes. The walls tremble. Lightning blinds me, and a shrieking gale whirls around the cabin, but none of that penetrates my brain. I grasp her ankles and hoist them onto my shoulders, then dive my head down to devour her flesh. Her cream smells like honey and tastes so bloody good that I scrape my tongue up and down her cleft to lap up every last bit of it. She clutches my head, clawing at my scalp, and unintelligible noises tumble out of her. I've barely gotten going when her body tenses, and she comes.

Her cries are nearly drowned out by the thunder.

I keep feasting on her flesh, and just when she seems like she's done, I suck her clit into my mouth so I can lash it with my tongue, wringing another orgasm out of her. She almost sobs, as if the second climax was even stronger than the first.

"Munro, please, don't stop. Fuck me with your dick."

The desperation in her voice makes my cock throb. Cannae stop myself. I pick her up and lay her across the coffee table, which places her thighs at exactly the right height for me to drive into her. But I need her a wee bit closer. So, I grasp her hips and drag her toward me, then claim her body with one powerful thrust.

Natalie cries out and claws at the tabletop, her nails scratching the glossy surface.

I pound into her so hard and fast that the movements create a sucking sound with every thrust. I blow out a breath when I push inside her and suck in a breath when I pull out. The table begins to shake and creak and slide across the floor, forcing me to crawl forward on my knees to keep shagging her.

She thrashes her head and wraps her legs around my neck.

"Bloody hell," I snarl. "Are ye trying to strangle me?"

Natalie seems to have lost the power of speech, since the only sounds she emits are not words.

In a lull between thunderclaps, the table creaks and cracks—and collapses.

"Are ye hurt, Natalie? Talk to me, please."

"I'm fine. Don't you dare stop now."

My cock is still buried inside her which means there is no way I will stop. I stand up and take her with me, cradled in my arms, while my fevered mind tries to come up with a solution to the problem of where to fuck her. My brain decides, and I obey.

I leap over the broken table and don't stop until her back slams into the wall. She has her legs locked around my hips, and I start pounding into her again. I grunt and growl and slap my palms on the wall while pistoning my hips, taking her so hard that she slides up and down the wall with every inward lunge.

A throaty, feral shout erupts out of me just as another lightning bolt blinds me and the thunder from it detonates like an atomic bomb. Spasms rack my cock, compelling me to unleash everything with three more thrusts. I throw my head back and roar.

Then it's over.

We're both fighting for breath, and I still have my *slat* nestled inside her. She feels so good that I don't want to move, but after the crazed way I took her, I know I need to make sure I haven't injured the lass. I walk to the sofa and carefully set her down on the cushions. Then I take a seat beside her.

"Natalie, are you all right?"

"Uh-huh." Her tits rise and fall, bouncing a little, thanks to the fact she hasn't caught her breath yet. "That was—Oh God—Never had sex like that before."

"How do you feel?"

"Fantastic." Her lopsided grin gives me a strange feeling in my chest. "Let's do it again."

I try to chuckle but don't quite have the breath for it yet. "Need a wee rest first."

"Me too. But promise me you'll do that again and make me come even harder."

"Harder? Better pace yourself, lass."

She lets her head fall back against the sofa, shuts her eyes, and smiles with deep contentment. "Mm, but I need more mind-blowing sex. Never had that before, and I think you've gotten me addicted."

I rise and kiss her forehead, then wander over to the porch windows. "Looks like the storm is moving away. The lightning isn't as intense, and the wind has let up too."

"Holy shit, Munro, I will never think of thunderstorms the same way again. Rain has always made me feel horny, but insane sex during a severe storm turns me into a maniac. I like it."

"Does taking a shower in a bathroom get you randy too?"

"Sometimes. And when it does, I always have to masturbate in the shower."

I turn around and stare at her. The lass I met this morning, who seemed to despise me, just told me the keys to inflaming her lust. She wants more of me too. I shouldn't have had a poke with her once, so I definitely shouldn't take her again. But I want to, and I swear my *slat* is already rising to the task.

Natalie still has her eyes closed with that sensual smile curling her lips, but now she drags her fingers down her chest, over her tits. She sucks in a sharp breath when her fingertips graze her nipples. Then the lass drags her palms down her belly and slips one finger between her folds.

"Ah-ah-ah," I say as I saunter over to the sofa and sit down. "No one makes you come except me."

She parts her lids a sliver. "Then do something, Munro. I'm already getting hot and wet and achy again. The rain is turning me on so fast that I won't be able to wait much longer."

"Neither will I."

"Are you always this…passionate?"

I've finally regained the ability to breathe normally, so I chuckle. "That's putting it mildly. No, I have never been quite like this with any other woman. Must be the weather."

Natalie shifts her attention to my cock. "How long until you're ready for more?"

"I want you now, but it might take a wee bit longer until I can make good on that statement." I settle a hand on her thigh. "But I can give you pleasure right now."

"Could we talk a little first?"

"*Bod an Donais.* All you've done for most of today is talk."

She leans in close. "If you ever want to 'have a poke' with me again, better stop insulting me."

"We don't need to like each other in order to shag."

"I'd like us to have a civil conversation. Is that such a horrible idea?"

"Depends on the topic of conversation." I sigh and give up, pulling my hand away from her thigh. "What would you like to discuss?"

"Why do you live way out in the boonies?"

"Because it suits me."

"Come on, that's not a real answer. Why do you live this way? There must be a concrete reason that explains your need to hide in the woods. Does it have something to do with why you quit being a river guide?"

The woman really won't give up, will she? As much as she loves to blether, she seems to relish harassing me even more. But she's in luck. I feel very relaxed right now after our monumental poke, relaxed enough to answer her question. "I stopped being a river guide for one simple reason."

"And that reason is…"

"I died."

Her face goes blank even as her eyes flare wide.

Aye, that's the reaction I received the only other time someone asked me why I quit my job as a river guide.

"I don't understand," Natalie says. "You died? But you're still alive."

And that's almost verbatim the response that other someone came up with when I answered that question. Might as well tell her. "I was taking a newlywed couple on a whitewater rafting trip through the Grand Canyon. They wanted to experience the roughest stretch of the river, which meant Lava Falls Rapid."

"How rough is that one?"

"It's a class nine on a scale of one to ten."

The lass's lips fall open, and she stares at me.

"After passing through dozens of rapids without incident," I say, "we finally hit the big one and everything went wrong. First, the raft nearly flipped, but I managed to right it. I thought the worst was over, but then the most powerful wave yet struck the raft, and I was thrown out into the raging river. I don't know exactly what happened next. All I remember is the wife screaming, then I passed out. The next thing I knew, I was waking up on the shore and everyone was amazed that I'd come back to life. A mate of mine had seen me go into the water and rescued me, then he performed CPR."

Natalie keeps on gawping at me.

I face the wall and bar my arms over my chest. "That's how I died."

"But you came back. It was a near-death experience."

"Don't get any daft ideas about me going into a tunnel, heading toward the light. I didn't have any visions. Everything went black, then I woke up. I was clinically dead for three minutes and five seconds."

"Minutes? Holy shit, Munro."

Talking about my death and resurrection always makes me uncomfortable. Maybe it's anxiety. I don't know. But I dinnae like discussing that event. My only way out is with distraction. "So tell me, Natalie, why would a lass who has never kayaked before suddenly decide to take a river trip alone?"

"I needed to get away."

"From what?"

Her face pinches up, and she compresses her lips.

"I told you my story," I say. "Now it's your turn. I didn't want to do it either."

"Yeah, I know." She bows her head briefly, then looks straight at me. "My ex-husband wants to kill me."

Chapter Nine

Natalie

Munro stares at me without expression, as if he can't understand what I said, as if I'd spoken gibberish. I know it sounds insane. My husband wants me dead. It's the plot for a bad TV movie, not something that happens in real life. But this is my life, and it's real. How can I convince Munro of that? Maybe I shouldn't bother, but we had sex a few minutes ago, and that makes me feel like I should explain.

Besides, he told me about his near-death experience.

"Why would your ex-husband want to kill you?" Munro asks, his tone measured. "You talk too much sometimes, but that's no reason to murder someone."

"It's not my personality that he hates. Elliot wants to do away with me because I discovered his dirty little secret."

"Which is what?"

"Elliot ran a puppy-smuggling cartel."

Munro stares at me, unblinking, for several seconds. Then he shakes his head and chuckles. "You're having me on."

"No joke. It's true."

"Puppy smuggling? You must be off your head."

At first, I could understand his skepticism. But now I'm getting damn annoyed. "Why would I lie about something that sounds totally ridiculous? I couldn't believe it at first, but then I had no choice but to accept it's true."

"How did you uncover this puppy smuggling cartel?"

I hesitate to respond, only because I've had my fill of getting laughed off as a nutjob. But Munro doesn't seem like he'll react that way, so I force myself to tell him the rest. "Elliot was always on the make, looking for the next big thing that he was sure would make us rich. I worked full-time while he pursued his goal of becoming an entrepreneur. Then one day, he announced he'd found his dream job—as a dog trainer."

"That isn't a puppy cartel."

"I'm not done yet."

Munro rests his elbow on the sofa's back and props his head on his raised fist. "Go on. I'm listening."

"Well, I believed Elliot at first. But when he started working odd hours and going on 'business' trips every other week, I thought he was having an affair." I accidentally glance at Munro's naked dick and lose track of my thoughts for a few seconds. Then I shake it off and continue. "The next time he left on a 'business' trip, I followed him to the airport."

"What did you see there?"

"Elliot and his buddies didn't go into the terminal. They drove their van to a cargo area and loaded crates full of puppies onto a plane bound for Indonesia."

Munro no longer seems amused by my story. Now he's clearly interested.

"I didn't understand what was going on," I say. "But when Elliot got home, I confronted him. Asked if he was a drug mule, somehow using innocent puppies as cover. He laughed so hard his eyes watered. 'Drugs? I'm not into that shit.' That's what he told me. Then he admitted he was smuggling puppies of rare breeds into countries around the world where rich jackasses would pay big time. He even smuggled dog semen too, and fertilized embryos."

Munro's lips curl into a disgusted slant. "Dog what?"

"Embryos. Do I have to explain what that means? Because I don't know all the medical terminology."

"No, I understand what you said. Just can't believe anyone would smuggle puppies or dog embryos."

"Apparently, there's big money in it."

He strokes his beard while studying me. "Still haven't explained why you say your ex-husband wants to murder you."

"Because I found out his secret. Worse, I went to the FBI to tell them about it. Of course, those jerks laughed at me. 'You married the Al Capone of puppy smuggling,' they said. And they laughed at me some more. Then they told me to go home and 'have some babies' to keep myself busy."

"If no one believed your story, your husband had no reason to hurt you."

"Of course he did. I knew his secrets. He blabbed it all to me because he arrogantly assumed I would never tattle on him. I moved out of our house, and he sent his goons to kidnap me. They admitted their job was to interrogate and then murder me. I managed to get away from them." I hug my knees to my chest as the old anxiety trickles through me. "After that, I realized I needed a place to hide where no one would be able to find me. A kayaking trip in Wyoming sounded perfect."

"How long were you planning to stay here?"

I shrug. "Didn't think that far ahead."

Munro just watches me, and I can't decipher his expression. Is he disgusted? Disinterested? Maybe he thinks I'm a whackjob. Puppy smuggling does sound like the plot for a zany comedy movie. But I need him to believe me. No one else would, so I shouldn't get my hopes up. To have one person on earth believe in me and stand by me, that would be a miracle for sure.

The naked Scot blows out a breath. "All right, I believe you."

"Seriously?"

He nods.

And I throw my arms around his neck to smack kisses all over his face. "Thank you, Munro. Thank you so much."

"For what?"

"Believing in me."

He delicately pats my back. "Ah, you're welcome."

I finally pull away and see his baffled expression. "I don't expect you to help me. Just thought you should know that having me around is dangerous."

"You are not a danger to me. I was in the army, and I battled the worst rapids in the Grand Canyon more times than I can count. Your puppy smuggling cartel doesn't scare me."

"Elliot's goons might try to kill you too, if they find me here in your cabin."

He chuckles again, but this time the sound is infused with menace. "Dinnae worry about that. I saw combat in the army. If I could survive that, I can handle those smuggling scunners."

"Yeah, I believe you. But I don't want anything to happen to you because of me."

"I can handle whatever comes. That's not arrogance. It's experience."

He spoke those words in a level tone, not like he's bragging. I believe he really can handle any situation. I met Munro this morning, yet I suddenly realize I trust him. If I've lost my mind, oh well. My life can't suck any worse than it already does. But since I had sex with Munro, I no longer feel like the universe is against me. I have him on my side. The man who terrified hikers and came back from death will never let anything happen to me.

Yeah, I've probably lost my mind.

"Don't worry about your ex-husband," Munro says. "Tonight is for shagging."

"Oh, that sounds wonderful."

"Let's go out on the porch where you can hear the rain better. You said that makes you randy."

"It does." But the thought of getting it on with him again makes me hornier than the rain or anything else on earth possibly could. "Let's go out there right now."

He stands up, but before I can do the same, he sweeps me up in his arms. "No need to walk, lass. Save your energy for the fucking."

I link my hands at his nape and let the beast-man carry me away. His eyes enthrall me with their deep-blue color and the dark lines around the rims. Or maybe it's the man himself who enthralls me. I don't even care if he somehow drugged me so I'd want to screw him. Tonight, I will do what Munro suggested. I'll forget about everything else and revel in the way he makes me feel.

Munro pauses near the front door. "Grab that blanket, would you?"

"Blanket?"

He nods toward a lump on the floor, then bends his knees deeply so I can reach the fleece blanket and snatch it up. He opens the door without my help and leaves it open. Then he sets me on my feet, so he can spread the blanket out on the porch floor.

"Lie down, lass."

I follow his command. Though I'm not the type who does whatever a man tells me, Munro's voice makes me so hot for him that I want to obey his commands, especially when I know he's about to give me incredible pleasure.

He kneels between my legs and skims his gaze over my entire body while pumping his cock in a leisurely rhythm. His dick had been firming up already, but the way he keeps stroking himself gets him hard even faster. Watching that happen reignites my lust, compelling my body to grow slick and achy in preparation for whatever he might do to me.

"Taking it slow this time," he says. "Ahm meaning to feel and taste every inch of you."

"Yes, I want that."

Munro lies down beside me, on his side, and trails his fingertips down my arm, eliciting a delicious shiver. "Close your eyes and listen to the rain."

I let my lids flutter shut.

He trails his fingers over my throat, down between my breasts, and finally to my navel, where he slips a finger inside it to tease me. I clutch the blanket while he cups one of my breasts in his hand, massaging it delicately, rubbing his thumb over the nipple until my neck arches and I moan. His mouth descends on that peak as he licks and suckles it. He moves his hand to my belly, swirling his palm in slow circles until my back bows up and I gasp.

All the while, rain patters on the porch roof.

I'd always loved the sensual sound of rain, but here with Munro, it gets me so aroused that I can hardly catch my breath. My skin has become sensitized, so much that even the faint puffs of his breaths make me squirm.

He moves between my legs again, kissing a damp trail from my throat down to my mound where he nuzzles the hairs and blows heated breaths over my flesh. When I gasp again, he drags his palms down my sides to my hips, pushes his hands under my ass, and lifts. The position seems to give him better access, allowing him to rake his tongue down my cleft and back up again, over and over while his nose nudges my clit.

I blindly reach for him and wind up shoving my fingers into his hair. He chuckles against my flesh, the vibrations driving me crazy. "Hurry, please, I need to feel your dick penetrating me so deeply that it feels like you've become a part of me."

"Ahm needing that too."

Munro lifts my hips higher and plunges into me to the hilt. "Open your eyes, Natalie."

I obey, and the sight of his nude body melded with mine sends a thrill through me. To feel him filling me up again, it's the most incredible sensation.

He begins a slow rhythm of pumping in and out, as if he wants to feel every inch of me the way I need to feel him too. I've grown so wet, more than I've ever done before. After a few minutes, he lies down on top of me and continues thrusting at a leisurely pace even while he claims my mouth, devouring me with his lips and tongue as well as his cock. I lay my hands on his back, gliding them down to his ass and back up to his shoulders. I love the feel of his muscles moving under my hands, powerful and controlled.

The rain grows heavier, pounding on the roof.

And Munro speeds up his pace. I lock my legs around his hips and dig my nails into his back, but he doesn't notice or doesn't care that I'm scraping his skin. He grunts with every powerful thrust, faster, faster, while my heart pounds and I can barely breathe with his mouth sealed over mine. At last, he tears his mouth away, gasping and grunting, his gaze locked on to mine.

Wordless cries erupt out of me.

Munro drops his head onto my shoulder. He bends his knees, which gives him enough power to thrust more deeply. Thunder rumbles in the distance just as I come. The spasms inside me seem to make him go wild, as he raises onto his straight arms to fuck me with even more power, and my body bounces. Waves of pleasure ripple through me, stealing my breath while I clutch his biceps and ride out the climax. Munro comes too, throwing his head back to shout. After two more thrusts, he pulls out and lies down beside me.

For a moment, neither of us moves. We look at each other, and Munro's mouth twists into a crooked smile. I can't summon the energy for any kind of smile, too dazed by what this man I barely know can do to me with his incredible body. And I finally recognize one inescapable fact.

I'm addicted to Munro MacTaggart.

Chapter Ten

Munro

I take a moment to appreciate how bonnie Natalie looks right after she comes, with her cheeks flushed and her lips swollen and rosy. The lass clearly loves sex, though it sounds as if she never enjoyed it as much as she wanted. Her *bod ceann* of a husband must not have cared about her pleasure. Now that I know more about her, I think I finally understand why she behaves the way she does. Her incessant talking is probably a nervous reaction, and she must've been terrified when she saw me leap out of the river.

I exhale a long, satisfied sigh. "We should always have a poke in the rain. It makes you wild with lust for me."

"Does the same to you. And you're much wilder than I am."

"Aye. My family calls me 'Wild Man,' and that's not hyperbole. Though I think my cousin Errol is the most insane MacTaggart. He blows things up, after all."

"He does what?" She pushes up onto her elbows. "Are you serious? He's some kind of pyromaniac?"

"No. Errol only uses those skills for a good reason, like blasting a hole out of the side of a mountain so we could reach the treasure hidden inside it."

"You went treasure hunting?"

"It's a long story. There was a legend about an ancient hoard in the Grand Canyon. Nobody believed it, except for my cousin Errol and Ashley Hartman." I think back on that expedition and everything we endured to liberate that prize. Sometimes I can't quite believe it actually happened. "Didn't you see the newspaper stories about the Grand Canyon hoard?"

"Now that you mention it, I did hear something about that. But nothing I read mentioned three Scots finding the treasure."

"Two Scots. Ashley is American."

"Did you get a reward for finding the hoard?"

"No. The United States doesn't give rewards to treasure hunters. We also might have broken a few laws in the process, though only to make sure no villains captured the hoard."

Natalie turns onto her side, propped up with one elbow. "Did you actually bump into villains?"

"Oh, aye. But that's a story for another day." I run my thumb over her bottom lip. "I need to feed you now."

"I am suddenly ravenous. Dinner wasn't that long ago, but I could eat a big old ribeye steak all by myself."

"Then it's time to go back inside the cabin." I pick her up and set her on her feet, then grab the blanket. "Maybe there will be another storm later."

"Do you think about anything other than sex?"

"That's a ridiculous question. Of course I think about many other things, like how to feed us and how to get all my work done when you're here distracting me."

"Oh, so it's my fault you're goofing off."

"Goofing?" I palm her erse. "No, lass, I'm performing my sacred duty as a Wild Man."

Laughter bursts out of her. "Are you seriously suggesting you're a sex god? I mean, you did just call screwing me your sacred duty."

"I'm no god. I'm a savage demon sent from hell to steal your virtue."

"You're too late. I lost my virtue a long time ago."

Clasping her hand, I lead Natalie back into the house. She searches for her clothes while I move the destroyed table into the far corner where it won't get in our way. I've now earned the right to brag to my cousins about how I shagged a woman so thoroughly that we broke a piece of furniture, but I will never share that story with anyone. I might be an untamed beast, but even I respect a woman's privacy.

We eat a hearty snack on the sofa, and Natalie keeps gawping at my body. I chose to remain au naturel. I don't think that bothers her anymore. She simply can't stop admiring me. I don't have the option to admire her body since she covered it up again.

The lass eyes me with curiosity. "Thought you didn't let anyone eat on your sofa."

"I never have before. But you might have been uncomfortable sitting on a stool after the workout I gave you."

"That was very considerate, Munro." Her gaze wanders over my body yet again. "Are you a nudist?"

"I'm nude right now, so I suppose the answer is yes."

"But are you officially a nudist? I've heard there are resorts for people who like to vacation in the buff."

"I know." Maybe I enjoy shocking her, and that's the reason I tell her, "My cousin Catriona got married at a nudist resort in Oregon. Most of the guests were naked for at least some of the time."

"Seriously? A nudist wedding. That's crazy." She leans toward me a wee bit. "Did you go naked at the wedding?"

"I didn't attend that event."

"Why not? Are you such a hermit that you wouldn't go to a family gathering?"

"Aye, I'm the worst hermit on earth." I try not to scowl at her but only half succeed. It's not her fault. I don't like talking about my past. "I'm sorry for growling at you again. But I didn't go to the wedding because I'd only just had my near-death experience. Couldn't handle seeing the whole clan."

"Have you seen them since then?"

I scratch the back of my neck and grimace. "No, I haven't."

"But you have seen your cousin Errol."

"That's right. He told me about the nudist wedding."

Natalie tucks her legs beneath her and wriggles around to face me. "So, we're both running away from someone, hmm?"

"I reckon we are. What should we do about that?"

She shrugs. "Nothing I can do. But you could go home and see your family. Don't your parents miss you? Or maybe your siblings?"

"Dinnae have siblings. My parents don't approve of my lifestyle choices and wouldn't want to see me."

"How do you know? Have you asked them?"

I fight back the urge to snarl at her. It isn't Natalie's fault that I'm a *bod ceann*. So instead of acting like a bear, I sigh and shake off my irritation. "I should ring them. Maybe I will sometime. What will you do? Can't hide in my cabin forever."

"Because you like your solitude. I'm infringing on your hermitage."

"No. But you belong out in the world."

She slants toward me. "So do you, Munro. At least I have a concrete excuse for hiding out."

I don't want to talk about this anymore, which means I need to change the subject in my own subtle way. That means I leap off the sofa and declare, "Time for bed. You take the sofa, and I'll sleep on the porch, just as we agreed earlier."

"We didn't agree. You commanded that's what we would do."

"And it is what we'll do."

She jumps up to stab a finger into my chest. "You can't sleep on the porch. What if there's another severe storm?"

"What do you suggest?"

"It's obvious. We share the sofa bed." She presses her body to mine, tipping her head back. "We've already had sex twice. Can't be shy about sleeping with me after that."

"Not shy. I was trying to be a gentleman."

A sly smile stretches her lips. "Interesting. So you think being a gentleman involves growling and snarling."

I grasp her erse. "It involves shagging too."

Natalie wriggles away from me. "I need sleep. How do we open the sofa bed?"

"Step back."

Her brows wrinkle, but she follows my order.

I fling the cushions toward the kitchen and yank the sofa bed open. "That's how we do it."

"You have no idea what subtlety is, do you?"

"It's a waste of time and effort."

Since I left the sheets and blanket on the bed when I folded it up last night, we don't need to do much to get it ready for use again. To my surprise, Natalie strips and crawls into bed with me completely nude. I guess the lass likes being naked with me, and she probably hopes I'll seduce her in the middle of the night. Maybe I will. If there's another storm, I will most definitely do that.

I never used to think thunder and rain were erotic, but Natalie changed my mind.

Hours later, I rouse briefly when I hear distant thunder and the light patter of rain on the roof. But Natalie doesn't stir at all. I decide not to wake her solely to satisfy my insatiable lust for her. Besides, she looks bonnie and sweet while she sleeps. I rise in the morning while Natalie still slumbers and whip up a good breakfast for her. I gave the lass quite a workout last night. After her ordeal when she lost her kayak, she deserves something more than oatmeal or toaster waffles.

She walks into the kitchen just as I've finished cooking our meal.

My brows shoot up. "Becoming a naturist, Natalie?"

"What?" she says while yawning. Then she glances down at herself. "Oops. I completely forgot I'm not wearing a nightie."

"Doesn't bother me."

"That's obvious." She hops onto a stool and smirks. "Unless your clothes are invisible. Do you often cook in the nude?"

"A man who lives alone in the wilderness can do whatever he bloody well pleases."

She folds her arms over her chest and raises her brows. Her skeptical expression tells me I need to confess.

"I generally wear clothes, in the house and outside. But I always bathe in the nude, even when I do that outdoors."

"Fair enough." She rests her arms on the island and scans me from head to toe. Her lips curl into a sly smile. "So, did you put on a nudie show strictly for me yesterday?"

"Not entirely for that reason." I lean across the island. "But mostly for your benefit. You do love it when I'm naked, aye?"

"Oh yeah, for sure."

"But we will need to dress after breakfast. My mate Owen should be coming this morning with the new transmission for my truck."

Natalie sits up straighter, her eyes alight with excitement. "I get to meet him?"

"No, I thought I'd lock you in the bathroom while he's here. I'll need to tape your mouth shut too."

"Ha-ha. I'm looking forward to meeting one of your friends."

After breakfast, we both dress for the monumental occasion. Natalie called it that. I don't consider it a grand event, though it is relatively rare for me to have guests. Maybe I have let myself get into a rut of not wanting to deal with other people. My time in the Grand Canyon with Errol and Ashley reminded me of how much I love an adventure, but despite that, I haven't made any plans to do…anything.

Have I become afraid to take risks? No, that's impossible.

While we wait for Owen, Natalie and I have a nice conversation about nothing of importance, just chatting and making each other laugh. It's possible I had become sort of a grumpy, growly grizzly bear. Natalie described me that way. I would never have used that phrase, though I can't deny she may be right. I feel much more relaxed since last night. Aye, an incredible poke has lightened my mood considerably.

Natalie seems more relaxed too.

"How old are you?" she asks. "I can't tell when you've got that big beard and long hair. You could be thirty or fifty. I'm thirty-eight, by the way."

"I'm forty-three." Why does she keep mentioning my beard and hair? I suppose she might be implying that she doesn't like my "scruffy" style. She didn't seem to mind last night.

"Have you ever been married? You know about my marriage."

Which means I should tell her about mine, even though I would rather not. "I was married once. The lass thought she could change me and convince me to take a corporate job. I'd been working as a hiking guide in the Highlands, and I made a good living that way. I refused to quit. So Eilidh left me."

"I'm so sorry, Munro."

"That happened years ago. By the time our divorce was finalized, I needed to get away, somewhere far from Scotland. I spent a large chunk of my savings on a holiday in America, visiting all the places I'd never seen before because I'd never visited this country."

Natalie is sitting right beside me, and I've had my arm across the sofa's back behind her. But now I feel the need to pull away. I won't do it, though. Until this morning, I had avoided thinking about why I hide in the woods, why I left Scotland in the first place, and why I avoid human connections. But being with Natalie has encouraged me to consider the reasons and come to terms with them.

"My divorce was bitter," I say. "Eilidh seemed to want to punish me for not changing myself to please her. I love the outdoors. She preferred the city. I should've realized how different we were before we married, but I've never been the most insightful man."

"Love is blind, right? I didn't realize what Elliot was like until it was too late."

"At least my ex-wife doesn't want to kill me." I slide a wee bit closer to her. "After a month in America, I reached the Grand Canyon and took a rafting tour. The whitewater rapids captivated me, and I knew I wanted to make a new life there."

"Until your accident."

"Aye. I'm not afraid of rafting these days, but I don't feel the thrill of it anymore."

She settles a hand on my knee. "But you aren't happy as a recluse either, are you?"

I shake my head. "Lately, I've been thinking…"

Chapter Eleven

Natalie

I wait for Munro to finish that sentence, but he seems like he can't quite do it. Well, he *can*. But maybe he feels like it would be unmanly to say whatever it is. Men can be so weird about emotional issues, especially if it involves their fears. Munro hasn't wanted to talk to me about his past very much, so I don't want to say anything that might make him clam up again.

Finally, he rubs his forehead and sighs. "I feel as if saying it out loud will make me sound like an eejit."

"Sounds like that means 'idiot,' but you aren't a moron. Please tell me what you've been thinking. I'd like to know."

He scrubs a hand over his face and groans. "I keep thinking about Scotland, about the Highlands where I grew up and lived for most of my life. And I…miss my family."

"You make that sound like it's a shameful thing."

"Maybe it is. I abandoned my homeland and my clan, from my parents to my many cousins, without any warning. How could they welcome me back after that?"

I inch closer. "Your cousin Errol didn't care that you'd left. He went on an expedition with you."

"Errol needed my help. But he did also try to convince me to go home with him and Ashley. I couldn't do it. Gave him a stupid excuse and ran away."

"But you want to go home. So just do it."

He lifts his brows. "Ye think it's that easy?"

"For the Wild Man, yes. If you can fight villains in the Grand Canyon and swim down a river to chase away the creeps who stole my stuff, you can definitely handle going home."

He stares at me for a minute or two as if he's struggling to figure out how much he should confess to me. I hope he feels like he can tell me anything, but honestly, we met yesterday and I wouldn't blame him for being reticent.

A breath blusters out of him, and his entire posture sags. He bows his head briefly, then meets my gaze. "Why do I feel stronger when I'm with you? I don't understand it. But your presence makes me feel as if I could climb Mount Everest or dive to the bottom of the ocean without any gear. Just having a conversation with you alleviates the worries I've lived with ever since my near-death experience in the Grand Canyon."

Holy shit. I didn't expect him to confess that much. No other guy I've ever known would have blurted out all that intensely personal information.

Munro scrunches up his face and averts his gaze. "I said too much."

"No. I'm still processing what you did say, though. Don't stop. Unburden yourself as much as you need to."

"Will you do the same?"

"After you're done talking, I'll share anything you want to know about me."

He tips his head to the side as if he's trying to figure me out, but he quickly gives up on that. "Here's what fashes me the most. Will my family accept me if I return to Scotland? The MacTaggarts never turn their backs on a family member. We are a fiercely loyal lot. But I've been gone for six years and haven't stayed in touch with anyone except Errol."

"Maybe you're comfortable talking to him because he's a wild man too."

He opens his mouth, about to tell me something that I sense I will really want to hear, when someone bangs on the front door.

"You in there, Munro?" a man shouts. "Got your transmission, if you still want that."

Munro and I stare at each other for a moment. The sudden arrival of his friend Owen seems to have burst the bubble we'd been cocooned in for the past twenty-four hours.

"Open up, Wild Man," Owen shouts as he pounds on the door again.

Munro jogs over there and yanks the door open. "Haud yer wheesht. Ahm-no deaf."

"Thought maybe you were busy showing your guest some Scottish hospitality."

Oh, yeah, our guest said that word in a tone that implies Munro was in the middle of screwing me when Owen arrived. We weren't doing that, unfortunately. I love getting down and dirty with Munro. But not in front of someone else.

Munro steps back and waves an arm. "Come inside. You are welcome in my abode."

I just manage to squelch a laugh. His abode? I assume he's being sarcastic.

Owen's brows knit together as he walks past Munro. Our guest shakes his head slightly while his lips form a cautious smile. "Never seen you in such a good mood before. Usually, you greet me with a growl and a grumpy statement about how you don't like visitors."

"Dinnae say that. You're exaggerating."

This time, I can't stifle the laughter that erupts from from me. I've still been lounging on the sofa, but now I jump to my feet and come up beside Munro while still laughing. I curl my arm around his. "You absolutely do behave that way. But it's part of your Wild Man charm."

"You two are off your heads."

"Says the man who terrified a group of hikers who mistook him for an alien Sasquatch from another dimension. No idea where they got that idea. I mean, it's not like you jumped out of the river completely naked with your long hair flying and snarled at them."

Owen grins. "This is great. The Wild Man finally got a girlfriend, and she's feisty. Congrats, Munro."

"What are you congratulating me for?" The Scot pushes me behind his body. "And don't be looking at her."

"Jealousy? That's new. You must really like this girl." Our guest leans sideways to peek around Munro's shoulder. "I'm Owen Metzger, by the way. Who are you?"

"Natalie Saari." I sidle away from Munro and thrust a hand out to Owen. "It's wonderful to meet you at last. Munro told me you're his friend and that you'd be bringing the new transmission. But that's all I know about you."

"Did Munro tell you what he does for me?"

"Nope. Not a peep."

The Scot blows out a breath through his nostrils, making them flare like an angry bull.

I nudge him with my elbow. "Take it easy. I'm curious, but I won't push you to tell me what you do for a living."

Owen arches his brows at Munro. "If she's your girlfriend, maybe you should tell her. It's nothing to be ashamed of."

"Natalie is not—*Mhac na galla.* You two are forcing me to share information, and it's verging on mental torture."

"Chill, Munro," Owen says, raising his hands palms out. "Your deep, dark secret is safe with me."

Munro bows his head, and his shoulders flag. "No, I should explain it to Natalie."

I throw my hands up. "Honestly, you don't need to do it on my account. We haven't known each other long."

The man who gave me incredible orgasms last night glances at me sideways. Then he pulls in a deep breath and raises his head. "I'm a freelance book editor. I do all types of editing—developmental, structural, content, line edits, copyediting, proofreading. Most of my clients want only copyediting and proofreading, though."

I might be gaping at him. Munro hasn't seemed like the kind of man who would want to be glued to a computer all day. I suppose he did what he had to do to make a living, but being a book editor is so far away from his previous jobs.

"You've shocked your girl," Owen says. "Better explain before she passes out."

Munro turns toward me and clears his throat. "I met Owen during my month-long holiday in America. When he told me about his chosen profession, I was very curious. We talked for quite a while, and Owen told me that he's had trouble finding a reliable copyeditor and would I like to give it a go. I knew nothing about editing."

"But Owen hired you anyway."

"Aye. He gave me five manuals on editing, and I studied them for six months before I would agree to try working on his newest book."

Owen grins. "And he rocked the editing. Munro might seem like an antisocial polar bear, but he can be pretty chatty sometimes. He has an innate understanding of language too, which I think most people wouldn't recognize."

"Yeah, I've seen that," I say. "Munro might spout Scottish-isms and Gaelic words now and then, but he's very eloquent."

Munro veers his gaze to me, his eyes wide.

I bump my shoulder into him. "It's true. You're eloquent."

"But I had never edited a book before. I wouldn't have tried to do it if Owen hadn't encouraged me."

"There was a bump in the road, though," Owen says. "Munro got a little bashful when it came to the, uh, special scenes in my books."

I glance from Owen to Munro and back again. "What kind of special scenes?"

Munro growls. "What does it matter?"

"You can tell me. Whatever it is, I won't freak out and run away."

"Owen writes romance novels." He winces. "And I edit all of them, including the explicit fucking scenes."

"The term is 'love scenes,' Munro," Owen says. "My ex-wife used to call them 'those dirty bits that everyone skips over,' but she didn't appreciate the romance genre. Or maybe it was my writing she didn't like."

Munro grunts. "Naomi sounds like a right bitch."

"We're all divorced?" I say. "No wonder you and Owen became friends."

"Your husband must've been a total dick," Owen says. "Why else would he let a beautiful, feisty woman get away?"

"We might be divorced, he hasn't let me go. My marital problems are way different than yours or Munro's."

Should I tell Owen that my ex-husband wants to kill me? It's one of those conversational gray areas, like whether to admit you're an exotic dancer. I'm not a stripper, and a murderous ex hardly compares to that.

Owen doesn't ask for more information, and Munro doesn't spill the beans. I didn't think he would. For reasons I can't explain, I trust him to keep my secrets.

While Munro and Owen go outside to begin replacing the transmission in Munro's truck, I get on the internet to do a teeny bit of snooping. First, I look up the Grand Canyon treasure and find quite a few articles about it. Errol and Munro are not mentioned, but he had told me they couldn't take credit for the find because they broke some rules in the process. After that, I search for the MacTaggart clan. I stumble onto the website of a metaphysical shop in the village of Loch Fairbairn in Scotland that's owned by Kirsty Turner of Clan MacTaggart. Is that one of Munro's cousins? More searching gives me additional names—Rory MacTaggart, a solicitor; Aidan MacTaggart, the owner of a construction company; and Evan MacTaggart, the billionaire owner of a tech company.

I also find several articles about Magnus MacTaggart, who is sometimes referred to as a bounty hunter and sometimes as a private investigator. Those articles also include mentions of Errol Murdoch. That must be Munro's cousin. He might have a different last name if his mother was a MacTaggart who married into another clan. The same could be true of Kirsty.

When I get bored with scouring the web, I head outside to see what the boys are up to out there. I bring with me a tray that holds three glasses of lemonade. I'd found a pitcher of it in the refrigerator.

Owen notices me first, waving and smiling. "Did you bring us refreshments?"

"Yep. I hope you like lemonade."

Munro lifts his head out of the depths of the engine compartment. "You put ice in it."

"That's the usual way to serve lemonade. It tastes fresh. Did you make this a few days ago?"

"No. I made it this morning. And aye, it is fresh squeezed."

I offer the tray to Owen and Munro, who both take a glass. Then I enjoy my first taste of Munro's lemonade. "Mm, wow. This is delicious."

"Can't believe I made it, can you?"

"Of course I can believe it. I'm surprised you would bother, that's all."

"I knew we'd be having a guest, and I thought lemonade would be a nice refreshment."

While I set the tray down, the men begin to discuss the logistics of replacing the transmission. I don't understand most of their conversation. Car stuff has never held much interest for me. But I enjoy listening to them and watching their hand gestures while they work things out. Apparently, they'd spent most of the time so far removing the old transmission or at least parts of it. I can tell they're good buddies just by their tone of voice and their body language. I bet neither man would admit to the other that they're close friends. Men can be so goofy about that.

Once they get going with installing the new transmission, I become fascinated by their interactions. They rib each other and laugh about it. Munro occasionally threatens to "skelp" Owen for minor infractions like dropping a wrench. Owen just laughs and slaps Munro on the back. I wish I had a friend like that. Nobody really wanted to hang out with me, but I only found out after the divorce that Elliot had been treating our neighbors like enemies, which drove them away. I think he wanted to keep me isolated, so I wouldn't tattle on him. I hadn't known about his nefarious activities back then, but he probably thought it was preemptive isolation.

Now, I am literally isolated—alone in the remote woods with two strangers. But I've never felt safer in my life.

Chapter Twelve

Munro

Natalie seems fascinated by the way Owen and I discuss the technicalities of replacing a transmission, and she even smiles as if she's watching a wonderful movie. She seems more interested in watching Owen than observing me, which does not matter to me at all. Let her become infatuated with the romance novelist. Dinnae care.

Owen glances at Natalie and smirks. Then he plunges his head deep into the engine compartment, an action that is completely unnecessary. "Hey, look. I found your missing sense of humor, Munro."

I rattle off a long string of the nastiest Gaelic curses I know. I'm not jealous. Owen annoyed me because…he's a damn eejit.

Owen chuckles. "Yeah, that sounds menacing when you growl stuff I don't understand. But for all I know, you're reciting your grocery list."

"Ahmno doing that." I glare down at the interior of the engine. "Need a torque wrench."

"Don't have one."

"I'll get it."

I jog back into the house. As I return from my mission to find a torque wrench, I hear Natalie and Owen talking.

"Hey, Owen, how many steamy romance novels have you written?"

"A hundred and fifty-two."

The lass blinks slowly twice, clearly baffled in the most adorable way. "Wow, that sounds like a lot."

He shrugs one shoulder. "I've been writing for fifteen years. Took a long time to develop a fan base and figure out how to market my books. And I was, uh, kind of embarrassed to be writing what my dad calls 'girlie' books."

"Does he read your novels?"

"Are you kidding? He has no idea what kind of stories I write. Everyone I know, except for my ex-wife, still thinks I write technical manuals for a living."

Though I can't explain why, I stop at the corner of the house where they won't see me and eavesdrop on their conversation.

"I hope I'm not offending you with my questions," Natalie says. "I've never met a real author in person."

He walks around to the front bumper, halting near her. "I don't mind if you ask. My family wouldn't understand why I love crafting a hot sex scene. Naomi, my ex-wife, used to make fun of me."

"That's awful."

"I've moved past all that. Mostly." He lays a hand on the truck, leaning into it while he gazes down at the truck's innards. "I write under a pseudonym so nobody will figure out what I do for a living. Only Munro knows about my pen name."

"What is it? Sorry, that's none of my business."

"That's okay. I can tell you're a trustworthy person. I write as Desiree Lachance."

"I love that pseudonym. It's perfect for romance." Natalie watches while Owen does something inside the engine compartment, then asks another question. "You said only Munro knows your pen name. But don't your agent and publisher know too?"

"Nope. I self-publish. Bad experiences with publishers and agents made me realize I want full control over my books." He raises his head to look at her. "I told you my secret. Mind if I ask what you do for a living?"

"I'm a landscape designer."

"Cool. My lawn could sure use your help."

Finally, I give up spying and stride back to where Natalie and Owen have been waiting for me.

Owen grins and slaps my arm. "You're one lucky guy. Natalie will whip your lawn into shape lickety-split."

"What are you talking about?"

"Your girl is a landscape designer."

Aye, I already knew that thanks to my eavesdropping, but I don't understand why she hadn't mentioned that fact to me before Owen showed up. I swerve my attention to the lass. "Why didn't I know that?"

"Because you never asked. Besides, I don't know if I'll ever be a landscape designer again."

Owen seems like he's about to ask a question. But I jump in and begin barking orders to Owen, distracting him from interrogating Natalie any further. I could tell she was growing anxious about what Owen might ask her next. She told me about her ex-husband and his vendetta against her, which is the reason why she might not have any need for a job soon. She shouldn't feel compelled to share that information. I know Owen didn't mean to back her into a corner, but he did.

Natalie aims a grateful smile at me. Then she watches with seemingly rapt interest while Owen and I wrestle with automotive parts. Soon, we're drenched with sweat and grease and other things I can't identify. Owen takes his shirt off and wipes his brow with it.

And Natalie sits up straighter, her lips curling up a wee bit at the corners.

Does she find him attractive? That thought spurs me to do a dead stupid thing. I strip my shirt off too.

Natalie rubs her palms together and licks her lips. "Ooh, man candy. I love that. Show as much skin as you want, boys. This is better than TV."

I might have appreciated that statement if she hadn't included both of us in it.

At lunchtime, Natalie offers to whip up some sandwiches for us. Owen barely notices what she said, too engrossed in working on the truck to pay attention to the sexy lass. I pretend not to notice when she leaves to make lunch, though I watch her peripherally. But when she returns carrying a tray full of sandwiches, potato chips, and beer, Owen and I both finally lift our heads out of the truck.

"I brought you lunch, boys, in case you want to eat. But if you'd rather gnaw on tree bark—"

"No, we'd love some sandwiches," Owen says. "I'm famished."

I drop my wrench into my trouser pocket. "I could eat too."

Natalie's lips pucker.

Maybe she has a right to be annoyed with me. I did sound less than enthusiastic about eating the food she graciously made for us. I'm worn-out from a long morning of working on the truck, but she must think I'm disinterested in her. That's rubbish. Am I behaving like a teenage laddie? I haven't felt his confused by a woman since before my divorce.

We all sit inside my truck to enjoy our picnic lunch, and Owen recounts bloody stupid stories about supposedly humorous things I had done or said or "growled about" over the years that we've known each other. If Natalie hadn't already thought I was a recluse, she must be certain of that now, considering the way Owen describes me.

After the laddie's ten thousandth anecdote, Natalie gazes at me for a moment. But instead of speaking to me, she turns to Owen. "I thought Munro was a hermit, but his relationships with you and his cousin Errol contradict my assumptions. How often do you and Munro get together?"

"Two or three times a week."

Natalie has frozen so completely that I wonder if time has actually ground to a halt in a wee bubble around her. But no, I decide it's abject shock that makes her behave that way. The only response she offers doesn't qualify as real words. "Whuh—huh?"

What is wrong with the lass? Owen announced that he visits me a few times a week. That's nothing so shocking that it should render her speechless.

Owen switches his gaze back and forth between me and Natalie, clearly confused.

At last, she regains the power of speech. "Munro said he doesn't like having guests. He's a loner."

"When did I say that to you?" I ask. "Never. You invented words that I did not speak."

"Oh, please. You were so rude to me yesterday, and it didn't take a genius to figure out you are a recluse. I mean, you hide in the desolate woods to avoid the rest of humanity, including your own family."

"That's bollocks. Maybe I prefer not to have guests, which doesn't make me a recluse. Owen is a friend, anyway, and that's different."

"Uh-huh, sure. What do you guys do together? Play poker?"

"We discuss Owen's books, and sometimes we blether about sports or current events."

Owen gives my arm a light punch. "The only sport you care about is Highland games."

"What else is there?" I huff. "Football is bloody stupid, whether it's the American version or the real sort."

"The real sort?" Natalie asks.

"He means soccer," Owen tells her. "Everywhere else in the world that's what 'football' means."

"Oh, right. I don't watch any kind of sports."

I lean over to wipe a bit of mayonnaise off the corner of her mouth. "You haven't seen Highland sports, have you? Now that's a true athletic competition. The MacTaggarts love a good round of games—caber toss, hammer throw, haggis hurling."

"I thought haggis was food."

"Aye, it is. But hurling a haggis has become a unique Scottish sport too."

"Okay. That sounds totally bizarre."

"It's not bizarre. It's imaginative."

After lunch, Natalie goes back into the cabin to stare at the wall while listening to music. Maybe I know that because I sort of followed her and peeked through the window. All right, I had my ear plastered to the glass. She plays her music so loud that I can hear hints of it. I suppose the boredom of being stranded in the back of beyond will drive a lass to do unhealthy things. That means more than ruining her eardrums, in this case. I watch with rapt fascination while she consumes an entire can of cashews that she found in a cupboard. When a few fall down between the cushions, the barmy woman excavates them and shoves the lot into her mouth.

"Are you done spying yet?"

Owen's whispered query jerks me away from my spying—ah, reconnaissance mission. I need to know more about the woman who's on the run from her criminal ex-husband. So I ignore Owen's question and quietly hurry across the porch to jump onto the grass where he waits for me.

"Kind of obsessed with her, aren't you?" Owen asks as we make our way back to the truck. "Secretly watching her through the window isn't the sign of a healthy mind."

"*Falbh dàirich fhein.*"

"Oh-ho-ho, I know I've hit a nerve when you bring out the Gaelic. What does that phrase mean?"

I throw him a sideways scowl that doesn't fash him at all. His only response is to grin and slap my arm again. He loves to do that.

And Natalie thinks *I'm* strange.

Maybe I did tell Owen to go fuck himself. He deserved it.

We spend three more hours working on the transmission, then realize we won't get it done today. I invite Owen to stay overnight in the cabin, and he accepts my offer. How will Natalie feel about it? Owen is too exhausted to drive home, so the lass will simply need to adapt to another guest in the house. But I haven't thought of her as a guest, not today. Not since last night, actually. Aye, not since we had a poke.

Owen and I waltz into the house, but Natalie doesn't notice. She's still playing her music too loud.

I step in front of her.

She yelps and jumps, which results in the cord for her earbuds getting stuck under her erse. That causes them to be yanked out of her ears and tumble onto her lap. Her eyes have gone wide, and she's breathing hard.

Natalie kicks my shin. "Dammit, Munro, I thought a Sasquatch was coming to kill me. But no, it's just a filthy Scot—and I'm not calling you names. You have oil and grease and who knows what else all over your face, arms, and clothes."

I squint at her. "What's fashing you now?"

"Oh, nothing, really. I had a heart attack, that's all." She lays a hand on her chest. "Do you have a defibrillator?"

"Dinnae be ridiculous."

Owen comes up beside me. "I don't know, Sasquatch. Looks to me like you gave her a serious fright. She might need mouth-to-mouth. I'm happy to perform that life-saving maneuver so you don't have to."

"Haud yer wheesht, ye *cacan*." I ram my elbow into Owen's side, pushing him away from Natalie.

"Are you boys done acting like teenagers?" she asks. "I hope there was a valid reason for scaring the shit out of me."

"You shouldn't play your music so loud," I say. "It's bad for your hearing."

"Thank you for your concern. But sending me into cardiac arrest is not a good solution."

I sit down beside her and clasp the lass's hand. "*Tha mi duilich, gràidh.* Scaring you wasn't my intention."

"What was that thing you just said?"

Owen rests his erse on the sofa's arm. "He was speaking Gaelic, but Munro doesn't like to translate for us Americans."

"I said I'm sorry, Natalie."

"So, '*gràidh*' is my name in Gaelic?"

No, it isn't. But if I tell Natalie that I called her "darling," she might get the wrong idea. I can't date the lass or whatever romantic rubbish women expect a man to give them. I have no intention of leaving the wilderness or my house. A woman like her needs to take part in society, while I have purposely removed myself from all that nonsense. I will never answer her question. She'll forget about it soon enough. The woman blethers so much that she can't possibly remember a passing comment for more than an hour.

But do I want her to forget?

Chapter Thirteen

Natalie

Munro scared the living daylights out of me when he leaped in front of me, but now he's holding my hand, seeming genuinely sorry for what happened. This man confuses me so much. He treated me like an unwanted guest, then we had amazing sex, and today he seemed jealous whenever I talked to Owen. Now he wants to comfort me.

"Do you forgive me for frightening you?" Munro asks.

I put on a sarcastic version of his scowl. But I can't hold that for long, so I let my features relax. "Yeah, I forgive you. But I need to apologize too. I called you a Sasquatch and a filthy Scot."

"That's all right. I forgive you."

"Wow," Owen says. "Munro definitely has a crush on you, Natalie. He still hasn't forgiven me for losing his crescent wrench, even though I bought him a brand-spanking new one."

Munro completely ignores Owen's comments, keeping his focus exclusively on me. His hand feels warm and surprisingly soft considering his rugged lifestyle. The blue of his eyes draws me in, and the rest of the world seems to fade away.

Owen clears his throat. "Should I wait outside?"

"No," Munro says. He releases my hand but doesn't move away from me. "I invited Owen to stay overnight. He's too exhausted to drive home. Do you mind?"

"No, of course not." I glance around. "But, um, where will he sleep?"

"On the floor. I have a sleeping bag he can use."

"And where will I sleep?"

Munro looks at Owen, who smirks and holds his hands up. "Your call, Sasquatch. I can bunk on the porch if you two need some alone time."

"Do ye think I want to shag Natalie with you ten feet away?"

"You and I will share the bed," I announce. "Platonically."

Damn, I wish we didn't have a guest for the night. I'm jonesing for more wicked-hot sex with the Wild Man. Okay, those are words I never imagined I would think. But it's true. I've been a prisoner of my fears, biting my nails every day while I wait for Elliot to catch up to me. Being with Munro makes me feel…free.

And I don't care how crazy that is.

Since the men still haven't reacted to my declaration, I go for the shock and awe approach to waking them from their trances. "The other option is for you guys to share the bed while I sleep on the floor.

Owen and Munro simultaneously take several steps away from each other. They both also shake their heads emphatically and throw their hands up as if I threatened to rob them. Did I mention their eyes are bulging too? Sheesh, they're weird.

With all the speed of sloths, the men lower their hands.

Munro picks me up, clutching me in his arms like I'm his favorite coat and he doesn't want his buddy to steal it. "Natalie sleeps with me. On the sofa."

"Yeah, of course," Owen says. "I'll be good on the porch."

"I'll give you my sleeping bag. You can spend the night on the floor *inside* the house. I don't want to wake up in the morning and find you dead on the porch, half-eaten by a bear."

"Thank you, Sasquatch. It's nice to know you care if I get mauled."

Munro still has me in his arms.

I poke his chest. "Um, are you going to put me down now?"

"No." He walks over to the front door. "We are going for a nature walk. Alone. You will stay in the house, Owen. Understood?"

Owen salutes. "Aye-aye, captain."

Munro lifts his gaze to the roof and shakes his head. "Americans."

He carries me out the door and manages to yank it shut without dropping me. The Wild Man doesn't set me down, though. Instead, he starts walking toward the trail we'd come down when he rescued me from that fallen branch.

"I can walk, you know," I tell him. "You can put me down."

"Not yet."

"But your arms will get tired."

He makes a derisive noise. "I jogged half a mile while carrying your backpack."

"Fair point. But I'd rather walk under my own power."

"Your backpack is awfully heavy for one wee lass to carry on her back." He halts and studies me for a moment. Then he carefully sets me down. "Do you feel more liberated now? Or should I carry you back to the cabin so you can hike all the way here on your own?"

"Getting grumpy again, I see. Do you always insist on carrying women through the woods?"

"No, only the ones I want to fuck."

"And how many of those have you brought here?"

"To this exact location?" He turns in a circle, seeming like he's deep in thought, but it's clearly sarcasm. "I'm fair certain I've only brought you to this precise spot. But this forest is probably littered with places where I shagged other lasses. Being a Wild Man, I can sniff out those spots."

I know he's teasing me, but what he just said makes me wonder. "How many women have you slept with?"

"Today? Since I moved to Wyoming? You'll need to be more specific."

"In your life."

He leans against a tree and thrusts his hands into his pants pockets. "So it's *that* conversation, is it?"

"What is 'that' conversation? Be more specific."

"Cheeky lass." He gazes into the distance, past my left shoulder. "I haven't kept count, but it isn't that many. I was married for nine years."

"Just give me a ballpark estimate."

He screws up his mouth. "Thirteen."

"That's kind of specific. A ballpark estimate would be more like ten or twelve."

"Fine, it's twelve."

Now he's getting grumpy again for sure. "Never mind. Where are you taking me?"

"To a good spot for fucking. Weren't you listening a minute ago?"

"I was hoping for a more specific answer."

He hisses a breath out through his nostrils. "You're obsessed with specifics, aren't you?"

"Yeah. My husband never told me anything concrete, just vague bullshit that I bought into because I loved him. And that's how I became a target."

He says nothing for a moment, though he keeps his gaze steadily on me. "I should have realized that's why you ask me nonstop questions. I'm an eejit."

"I assume that means 'idiot,' but I've never thought you were stupid. How could you guess that I'm traumatized? Even after I told you about Elliot, it couldn't have been obvious."

Munro saunters up to me and pulls me into his arms. "Maybe I'm not an eejit, but I am blind. And I will never let anyone harm you."

I don't know what to say. The Wild Man seems determined to comfort and protect me. After all his grumpiness, I never would have expected him to react this way. But as I stand here now, cocooned in his arms, I feel safer than I have in years. I've known Munro for two days, yet I trust him and want to stay with him.

So what if that's crazy? Maybe I need a little insanity in my life.

"You don't need to be jealous," I say. "I'm not attracted to Owen."

"I haven't gotten involved with a woman in such a bloody long time. Just sex, that was all I thought I wanted." He combs his fingers through my hair. "But I was lying to myself."

Neither of us speaks for a while. We sink into a comfortable silence and the comfort of holding each other. I close my eyes and listen to the wind rustling the leaves on the trees, the rushing of the river in the distance, the songs of various birds, and the beating of Munro's heart. I have my cheek on his chest, so I can count the thump-thumping of his every heartbeat.

A car horn blares.

Both our heads pop up at the same time, and we swivel our heads toward the sound. The horn blares on and on without a break.

"Car alarm?" I ask.

Munro shakes his head. "That's my truck. It doesn't have an alarm."

The horn stops.

Every hair on my arms and at my nape stiffens, and goosebumps raise up and down my skin.

"Stay here," Munro hisses, and he drops into a half-crouch as he sneaks up the trail to the house.

I follow him.

He flashes me a scowl over his shoulder but doesn't try to stop me from going with him. He probably realizes I won't hide in the woods while he walks into who knows what. Maybe Owen wanted to summon us back to the cabin because the sun is sinking lower.

Munro halts at the periphery of the woods, close enough that we can see the cabin but far enough back that shadows cloak us. When I try to come up beside him, he gently pushes me behind him again.

Three men stand on the porch. One peers through the window. The other two seem to be having an intense conversation. I don't recognize any of them.

"Do you know those guys?" I ask, whispering into Munro's ear.

He shakes his head.

One of the men sets his hand on his hip, which pushes his suede jacket back just enough to reveal the gun holstered there. I assume the others must have weapons too. Something about their demeanor convinces me they mean business, and their pristine clothing suggests they aren't lost hikers.

The armed man in the suede jacket pounds his fist on the door. "Come out now! We'll shoot our way in if we have to, so make this easy on yourself."

He must be talking to Owen. But I assumed he was the one blaring the truck's horn. Owen must have slipped back into the house after that. Is he a former commando or something? Munro told me he had been in the army, so even if Owen hadn't served, the Scot must have the right skills to deal with whatever is going on.

Munro looks at me over his shoulder and whispers, "Stay here. Please."

"What are you going to do?"

"Find out what's going on and stop it."

His commanding tone convinces me that he means what he said and he will succeed. But I can't hide here while he confronts at least three bad guys. What if more are hiding somewhere nearby?

I don't get the chance to voice my concerns to Munro. He slinks through woods while keeping an eye on the bad guys. And I follow him. He throws me an annoyed look. I stay close to Munro but keep myself behind him since he has military training and is freaking scary when he wants to be. The only weapon I have is my fists. Munro has all those muscles and who knows what else.

Once we reach a spot that's directly across from the cabin but just to the side of the porch, Munro halts. He holds up a hand to preemptively stop me from talking. Then he slinks toward the cabin, walking in a manner that seems to prevent his footfalls from being heard. I try to imitate that, and it actually seems to work for me.

At the edge of the trees, he halts again and pulls an object out of his back pocket, flipping the switchblade open to reveal its wide blade with a serrated edge at one end and a smooth edge at the top. I think it might be a hunting knife.

Yeah, that looks like a nasty weapon.

Munro gestures for me to follow him. We creep up to the house without making a sound, and the men on the porch don't seem to have noticed us.

"You have five seconds to come out," the leather-jacketed man hollers to Owen. "Then we'll break down the door."

We've just reached the house, and Munro sidles up to the wall. I do the same. He listens for a moment, his head cocked, then clasps my hand to lead me around the back of the house. We keep walking in the stealthy way I'd picked up from him. At the corner of the house, we stop again so Munro can surveil the area. Yeah, I'm now an expert on covert stuff. Not even sure I used the right word.

Once Munro is satisfied, he leads me behind the house to a door I'd noticed before but hadn't known where it led. Now, he cautiously turns the knob and eases the door open. After a brief hesitation—to listen for more bad guys, I think—Munro starts down the stairs while still holding my hand. Luckily, the stairs don't creak. Our stealthy walking method might have prevented that, I guess. Can't ask Munro right now.

We step off the stairs and onto the earthen floor of a basement. Wooden boxes housed on shelves seem to hold various kinds of tools. It's pretty dark in here, with only the light coming down from the open door to guide us, but Munro clearly knows this basement like the back of his hand.

He stops halfway across the space.

"What now?" I ask.

"There's only one way into the house from down here."

"And what's that?"

"The crawlway."

Whatever that means, I don't care right now. Munro knows what he's doing, and I have no clue how to deal with a hostage situation. So, I'll defer to his expertise. A "crawlway" doesn't sound appealing, but this is an emergency. Time to suck it up and do whatever is necessary.

Chapter Fourteen

Munro

I snag a headlamp from one of the shelves and strap it around my forehead, then switch the light on. I drop to my knees in front of an old mirror that leans against the wall, right where I'd positioned it on purpose to hide my secret. Shifting the mirror to the side, I expose the wooden panel in the dirt wall that has a small handle attached to it. Aye, this is my secret. I grasp the handle, tugging until it comes loose. Now the tiny hinges attached to one side are visible, but only if a person squints at them.

Once I've eased the hatch open, I crawl inside the three-foot-square space behind it. Natalie crawls in after me. I reach past her to pull the hatch closed, and she cringes a wee bit.

"Are you claustrophobic?" I ask.

"Never used to be, though my ex-husband was. He would freak out in this tunnel, and I can't deny it makes my skin prickle. The only light comes from your headlamp, and that doesn't go very far."

"Just focus on me and stay close."

"You mean I should focus on your ass."

I smirk. "If that's what works for you."

As we crawl forward, I glance back and see that she is indeed focusing on my erse to distract herself from thinking about the close quarters. The smell of dank earth surrounds us. I don't have the luxury of watching her erse while we crawl down the tunnel, but even if she were in front, I would still need to concentrate on getting to our destination. At last, we reach the end of the tunnel.

I point upward.

She tips her head back to stare up at the hatch above our heads. It looks almost identical to the one we'd crawled through in the basement. "What's up there?"

Natalie spoke in such a soft whisper that I doubt anyone more than three feet away from us could have heard it.

I employ an equally soft voice when I say, "You'll see."

This time, I take even greater care in opening the hatch, and it comes loose with only the faintest click. I slowly lower the wooden panel, letting it hang down.

Then I plaster my mouth to her ear. "Stay right here."

"Where are you going?"

"Up there is the storage closet in the bathroom. I'm going to peek out the door to see if Owen is still alone in the house."

This time, the lass doesn't argue about my orders.

I remove the headlamp and put it on her head. She gives me a shaky smile. I plant a quick, firm kiss on her lips, which seems to perk her up. Then I hoist myself out of the tunnel and into the bathroom.

Natalie pops her head up just enough to see me.

I'm still inside the closet, though I've pushed the door open. Now, I reach into the cabinet above my head to retrieve a leather case. Natalie's brows furrow as I remove a silver-colored metal object and hand it to her.

She accepts the weapon—a .38 caliber revolver.

I duck my head into the tunnel to whisper to her again. "Have you ever used a gun before?"

"No."

"A revolver is easy. Pull the trigger. You've got six rounds of jacketed hollow-point ammo."

"Okay."

I doubt she knows what jacketed hollow-point ammo is, but I don't have time to explain.

She swallows hard as she eyes the revolver, with curiosity rather than fear. I doubt the lass would have volunteered to hold a gun and potentially shoot someone, but she realizes our situation bears all the hallmarks of a life-or-death struggle. Her composure under these circumstances is extraordinary.

I glance at her one last time, then move away from the closet, out of view of Natalie. I ease the bathroom door open a wee bit, barely enough to peek into the unknown. At first, I don't see Owen. But then I notice a small brown something sticking out from behind the kitchen island. I doubt the men outside can see it from their angle. Is that a brown boot? Could it be Owen's foot?

One way to find out.

I cup my hands around my mouth and hiss, "Owen."

No response.

"Owen," I hiss again, slightly louder this time.

He leans around the island, though not enough for the bastards outside to notice him. I can see him, though. He seems puzzled, so I wave at him. That only increases his confusion.

Owen speaks in a voice equally as hushed as mine. "Munro? How did you get in here?"

"Never mind. Are you all right?"

"Yeah. Did you see those guys out there?"

"Aye."

"Who are they?"

I shrug. "Not sure, but they could be working for Natalie's ex-husband."

"Damn, that guy must be a monumental prick like his dickwad friends out there."

"Can ye get over here without alerting them?"

Owen puckers his mouth as if he's considering his answer. "Don't think I can sneak over there without them seeing. They keep peeking through the windows."

How can I get Owen out of here? I need time to consider the options, but I doubt we'll have that much leeway.

"Where the fuck did you go?" one of the men outside shouts. It sounds like the *cacan* in the suede jacket. "All right, no more pussyfooting around. We're coming in."

An explosive bang reverberates through the house.

No time to formulate a plan. I shout, "Get over here, Owen!"

He scrambles across the floor on hands and knees while the villains race into the cabin. Their footfalls pound. The second Owen scurries into the bathroom, I yank the door shut and lock it from the inside. Natalie's head still pokes up out of the tunnel.

I snarl, "Get down!"

She disappears from view.

Owen jumps into the tunnel, and I'm right behind him. Natalie scrambles to get out of our way. I reach up to shut the door to the bathroom cabinet, then duck into the tunnel again, pulling the overhead hatch closed, securing it with the latch.

I snatch the headlamp from Natalie. "Let me go first. We're heading back to the basement."

"Won't they think to look there?"

"Aye. We'll need to move fast to get out of the house before they realize we've gone."

Those men can't know the layout of the house or that I installed a crawlway. They don't seem particularly motivated either, considering how long they waited to breach the cabin, so we might have enough time to escape.

I sidle past Natalie and take the lead as we hustle down the tunnel. No need to go slow this time. I push the hatch open and climb out, then help Natalie do the same. Owen gives me an exasperated look when I offer him my hand—and he winds up falling facedown onto the dirt floor.

Once I've shut the hatch, I move the mirror in front of it again.

"What do we do now?" Owen asks.

"Go up the stairs and outside, of course. Did ye think we'd sit on the floor and hold hands to sing a song together?"

I start up the stairs, taking great care with my footsteps to avoid making any sound. Natalie follows me, adopting the same walking style, and Owen brings up the rear. He also follows my lead in how to mount the stairs. We reach the top without incident, and since I can hear those men stomping about above us, I feel relatively confident we can make it to my truck or Owen's and effect our escape.

As I grasp the doorknob, the hairs at the back of my neck stiffen.

The door is wrenched open.

I almost stumble backward into Natalie.

A man with salt-and-pepper hair stands before me, still clutching the knob. He swings the door open all the way and points a Glock .9mm pistol at us. His gaze flicks to the lass behind me, and lines fan out from his eyes when he smiles with nothing close to friendliness. "Natalie, you sneaky little minx. Did you seriously think you could get away from me?"

"Yeah, I did think that." She leans around me to glare at him. "Because I got away from you."

"Not far enough away. Here I am, and you are about to die."

I ball my fists and grit my teeth. "Who the fuck are you?"

"Elliot Rudaski. I'm Natalie's husband."

She tries to push past me, seeming like she wants to throttle the bastard, but I thrust an arm out to stop her. "You are my ex-husband. And I wish I'd never married you in the first place."

Elliot chuckles. "Aren't you cute when you try to play the tough chick."

Fuck this asinine conversation. I hurl my entire body at Elliot, knocking him backward onto the ground with me on top. I clinch his wrist and pound it into the ground until he loses his grip on the gun, then I stuff the weapon into my waistband. I punch him in the face three times, though I could've subdued him without doing that. But I enjoyed pummeling the *bod ceann.*

Because he wants to murder Natalie.

I hoist Elliot onto his feet, though he's too dazed to hold himself up.

Natalie and Owen gawp at me.

"Out of the way," I snarl as I haul Elliot through the doorway and hurl him down the basement stairs. Then I slam the door shut and face my companions. "Into the truck. Now."

"Which one?" Owen asks.

"Mine. It's closer." I stalk over to the vehicle and tear the door open. "Hurry up, would you? This isn't a game of hide and go seek."

The three of us jump into the truck, and I reach for the ignition.

"Where's the key?" Natalie asks.

"*Bod an Donais.* It's in the house."

Owen throws the passenger door open. "Come on, I've got my keys in my pocket."

We race for his truck, which he'd parked on the far side of the house. Just as we reach the vehicle, Elliot starts to scream for his mates. The pounding of footfalls approaching from the front of the house tells me we don't have much time. I take the wheel, and Owen doesn't complain about that. He knows I can drive faster and more aggressively without causing an accident than he can. Since Owen's truck has a backseat, I order Natalie to sit back there.

"Do up your seatbelt, lass," I say. "This won't be a gentle ride."

Owen and I secure our seatbelts too, and I gun the engine. Instead of trying to back out from behind the house, I aim for the front yard. We rocket around the corner of the house and across the lawn, then swerve right to head down the driveway.

Elliot's men leap out of the way and fall down. In the rearview mirror, I see Elliot stumbling out of the basement with blood trickling down one side of his face.

That's the last look I get at the bastard. Soon, the trees block our view of the cabin and the villains. None of us speak during the bumpy ride down the long dirt road. No one lives out here except for me. That means we must rely on each other to get to safety, if such a thing actually exists. I don't have a mobile phone, but maybe Natalie or Owen has one we can use to call the authorities, once we enter the vicinity of a cell tower.

I steer the truck around a curve in the road—and slam on the brakes.

A large SUV blocks the roadway, positioned sideways. We don't have enough room to drive around it. Slamming my fist on the steering wheel, I spew a litany of Gaelic curses.

"We're trapped, aren't we?" Natalie says. "Is anybody in that vehicle?"

I peer through the windshield of our truck and the SUV. "Can't tell for sure."

"What should we do?"

"You and Owen should run." I dig an item out of my pocket and hand it to Owen. "Use my compass and keep heading northwest. You'll reach the town that way."

"Are you sure about this plan?" he asks.

"Yes. Take Natalie and go."

He climbs out and opens the back door, but the stubborn lass refuses to move.

I twist around to glare at her. "Go with Owen. I'll have him throw you over his shoulder if that's what it takes."

She locks her arms over her chest and lifts her chin.

"Do it, Natalie, *now.*"

"No."

I glower at her harder, but she seems unaffected by my expression or the way I snarled at her.

"Uh, you better do something quick," Owen says. "I hear a vehicle coming up the road."

I glance out the rear window and see movement. That must be the villains coming around the curve, heading our way. I hiss another Gaelic curse. "Go, Owen. Get help. I'll take care of Natalie."

"You sure?"

"Aye. Go, before they see you running away."

He hesitates for only a second, then sprints into the forest.

Natalie climbs over the center console and drops onto the passenger seat. "You saved my life once, and I will not abandon you now."

I could point out again that she wouldn't have died because a branch fell on her and that she would have summoned the strength to lift it off herself eventually. But we don't have time for another argument.

So I push my door open. "Might as well get out. We have nowhere else to go."

And I pray Owen will make it to town.

Chapter Fifteen

Natalie

I must have gone crazy because nothing else explains why I refused to run away. My ex-husband has come here to kill me, so I
should be sprinting through the woods right now. Instead, I vowed to
stay with Munro. Why wouldn't he leave? Maybe we could have all escaped
into the woods, but he seemed to be convinced that someone needed to stay
behind to distract Elliot and his goons.

Maybe Munro was right. I don't know. But I will not abandon him.

Yeah, I'm certifiably insane.

I stuff the revolver into my waistband, snug against my spine, and climb
out of the truck to walk around to the rear bumper, where Munro already
waits for me. He clasps my hand as a truck barrels toward us, and I suddenly
recognize that vehicle. "Isn't that your truck?"

"Aye. They must have found the key or hot-wired the ignition."

"Why would they steal your vehicle? They must have brought their own
cars."

"Did you see any other vehicles at the cabin?"

I try to rewind my thoughts to remember if he's right. "Now that you
mention it, I don't remember seeing any other cars. Elliot and his men must
have walked all the way to the cabin. Do you think there's anyone in the
SUV behind us?"

"Probably not. It's their road block."

The truck halts several yards away. Elliot jumps out first, followed by
two of his men. The third stays inside the vehicle, behind the wheel.

My ex-husband moves in front of the truck and leans back against the vehicle. He rests one arm casually on the hood as he aims his gun at me. "You really are the dumbest bitch on the planet, aren't you?"

"Haud yer wheesht," Munro says. He sidles in front of me. "That means shut your trap and tell us what you want."

Elliot laughs. "My wife's corpse lying bloody on the ground, of course. That's all I want."

"Then why haven't you shot her yet?"

Is Munro trying to get me killed? No, he wouldn't do that. He must have a plan of some sort.

Elliot lowers his hand, his expression turning thoughtful. He taps the gun's barrel against his thigh. "What makes you think I have an ulterior motive?"

"Because ahmno blind or stupid. So I'll ask you again. What do you want?"

My ex-husband studies me. "I'm going to kill you either way, sweetheart, but you can make it easier on yourself if you give me the information you stole."

"What information?" I ask. "Why on earth would I steal anything from you when I don't even know what it is?"

"Come on, cupcake. You know you have what I need."

Did he seriously call me "cupcake"? He had never used any pet names for me before, not even "sweetheart." If he's trying to piss me off, well, he gets an A-plus on that exam. But I still have no clue what he thinks I have. I'd walked away from our marriage with nothing, not even alimony. His high-priced lawyers made sure of that.

"If you think I've got something of yours," I say, "describe it to me. 'Information' is too vague, and I'm not psychic."

"All right. Let me elaborate." He taps his finger on the gun's barrel in a slow cadence. "Since the day you poked your little nose into my business and demanded to know everything, you became a repository of information. *My* information."

A chill sweeps through my body because I can guess what he's about to say.

"I can't take back what you learned, but I can erase that knowledge." Elliot raises his gun. "By erasing you."

Munro looks at me, and I glance at him sideways. He grips my hand more tightly and keeps staring at me. If he's trying to tell me something, I can't figure it out.

"Your erse," he murmurs while barely moving his lips.

I still don't get.

He shoves his hand into the back of his jeans, and I finally understand.

"What are you doing there?" Elliot demands. He veers his gun toward Munro. "Do you have a death wish? I'm happy to fulfill that desire unless you remove your hand from behind you—slowly—and raise both hands above your head."

Munro complies.

I know he's only doing that because I have the gun. Does he want me to shoot Elliot? I never used to think of myself as the violent type, but I will eighty-six my ex-husband if he doesn't shut his fucking mouth and stop threatening me and Munro.

"Okay," Elliot says in a cavalier tone. "Time for a game of Russian roulette. My version. That means I'll shoot you six times."

I swing the revolver up and train it on his chest, then pull the trigger. The deafening boom of the shot echoes through the woods. While my ears ring, Elliot stumbles sideways and drops to his knees.

Munro seizes my hand and drags me into the woods. We run and run and run as my hearing gradually returns to normal and I can detect male voices shouting behind us. Did I kill Elliot? Not sure. He stumbled and fell but didn't seem to be bleeding. His white dress shirt looked fine, but I hadn't gotten a good look. Munro and I started running while Elliot's lackeys still seemed to be in shock.

Gunshots reverberate through the woods.

"Cut that out, you morons!"

That sounds a hell of a lot like Elliot.

Damn, I thought I'd sighted in on him well enough to at last hit some part of his torso. Shouldn't hitting anywhere on his body slow him down? Maybe I missed.

We're running so fast that my legs have started to ache and I'm out of breath. Munro sounds like he's breathing hard too, and his cheeks are flushed. My face feels warm, so I'm probably having the same reaction. The ringing in my ears has come back, but I don't think it has anything to do with when I shot Elliot. My lips feel numb too, and coldness is seeping deeper into me minute by minute.

I trip and fall to my knees.

Munro crouches in front of me. "What's wrong, *gràidh*?"

"Can't run anymore. I'm sorry. You should go on."

"Not without you." He slings me over his shoulders. "I'll get us there."

Where are we going? I have no idea, and asking seems pointless right now. If he can't carry me all the way to wherever we're going, we are both screwed.

His pace seems to be slowing, and his chest is heaving.

"Stop, Munro, you'll kill yourself with a heart attack."

"Cannae stop." He stumbles but catches himself, determined to keep going. "Need to get there."

I wriggle out of his grasp and slide down his body until my feet touch the ground. "Get where? Elliot and his goons will find us if we go to the cabin."

"No choice." He bends his knees, resting his palms on his thighs, and takes five slow, deep breaths. He has less trouble talking now. "I'm heading for the river. We'll come up the trail where I found you caught under that branch. Then we'll get your backpack and anything else we have time to grab."

"But then what?"

"We run. I'll carry you and your backpack if necessary, as well as my rucksack."

If anyone else had made the claim that he could sprint through the woods with all that weight on his shoulders, I would've laughed. But I believe Munro can do it. The man is a real-life superhero. So I accept what he said and move on. "How far ahead of them do you think we are?"

"Not as far as I'd like."

"Could we somehow trick those creeps into going down into your tunnel? Then we could lock them in."

Munro straightens and studies me, then his lips twitch into a sly smile. "You are brilliant, Natalie. But your idea needs a wee bit of tweaking. Let's get back to the cabin."

"That means more running, doesn't it?"

"Aye. But we should be almost there." He touches my cheek. "Think you can keep going?"

"To make sure Elliot gets his comeuppance? Yeah, I could run a hundred miles for that."

He clamps his hand around mine, and we take off.

Our rest stop in the wilds, combined with our new plan, seems to have reinvigorated us both. I stop thinking about what or who lies behind us and focus on reaching our destination. We burst out of the trees into the little clearing where I'd first seen Munro, pelting down the trail and straight to the open area around the cabin. We don't stop until we've raced up the porch steps and through the open door.

We rest for about thirty seconds.

"Time to enact your plan," Munro says. "We need to concoct a way to lure those men into the bathroom. I have an idea for how to keep them in the tunnel. The hatches aren't designed to lock anyone in, so I'll need to do some shoring up."

"I'll leave that to you. As for capturing them, you could hide behind the bathroom door, right next to the cabinet that hides the tunnel. Then I could lure them in one at a time."

"Too dangerous. I willnae leave ye alone with those men."

"There's also the problem of how you'll keep them down there while you round them up."

He chuckles with dark delight. "Dinnae worry about that."

Yeah, I should never underestimate Munro MacTaggart. "I have no clue how to trick them into doing what we want."

Munro compresses his lips and holds perfectly still. I think—or maybe hope—he's dreaming up a plan. Without even glancing at me, he stalks into the kitchen and roots around in one of the lower cabinets until he finds what he wanted. He straightens and holds up his prize.

"Walkie-talkies?" I say. "What are we supposed to do with those?"

"Let me tell you my idea."

I listen while he quickly lays out the scheme, and I have to admit it sounds perfect, assuming everything goes according to our plan. I take one of the walkie-talkies and head back to the location Munro had described to me. Then I switch the radio on and wait.

Please, please, please let this work.

From my vantage in the woods, crouching to reduce my "profile" as Munro called it, I can see the cabin. Munro had assured me no one else will spot me. He knows these woods, and I trust he wouldn't have sent me out here unless he was sure I'd be hidden. I have the .38 revolver too. Munro has no weapons as far as I know, since he gave Elliot's bigger gun to Owen. Maybe Munro has other weapons I haven't seen yet. Or he might be so damn tough that he doesn't need a gun, a knife, or anything at all.

Yeah, I can believe he's that tough.

The noise of pounding feet and cracking branches, hard to hear at first, grows louder every moment. Elliot and his men are getting closer. Has Munro set up his barricades or whatever he planned to do to confine the bad guys? I'll find out soon, because those bastards are getting closer. They don't seem to care about stealth. I bet they assume their bigger guns and strength in numbers will be all they need to subdue me and Munro.

I can't help smiling. Those jerks don't know the Wild Man.

Elliot's goons burst out of the woods first, but the man himself lags behind. He emerges just as his men halt in front of the cabin. They engage in a whispered conversation that I can't hear and then spread out.

I hold the walkie-talkie to my mouth, press the button, and whisper, "Get ready, Munro. They're here, and they're surrounding the house."

We had agreed he wouldn't respond and I should assume he hears whatever I tell him. Responding could alert the bad guys to my position.

Two of the goons jog behind the house, while Elliot and another man head for the porch. The door hangs ajar, another of Munro's ideas. The intruders position themselves at either side of the door and wait, apparently listening for something or simply waiting for the Scot to reveal himself.

Only one thing left to do—pray.

A gunshot explodes, echoing in the clearing. My pulse shoots into the stratosphere, and I take slow, deep breaths to calm myself. I want to call out to him through the walkie-talkie. But Munro knows how to take care of himself. He hasn't been shot. I feel it in my soul.

Elliot peers through the window beside the cabin's door. "Ramsey! Peters! What's going on?"

Way to be stealthy, moron.

A man screams.

Elliot says something to his buddy, who nods. And they both storm into the house.

Chapter Sixteen

Munro

"Your turn, Natalie," I whisper into the walkie-talkie. The next part of our plan centers on her, though she will come nowhere near the cabin. One of the two men who breached the house had shot at a shadow, literally. I've been hiding behind the kitchen island, and outside the window, tree branches shivering in a breeze had cast their shadows on the floor. The writhing darkness and light apparently terrified one of the villains. He shot wildly. I can see the hole where the slug slammed into a cabinet.

Will the idea Natalie and I came up with work? The time has come to find out.

"Help! I'm trapped!"

Natalie's voice emerges from the half-closed bathroom door.

"Munro! Where are you? I fell into the hole and can't get out."

She's displaying acting skills I never would've imagined she would have. Desperate times can make people pull things out of their psyches that they had no idea they could do.

I hear the footsteps of the two men approaching, and I can see their shadows. That's how I can tell they're coming closer. Our plan banks on the fact that Natalie claims to be in the tunnel and the villains won't realize she isn't. They can't hear her very well.

"Please help! Is anyone out there?"

The shadows of the men move away from the kitchen. They seem to be heading toward the bathroom, the only other room in the cabin. I don't have a weapon, but I don't need one. When I'd told Natalie that, she seemed shocked only for a second or two, then she accepted it's true. My cousin Errol can confirm it.

And these bastards are about to learn one of the many reasons why my family calls me the Wild Man.

"What the hell is that?" one man says. "Is it some kind of septic system?"

"Those aren't in the bathroom, you moron." That is Elliot speaking.

Natalie's voice emerges from the tunnel. "I've hurt my leg and need help. Please."

"Should we go down there, boss?" the man who isn't Elliot says. "That sounded like your wife."

"Yes, it did." A pause follows. "You go down there and see what's happening."

"Down into the dark hole? What if it's a hundred feet deep or something?"

The sound of a slap suggests the "boss" just smacked his underling. Elliot snarls, "Do it now. I need to check the other two. They've been out there for too long." Another slap ensues. "What is wrong with you three? You're a bunch of fucking children."

Footfalls clomp as Elliot exits the cabin.

Time to take down lackey number one.

I peek around the island, through the open front door, to watch Elliot leap off the porch and head toward the back of the house. Then I rise into a half crouch and tiptoe out from behind the island. The *cacan* in the bathroom hovers at the edge of the tunnel hatch, knees bent, hands on his thighs, too consumed with figuring out what lies below to notice my approach.

"Lady, are you okay?" the *cacan* asks.

Aye, I've suddenly lost all sense of reality and believe he really gives a damn. That means no, I dinnae believe him at all.

I barrel toward the man and slam my head into his lower back. He stumbles forward, shouting as he trips and falls into the tunnel. My job isn't over yet, though. I have three more bastards to capture. But first, I leap into the hole and snag the stunned man's wrists while he's still struggling to understand what happened. I bind his wrists and ankles with duct tape, then seal a strip of it over his mouth.

His eyes are bulging. His face has gone pale.

That reaction is nothing new for me. I'd seen similar expressions from the men I'd taken down in the Grand Canyon. Maybe I'll tell Natalie that story once this emergency situation has ended. It's an emergency for this gang of scunners, not for me.

After dragging the man deeper into the tunnel, I climb out again and make sure my walkie-talkie is still in position in the crawlway. I might have accidentally kicked it out of the way, or the *cacan* might have done that. But it's right where it should be. Time to grab another villain.

I peer out the bathroom window but see no one there. Then I return to the kitchen to check out that window. No one there either. I crouch behind the island once again and cock my head, listening for footsteps. I let my jaw fall open a wee bit to help me hear better. Ah, there it is. The faint sound of someone approaching. I can't detect their footsteps, but I can hear the rustling of their clothes and the whispering of their breaths. It's a distinct sound unlike the rustling of leaves in the trees.

Despite their efforts to remain stealthy, my ears pick up the light creaking of the porch boards as they step onto that surface. Elliot's leather jacket makes a distinct noise too. He must have just bought it recently and the material hasn't gotten broken in yet.

"Peters, where are you?" Elliot calls out.

The only response he receives is silence.

"You two check the bathroom," Elliot says. "I'll check the woods. Maybe Peters is a coward and ran away."

Ah, so the man in the tunnel is called Peters.

"I said go, Ramsey," their leader barks. "You and Watkins should be able to handle scoping out a bathroom on your own. Or do I need to remind you of what happens if you screw up?"

The shadows on the floor tell me the two lackeys have gone into the bathroom. Elliot leaves to "check the woods," though I doubt he has any idea how to do that. Natalie is well hidden, and she's clever enough to know how to stay out of her ex's path.

Still, I need to move quickly.

Keeping low to the floor, I hurry toward the open bathroom door. The two men seem to be studying the hole in the floor, just like their mate had done. They whisper to each other about what the hole might be, and one laddie actually wonders if their friend Peters had fallen into the dark, dank space below. Maybe they aren't complete eejits, but they do seem like city people who know nothing about survivalist skills.

I ram my head into the nearest man's backside.

He trips, and one leg drops into the abyss. But his other leg gets caught, holding him halfway into the hole. The other laddie reaches for his friend.

And I kick him squarely in the back.

The pair tumble into the tunnel while shouting and grunting. I turn on my headlamp and jump into the hole. It's a tight squeeze with three of us huddled just inside the opening. But I have the advantage against the confused men. While I bind the one laddie, the other tries to scramble away down the tunnel. I hurry after him and catch the bastard in a choke hold, then flip him onto his back on the dirt floor. Soon, I have him bound too.

Duct tape is a versatile tool.

Now I have only one more man to subdue—Elliot, the murderous bastard. I sneak outside and study the tracks Elliot left behind. He and his men are not experts at man tracking, otherwise they wouldn't have left so many signs for me to read. I follow the footprints to the edge of the trees, but then the grass makes it trickier to track Elliot that way. Still, I have no trouble detecting the signs he left behind.

I move quietly and quickly, coming up behind Elliot while he stops to rub his back and survey the area. This is my chance. I rush up behind him and tackle the bastard to the ground.

He tries to fight but winds up only flailing his arms. My body pins him to the ground. I yank his wrists behind his back and use more duct tape to bind them. He snarls nasty curses and keeps trying to thrash his legs, but I pin him down with one knee on his spine while I tape his ankles together.

"Quit your bawling," I say as I smack the back of his head. "I could've killed you. Might want to thank me for sparing your worthless life."

"I'll get you. Just wait."

Och, how that threat terrifies me. I resist the impulse to laugh in the *bod ceann's* face. Then I throw my head back and shout, "Natalie! You can come out now. I got them all."

The crashing of her footfalls confirms that she heard me, and that she knows it's safe to come out of hiding. The lass bursts out from behind a small bush and halts beside me, gasping for breath. She glares at her ex-husband, then kicks him in the erse.

"Easy," I say. "You want him to live to go to prison, don't you?"

"Not sure. Maybe he deserves to die right here. Might be better if we dragged him onto a pile of bear shit, then killed him."

I assume the lass isn't serious about that. Though I would have no qualms about dispatching the bastard who wanted to murder her, she doesn't seem like the sort who would do that. I was a commando in the British Army. She is a landscape designer. Of course, she has surprised me again and again with her resolve and fortitude.

"Did you wear a bulletproof vest?" Natalie asks. "I shot you in the chest, but that didn't stop you."

Elliot narrows his gaze, which is the only sort of expression he can manage with his mouth taped shut. He tries to wriggle too, but my knee on his spine prevents him from doing anything more than thrashing his head and bending his knees. I stop him from doing that by placing my other leg on his calves.

"Yes," Elliot says through gritted teeth. "I wore a Kevlar vest."

I smack the back of his head. "This laddie needs a skelping more than anyone else I've ever met. Even the antiquities thieves in the Grand Canyon weren't as irritating as this one."

"Yeah, he's used to getting his way," Natalie says. "Elliot never did believe in sharing our marital assets. We had separate bank accounts, and he insisted that I should keep my maiden name instead of taking his."

Why would he do that? I can think of one reason, based on his actions today. So I flip him over and bar my leg over his thighs while I grasp his bound wrists and give them a hard tug that makes him wince. But I speak to Natalie, not him. "Did he know all your financial information? Bank passwords and the like."

"Oh yeah, he did. Elliot insisted I was too dumb to understand financial matters. He never would explain why he didn't want me to take his name, though I'm glad for that now. He told me some bullshit about saving my own identity." She sucks in a shaky breath, her eyes glistening. "Can't believe how stupid I was."

I can reassure her later that she's wrong about that. Right now, I want answers from the *bod ceann*. I seize his wrists and yank him up into a half-sitting position. Spittle sprays his face as I snarl my words at him. "Tell me what the fuck you were doing with your wife's financial information? I'd wager everything I own that you made her keep her maiden name so you could sign her up for secret bank accounts to hide your ill-gotten gains. Nod if you agree."

Elliot glowers at me.

"Stubborn, eh?" I haul him to his feet and drag him over to a large tree, then slam his backside into the trunk, making him wince again and issue a muffled cry. "Tell me now, or I'll show you what I do to bastards who try to hurt women."

Natalie comes up beside me. "He can't talk when his mouth is duct-taped shut. I like him better this way, but we won't get any information out of him."

"Fair point." I aim a wicked smile at Elliot. "Tear it off, Natalie."

She rips the tape off his lips.

He screams like a wee bairn while tears dribble down his cheeks. "I'll get you both for this. My men will find you and—"

I chuckle darkly. "Your men are in the crawlway. That's a dark, narrow tunnel under the house. I bound them so they can't come to rescue you."

Natalie slaps his cheek hard enough to make his skin red. "It's over, you rotten, conniving, sleazy son of a bitch."

A rumble in the distance gradually resolves into the distinctive sound of a helicopter's rotors whirling.

I tilt my head back and scan the sky. Then I see it. The helicopter is coming from the other side of the clearing around the house, swinging around from the direction of the dirt road. The sheriff's department logo is emblazoned on the side of the craft. Had they seen the SUV blocking the road? Owen must have reached someplace where he could call for help.

I sling Elliot over my shoulder, which spurs him to spew a string of nasty curses.

Natalie gazes up at the sky too.

"Looks like his confession will have to wait a wee bit," I say. "The authorities are here."

Chapter Seventeen

Natalie

Munro must be some kind of god, like Zeus or Thor, and I'm not talking about characters in superhero movies. No, I mean the real gods that cultures around the world worshiped and to whom they made offerings to appease those beings. I don't believe in those kind of gods, but I know with complete certainty that Munro is no ordinary man. He's incredible.

And I want to screw him right now. But I can't. The cops are here.

Their helicopter lands right in front the house, just as we return from the woods with Elliot. Munro carried my ex-husband over one shoulder the whole way. The chopper's rotors are winding down, and the cops—who I can now tell are sheriff's deputies—hop out of the helicopter and jog toward us. We've stopped near the porch. Elliot bitched and whined during the swift journey back to the homestead, but he shut his mouth when he saw the sheriff's helicopter.

The last man to exit the chopper is someone we know.

Owen trots over to us, arriving ahead of the deputies. "I'm so glad you guys are okay. What happened to the other thugs?"

"They're in the house," Munro says. "Well, more below the house than in it."

"I don't get it."

"You'll see."

The three deputies finally reach us. The man who wears the sheriff's badge speaks to us. "I'm Sheriff Dan Holzer, and these are my deputies,

Sam Folger and Bobby Santos. Mr. Metzger told us there was a dangerous situation going on here. What can you tell us?"

Munro sets Elliot down on his feet and shoves him toward one of the deputies. "This laddie, Elliot Rudaski, came here to murder his ex-wife. That's the woman standing beside me. She learned that her husband had been involved in a smuggling scheme, but you should let Elliot explain about that."

I guess Munro doesn't want to explain puppy smuggling to these tough-looking law enforcement professionals. I don't blame him. They'd probably laugh and walk away.

Sheriff Holzer looks at me. "You're the wife?"

"Ex-wife. I'm Natalie Saari."

"Let's go inside to talk about this."

"Okay, but you should know there are three more men who are locked in a tunnel under the house. They're Elliot's henchmen."

The sheriff stares at me, unblinking. "There are who in the what now?"

"Men in the tunnel under the house. If you come inside, we can show you."

"Yeah, I really think you'd better show us." He glances at Elliot and grimaces. "Better remove all that duct tape too. Just until we decide what the situation is."

He must mean that he doesn't know for sure who the good guys and bad guys are. I hope he'll have no more reservations once we explain fully, but holding three men hostage in Munro's crawlway might make it more difficult to convince the sheriff. The fact we duct-taped Elliot probably doesn't bolster our case either.

Munro rips the tape off Elliot's wrists and ankles. Naturally, he acts like a big, nasty baby. Sure, duct tape must hurt. But he deserves way more pain than that. Deputy Folger takes control of the prisoner while Munro leads our three new guests into the house and over to the bathroom. Owen and I follow behind them, but we loiter near the kitchen to give the other guys plenty of room to look at what's in the bathroom. I can mostly see what's going on in there. Munro has lifted the hatch in the closet.

"Here it is," he says. "You'll find three of Elliot's men down there, all of them with their mouths, wrists, and ankles duct-taped. I have a headlamp if you want it."

"We've got flashlights," the sheriff says. Then he swivels his head toward his deputies. "Folger, you and Santos go down there to retrieve our suspects."

Sheriff Holzer and Munro step out into the main area of the cabin. Munro comes over to me while Holzer hangs out on the other side of the open bathroom doorway. He says nothing while we wait for the deputies to bring out Elliot's goons. It doesn't take as long as I'd thought it might. The five men emerge from the tunnel within a few minutes and halt just beyond the bathroom threshold.

"Got 'em," Santos declares. "What now, boss?"

"We need to take them in for a nice little chitchat." He eyes the rather dazed and shell-shocked bad guys. "Why don't you take these three out onto the porch? Cuff 'em and read 'em their rights. We'll figure the rest out after I deal with these folks."

He means me, Munro, Owen, and Elliot. Is he going to interrogate my ex right here with three witnesses?

"Wait," Holzer calls out to his men. "Better take this one too. Use my cuffs for him."

The sheriff tosses his handcuffs to Folger, who corrals Elliot, and the deputies head outside with their prisoners.

It's fully dark now, and I can just make out the stars beyond the kitchen window. Tree branches conceal most of the sky, though the sliver I can see is beautiful. But it can't lessen my anxiety. With no concrete proof that Elliot planned to kill me, our story hinges on whether the sheriff believes us.

Owen, Munro, and I sit on the sofa. Sheriff Holzer drags the desk chair over here, so he can sit facing us. His gaze gravitates to the broken table tucked into the corner, and his brows rise briefly, but he doesn't ask about that. What a relief. I don't care to tell the sheriff that Munro and I fucked each other so hard the table shattered.

Holzer sets a hand on each arm of his chair and gives us The Cop Stare. "Tell me your side of the story. All of it."

"Do you want to hear about my past with Elliot first?" I ask. "Or would you rather focus on today's events?"

"Let's go from today."

"It started earlier, right before dusk. Owen and Munro had worked hard all day trying to install a new transmission is Munro's truck. After dinner, Owen wanted to rest. But Munro and I decided to go for a walk." I resist the impulse to glance at the men who sit at either side of me. That might make me look guilty or…something. "Munro and I had just reached a nice little spot along the river when we heard a car horn blaring."

Owen raises his hand. "That was me."

Holzer aims his steely stare at Owen. "Why were you blaring a horn?"

"I'd gone behind the house to check if I'd left Munro's torque wrench out in the vehicle we'd been working on. My friend can be kind of anal about where I leave the tools he lets me use." Owen glances at Munro. "No offense."

Munro grunts.

"Go on with your story," the sheriff says. "I'm all ears."

Owen clears his throat. "Well, I thought I heard a noise in the woods, like people creeping around. But it was coming from down the road, not the direction where Munro and Natalie had gone. Then I saw figures coming this way. Considering the way they were sneaking around, I thought they might be bad guys. Since Natalie had told us about her ex, I had reason to think that. I blared the horn to alert my friends."

"I see." Holzer nails each of us with his hard stare, though it doesn't faze Munro. "What did you do next, Mr. Metzger?"

"Ran inside and locked the door. Then I hid."

"Did anything else happen?"

"Those guys came up onto the porch and tried to open the door by kicking it. When that didn't work, they started yelling about how they were going to break down the door and beat me up."

"Hmm." Holzer turns to me. "Tell me your side of things."

"Munro and I heard the horn, so we hurried back to the house. Munro was in the British Army, so he knows how to avoid detection. I followed his lead."

The sheriff relaxed a little when I mentioned Munro's military background. Maybe he'll believe us now. We go on with our stories, explaining everything that happened, and I admit that I shot Elliot. I also point out that my ex admitted to wearing a bulletproof vest. Munro takes over to lay out our escape and how we captured Elliot's goons. The only thing left to do is for him to hear Elliot's take on those events.

Holzer spears each of us with his sharp gaze. "I'm trusting you three to stay in here while I'm outside with my guys and the suspected perps."

"We will stay put, absolutely," I say.

Munro and Owen proffer their agreement too.

The sheriff orders us to wait inside the cabin and not touch anything while he goes out onto the porch and shuts the front door behind him.

Elliot will lie, of course, through his nose and his teeth and any other part of his body that will help him invent sleazy falsehoods. But as I watch Holzer interrogating Elliot out on the porch, I get the impression the sheriff isn't going to let my ex-husband snooker him. No, Dan Holzer seems too smart to fall for that.

We wait. And wait. I can't hear what's being said out there, so I wind up literally twiddling my thumbs to stop myself from chewing my nails. Elliot had always been great at schmoozing, and he can be remarkably nice when he feels like it. He only felt like it until the day I discovered his secret. Then his dark side reared its head.

"Of course I wanted to kill her!" Elliot shouts. "The stupid cow stole from me. She deserves to die, and I don't care if I go to death row for murdering Natalie."

The door to the cabin swings open, and Sheriff Holzer waves for us to get up. "Come on, we've got a few last things to discuss."

Munro leads the way with Owen and me following him onto the porch. The deputies are herding Peters, Watkins, and Ramsey into the helicopter.

"I believe your story," Holzer says. "So I won't take you in along with these guys. But you need to leave the cabin and find a place to stay in town until we've processed the scene and gathered any evidence."

"Sure, we can do that," I say.

"Two of those jerks in the chopper are fugitives, and the other is under investigation in Montana. That gives me plenty of reason to trust what you say over anything they might claim. Rudaski confessed too, which leaves no doubts in my mind." He hands me a business card. "Call me when you get settled in at a motel or wherever."

"Will do."

He grabs Elliot's bound wrists and forces the creep to stand up. Then Holzer frog-marches my ex off the porch and toward the helicopter. Despite his situation, Elliot wears a smug expression.

The sheriff pauses halfway to the chopper and lays a hand on the butt of his gun, though it's still holstered. "I know whose story I believe, and it's not this jackass. Every word that came out of his mouth smelled like bullshit, and he clearly thinks he's the smartest kid in school. But he's far from it."

"My lawyer will rip you to shreds," Elliot says. "You should arrest these three for assault and attempted murder. My wife admits she shot me."

"Self-defense, in my book. But the courts can hash that out. My job is to take you in." Holzer grips Elliot's shoulder so firmly that my ex winces. "You can go easy, or you can go hard. Your choice."

Elliot lifts his chin. "I want a lawyer."

"And you'll get one. Eventually. We're kinda busy, you know."

"Do we need to come in to give statements?" I ask.

"You can do that tomorrow. Think you guys have been through enough today."

"That's it?" Elliot says. "You're letting them roam around free?"

"Yeah, I am. If you don't like it"—Holzer leans in to aim his steely glare straight into Elliot's eyes—"call a lawyer."

My ex pouts. Really, he does that.

Holzer marches to the helicopter's open passenger door. "Take the ring leader. I'm coming around the other side."

"Hey, sheriff," Owen says. "I live in town. Munro and Natalie can bunk at my place tonight. I'll call you with the address."

"Sounds like a plan." Holzer turns to Munro. "Do you need help moving that SUV out of the way? You can't drive into town otherwise."

"I can move it. Dinnae worry."

"Okay. Take some pictures of the scene before you move that vehicle. And try not to leave any fingerprints on it."

"Aye, we will." Munro hesitates, then asks, "Why aren't you worried about us contaminating the scene?"

"Mr. Metzger told me you're ex-military, and he also mentioned your cousin Logan who's former MI6. I called a friend at the Home Office back in the UK. He knows Logan and gave me his number. So I called him and confirmed your identity that way."

Wow, Munro's cousin must have serious creds. I wonder if he was a real-life James Bond. But I'm too tired to ask Munro about that.

The three of us hang out on the porch while Folger stuffs Elliot into the backseat with his buddies and the helicopter takes off. I can't believe what's happened. I must be in shock, though I don't feel that way. Does a person know when they're suffering from shock? Not sure. We grab our stuff, careful not to disturb any evidence, and climb into Owen's truck for the long drive to his house. Once we get there, Owen offers to sleep on the sofa so Munro and I can share the bedroom. I fall asleep cocooned in Munro's arms. But as I succumb to slumber, one thought keeps repeating in my mind.

Is it really over yet?

Chapter Eighteen

Munro

How could any of us have slept last night? Because we were exhausted, I suppose. The moment Natalie and I crawled into bed, we sank into a deep slumber. Well, I did. Can't say for sure that she did, but it seemed like it. In the span of a few hours, we went from enjoying dinner to being chased by Elliot and his three mates. Now, we're staying in Owen's house because mine is a crime scene. So are the woods around it.

During the helicopter flight to the cabin, Owen had pointed out to Holzer and his men where Elliot's vehicle had blocked the road. After the sheriff and his deputies left with Elliot and his lackeys, I had indeed shifted that SUV out of the way. Owen offered to help, but I assured him I didn't need it. All I had to do was move the gear shift lever into neutral and push the bloody thing into the roadside ditch. Someone else can worry about how to remove the vehicle.

I woke up this morning feeling good, all things considered. To rouse from a sensual dream with a bonnie lass cuddled against me feels even better. I carefully sneak out of bed, not wanting to disturb Natalie after the events of yesterday, and wander into the attached bathroom to have a shower. By the time I walk out again, the lass is sitting up and yawning.

"Good morning, *gràidh*. Did you sleep well?"

"Surprisingly well. What about you?"

I saunter over to the bed and sit down beside her. "I had a remarkably good night's rest. We must've both been exhausted."

"For sure."

"And I had an erotic dream about you. That's sure to make a man feel good in the morning."

"I dreamed about you too." She skims her gaze over my naked body and rubs her lips together as if she's imagining all the naughty things she wants to do with me. "I know you didn't sleep in the nude."

"No. I undressed and took a shower. Now I need to put on some clothes or else Owen will be horrified."

"I kind of doubt that. He doesn't seem like the sensitive type. If he saw you buck naked, he'd probably make a joke about it."

"Aye, you're right." I lean toward her, slide a hand into her hair, and draw her in for a kiss. "Ye taste even better this morning."

"Must be the flavor of leftover adrenaline." She throws the covers back and hops off the bed, raising her arms to stretch and moan with satisfaction. "What should we do now? I guess we need to stick around for a while, until the legal stuff is taken care of. I hope they keep Elliot locked up until his trial."

"So do I." When I recall last night, I can't help shaking my head. "Still can't believe the sheriff accepted your story about a puppy smuggling cartel. It sounds like rubbish, even though I know it's true."

"Yeah, I was kind of amazed too. But Sheriff Holzer is a smart man with loads of experience as a cop. I'm sure he could sniff out bullshit from ten miles away."

"Aye, I'm dead certain he could." I slap her erse. "Get dressed, lass. I'm fair starved."

Natalie digs items out of her backpack and gets dressed while I pull on my clothes. Then we amble out into the living room where Owen had spent the night on the sofa. He's awake now, and seems to have been awake for quite some time.

"Hey, sleepyheads," he calls out to us from the kitchen. "I made scrambled eggs, bacon, and French toast. Hope you guys like that kind of thing."

Natalie rubs her palms together. "Ooh, that sounds yummy."

"Aye, it does sound good," I say. "And it smells delicious too."

Owen has an actual dining room with an actual table in it, so we take our food in there to enjoy a meal and camaraderie. Considering our ordeal yesterday, I'm amazed that we can all manage to laugh and joke with each other. We avoid talking about the siege at my cabin, but I think that's a good idea right now. Later, we'll need to deal with it. But for the moment, laughter truly is the best medicine.

Natalie and I help Owen clean up after breakfast. We've just settled onto the large L-shaped sofa when Owen's landline rings. He had gone into the bathroom, so I follow the ringing through the living room and into the kitchen, following the sound until I stumble onto the cordless unit and its handset. Owen comes into the living room while I answer the phone. He and Natalie can see me, since the kitchen features an open design similar to my cabin.

I answer the phone. "Hello?"

"That sounds like Mr. MacTaggart, not Mr. Metzger."

"Aye, it is."

"This is Sheriff Holzer, by the way." His grave tone doesn't bode well, but for once, I decide to be optimistic.

"Do you need our statements now?"

"No." Holzer hesitates for a second longer than I'd like. "I'll get straight to the point. Elliot Rudaski escaped from county lockup early this morning."

"How the bloody hell did that happen?"

"Not sure. We're looking into it, and the state police are getting involved too. Rudaski assaulted Deputy Santos, who is still unconscious and can't tell us what went down." Holzer sighs heavily. "You three should come to my office so we can put you in protective custody."

"What does that mean? We'll get locked up while he roams free?"

"No. We'll find a safe house and have my deputies patrolling the grounds twenty-four seven."

"Elliot might have other cohorts besides the three you arrested." I glance into the living room where Natalie and Owen are watching me. They must've heard what I said and suspect something has gone wrong. Though I want to assure them we aren't in danger, I feel less than convinced that protective custody will live up to its name. "I appreciate the offer, Sheriff Holzer, but there's only one place I know we will be safe."

"Where's that?"

"Scotland. The MacTaggart clan takes care of its own." When I glance back again, Natalie's eyes are wide. "I'll give you the information about where we'll be going before we head out of town."

"That's not standard protocol."

"Aye, but my clan has more than two people. We are a small army of determined Scots including a former MI6 agent, as you well know. Several of my cousins and uncles were in the army, and a number of others offer a variety of talents and skills that will be very helpful."

"I see." Holzer falls silent, probably considering my suggestion. "Okay, I'm going to allow it. I only have two deputies, and your family sounds capable. I will need you to check in with the local police when you get to Scotland."

"Aye, we'll do that. Thank you, Sheriff."

"Good luck, Mr. MacTaggart."

I disconnect the call and walk over to the sofa, sitting down on the coffee table so I can look at both Natalie and Owen. "You heard what I told Sheriff Holzer."

"Yeah," Natalie says. "Are we really going to Scotland?"

"Aye. Dùndubhan is the only place where I know I can keep you safe—with my family's help."

"What is Dùndubhan?"

"It's a medieval castle that's been refurbished. It used to be my cousin Rory's home, but now it's mostly a museum. Family members often stay the night there too." I look at Owen. "You can come with us if you like. Or you can go into protective custody here."

"Think I'll do the protective custody. No offense to your family, but I've got work I need to do and I write better when I'm alone."

Natalie hugs Owen and kisses his cheek. "Be safe. I'll miss you."

My friend seems a wee bit embarrassed. "Uh, yeah, you too."

Owen looks at me and makes a pained face.

"Ahmno jealous," I say. "Natalie might have kissed your cheek, but she sleeps with me."

Natalie and I grab what we'd been able to bring from the cabin while Owen collects what he might need in protective custody. Then we stop off at the sheriff's office. I provide Holzer with the information he wants about where I'm taking Natalie and then we say goodbye to Owen. A taxi takes us to the airport.

When we bypass the terminal and head straight for the tarmac, Natalie tugs my arm to stop me. "Where are you going? We have to go into the terminal."

"No, we don't. While you were in the restroom at the sheriff's station, I called my cousin Rory. He informed me that our cousin Evan is currently in Utah. So I called Evan, and he sent his jet to pick us up and fly us to Inverness."

"A private jet? Wow, I didn't know those kind of planes got to skip security."

"They do. And we will reach Scotland faster this way."

I keep a hand on her back as we swiftly walk across the tarmac and mount the stairs to board the jet. Natalie's eyes widen a wee bit when she sees the luxurious interior, and she turns in a circle to take in the surroundings. Well, Evan's jet does have butter-soft leather chairs, a plush sofa, a huge television with surround sound, and a wet bar too.

When I show Natalie the bedroom, she laughs.

I shake my head. "You think a huge bed is hilarious."

"No. I'm not laughing because I think this is funny. I've never seen a plane this luxurious before, that's all."

"So, you laugh when you're amazed."

"Yes." She spins around and flops onto the bed on her back. While she skates her palms over the blanket in a snow angel motion, she smiles with ultimate satisfaction. "Could we live on this jet? Elliot wouldn't be able to find me if we never touch down. Plus, you and I could have sex for days on end."

I chuckle. "We might need breaks to eat and shower. We would also need to touch down to refuel on occasion. And there's no laundry service on this jet."

She props herself up on her elbows. "Okay, we won't live on the plane. But we could get naked in this room."

"Have you ever fucked on a private jet?"

"No. I've never even been on one before. What about you?"

I sit down beside her. "I haven't flown on this jet before, but I have been on the one Rory and Lachlan share. It was several years ago. I haven't seen any of my family except for Errol since then."

"Not even your parents?"

My entire body suddenly feels itchy, but I resist the urge to scratch. "I haven't seen them either. Ma and Da occasionally call me."

"Are you friendly when they call? Or do you grunt and growl at them?"

I could lie, but I don't want to do that anymore, not with Natalie. "Sometimes I grunt and growl. But Ma and Da are used to it."

"Did you inherit your grumpiness from one of them?"

"You would need to ask my parents about that."

Natalie sits up straighter and leans against my shoulder. "How can you not know whether one or both of your parents are grumpy?"

"Since I've been accused of being that way, I can't be objective."

"You are so weird, Munro." She kisses my cheek. "But I like that about you."

"Not sure if I should thank you for the compliment or snarl at you for harassing me."

She laughs in the sweetest way. "Come on, admit it. You like it when I harass you."

"It does make me randy. Maybe we should have a poke after all."

A throat-clearing draws my attention to the doorway, where the co-pilot stands on the threshold. "Sorry to disturb you, sir, but we're about to take off. Just wanted to let you know."

"Thank you."

"Once we're in the air, the chef will be happy to cook something for you if you're hungry."

"Aye, we might do that."

The co-pilot nods crisply and leaves us.

I slide an arm around Natalie's waist and tip my head down to nuzzle her cheek. "What do you say about that poke?"

She yawns. The action makes her mouth gape open while her eyes are squeezed shut.

I pat her thigh. "How about a wee nap first?"

The lass yawns again. "Yeah, a nap sounds good."

We kick our shoes off and lie down on the bed on top of the covers. Natalie snuggles up to me, draping an arm over my chest, while I wrap my arms around her. Soon, she drifts off to sleep. I lie awake for a while, but once the jet reaches altitude, I give in and go to sleep too.

I might not have a bloody clue how I feel about Natalie, but I know one thing for certain. My life will never again be the way it was before I met her.

Chapter Nineteen

Natalie

Who knew a jet could fly from Wyoming to Scotland in less than half a day? I never thought about how fast a private jet could go until I stepped onto this plane. When I woke up after my nap, Munro was still sleeping. So I just lay there in his arms watching him and wondering what will happen next. We'll go to the castle he'd mentioned, I assume. Munro didn't explicitly say we would hide out there, but I assumed that was why he mentioned that place.

I doubt I'll be able to pronounce that castle's name without mangling it. Dun-doo-in? Not sure if that's right. I'd wanted to ask Munro about the pronunciation when he woke up, but we were both too hungry to have a conversation. By the time we had finished off our meal, cooked by a real chef who actually wears one of those poofy hats, I'd forgotten about the question I'd wanted to ask.

Oh, well. We have more pressing issues to discuss than how to pronounce a castle's name.

Like what my ex-husband might do next.

But Munro and I agreed not to discuss the woolly mammoth in the room until we touch down in Scotland. Yeah, Elliot is now a big hairy beast from the Ice Age. Comparing him to those creatures might be an insult to woolly mammoths.

As our jet approaches the UK, at first I see nothing but water below us. Then I spot the first glimpses of land ahead and wriggle closer to the window for a better view. Of course, I can't really see anything yet. But as we descend, heading toward Inverness, I spot craggy mountains and dark lochs that spread out toward the sea to the west and north. That's the Highlands. I'm about to set foot on Scottish soil for the first time in my life.

Munro is sitting across from me, but now he slants forward to point out the window and tell me the names of the various natural landmarks. I can't pay attention to what he says, though. I'm too excited. When we touch down on the runway, I feel like whooping and clapping. But I don't do that. It would be dumb.

As soon as the stairs are wheeled up to our jet, the pilot comes out to swing the door open so we can exit the plane. He also carries our bags for us. We descend the steps first, and I suddenly notice the large group of strangers who have trotted onto the tarmac—to greet us, I assume.

"Is that your family?" I ask. "Seems like a lot of people."

"Aye, I told you my extended family is large."

"Yeah, I remember. But are your parents here? Or just your cousins?"

"Ma and Da must be here somewhere." He clasps my hand as we approach the crowd. "Get ready. The horde is about to descend on us."

"You make your family sound so friendly."

"They're good folk. But they can be a wee bit…overenthusiastic."

I don't get the chance to ask him what he means by that because the horde does indeed descend on us like a smiling, laughing, super-friendly swarm of locusts. I get kissed on the cheek by several women and some of the men too. Even Munro seems to have trouble sorting out the crowd, and if he weren't holding on to my hand, I might get swept away on the human tide.

"Haud yer wheesht!" Munro hollers. "We can't all talk at once."

The boisterous crowd settles down enough that at least my eardrums won't rupture.

Munro drapes an arm around my shoulders. "This lass is Natalie Saari. She needs our help. Her ex-husband wants to murder her, for reasons we will explain later once all of you lot have calmed down. I explained the situation to Evan and Rory, but I only gave a bare outline. If you let us get settled in, we will tell you everything."

The MacTaggarts nod.

Amid a flurry of whispering, the crowd parts to allow an older man and woman to approach me and Munro. They halt an arm's length away and seem far from thrilled to see us.

"So, I reckon you expect a homecoming parade," the man says. "We haven't seen ye in years, but you bring a girl with you and don't explain how long you've been with her."

"I know we haven't seen each other in a long while," Munro says. "But we have talked on the phone. And I'll tell you all about Natalie in the car on our way to Dùndubhan. All right?"

The woman bursts into tears and throws her arms around Munro, babbling things I can't understand.

He pats her back and looks at me. "This is my mother, Kenna. And that scowling man is Peadar, my father. Ma, Da, say hello to Natalie."

Kenna releases her son only to latch on to me and start crying again. "Yer so bonnie, lass. And I can tell you're sweet too. We're so happy to meet you, Natalie."

"I'm happy to meet you too." My words come out sort of breathless thanks to how hard she's hugging me.

The second Kenna backs away, her husband takes one step toward his son. They now stand inches apart, each eying the other as if neither knows what to do now. After a moment, Peadar's hard expression melts away.

And he drags his son into a bear hug. "At least ye didn't get yourself killed going down the river in the Grand Canyon."

Munro slaps his father's back. "Aye, I'm glad for that too. Da, don't ye want to meet Natalie?"

"Och, of course I do." Peadar releases his son and gives me a softer hug. He kisses my cheek too. "Welcome to the family, Natalie. Never thought my son would settle down."

Munro aims an exasperated look at his father. "Da, let Natalie recover from the flight before you start planning the wedding. There won't be one. We are not engaged or even officially dating."

Not officially? That's what he said. Munro couldn't mean that we *are* dating, just not going out on actual dates. We haven't talked about that at all. Now is not the time to broach the subject. We have fantastic sex and have developed a closeness I hadn't expected, but none of that gives me any insight into what Munro feels.

How do I feel about the Wild Man? I haven't had time to sort that out.

The rest of Munro's relatives approach us in pairs and introduce themselves as his cousins and their wives or husbands. I meet some of the people I'd come across during my nosy internet search, and they're all so nice and so kind in their determination to help me despite having just met me minutes ago. They don't even know all the details, yet they still want to pitch in. When Kirsty and Luke Turner introduce themselves, I can't stop myself from asking a question.

"I saw your shop online," I tell her. "It looks amazing. Are you really a witch?"

"Wiccan. I have *da-shealladh*, the second sight. But my witchy powers aren't infallible. I never had an intuition about Munro and you."

"Maybe I could visit your shop sometime."

"That would be lovely."

Luke pulls his wife close and kisses the top of her head. "Kirsty might be nuts, but it's the cutest kind of insanity."

He smirks, and I can tell that's because he's teasing Kirsty. Their love for each other is evident—and the same goes for every couple I've met.

Now, I want to know what on earth Munro was talking about earlier. So I turn to the couple who have just walked up to us—Rory and Emery MacTaggart. "Munro mentioned something called the American Wives Club. Do you know anything about that?"

Rory chuckles. "Do we know anything? My wife is one of the founding members of the American Wives Club. She gave the group its name."

"Somebody had to do it," Emery says. "We couldn't call ourselves the No Name Brigade."

Her husband rolls his eyes. "Why must women give silly titles to everything?"

"Because it's fun." Emery leans toward me and speaks in a fake whisper. "You could join the club now as a provisional member. That way, once you and Munro tie the knot, you'll already know what to expect."

Tie the knot? I've known Munro for a few days. "That's really sweet of you. But I think it's too early for me to join your club. Besides, I have serious problems that need to be dealt with."

"Of course. Rory told me that Munro said your ex-husband wants to murder you. The MacTaggarts will never let that happen."

"Elliot is dangerous and ruthless. I don't want anybody to get hurt trying to protect me."

"Don't worry. We've got every kind of expert you could possibly need or want right here in the Highlands. And this will hardly be the first time some jerk-off tried to lay siege to Dùndubhan. The castle has survived for hundreds of years because it's virtually impenetrable." Emery winks. "We've got your back, sweetie."

That sounds wonderful, but I worry about who might get hurt and how badly if Elliot brings more goons and bigger guns when he finally tracks me down. Yeah, I assume he will succeed in finding me. Maybe I feel that way only because of how thoroughly my ex managed to terrify me.

As the other MacTaggarts disperse and climb into various vehicles, we follow Emery and Rory to their Mercedes. We keep a little behind them, and I soon find out why. Munro wants to talk.

"Are ye all right, lass?" he asks. "I know my family can be a wee bit overwhelming."

"Well, yeah, there are so dang many of them. I'm an only child of two only children."

"I'm an only child too, but as you've seen, I come with a herd of stampeding cousins, aunts, and uncles."

"Everyone I've met is so nice. They don't even know me, but they swear they'll defend me at all costs."

He wraps an arm around my shoulders. "They mean it too. MacTaggarts are dogged and fiercely loyal."

"Are we going to the castle now?"

"We are."

Munro and I climb into the backseat of the Mercedes while Rory holds the door open for us. Then he shuts the door and gets into the driver's seat with Emery seated beside him.

Rory twists around to look at me. "Have you ever seen a medieval fortress in person?"

"No. But I thought we were going to a castle."

"Dùndubhan is both a grand castle and a powerful fortress. No one has ever taken Dùndubhan in battle, and no one ever will."

While Rory steers the Mercedes out onto the road, I snuggle up to Munro. He settles his arm across the seat's back. How can being with a man I barely know feel so comfortable and so…right? After everything I've been through, I don't want to second guess anything about my relationship with Munro. It's the best thing in my life.

During the three and a half hour drive to Dùndubhan, Rory and Emery point out every touristy thing we pass along the way. We don't stop at any of those points of interest. We need to figure out a plan for protecting me from Elliot. Can these wonderful people really do what they say they will? I have my doubts, until we turn off the paved road and head down a dirt two-track through the woods. The forest is so deep that I can't tell how far away we are from the castle. Just when I decide Rory must have gotten lost on his own land, we pass through an open metal gate, and the dirt gives way to gravel. And up ahead, I can make out the lines of a hulking gray shape.

Dùndubhan. It must be.

The woods open up, revealing the castle.

My jaw drops. Literally. It's no exaggeration because I can feel a draft blowing into my mouth. Ahead of us hunkers a large, boxy structure constructed from grayish-brown stones. I see two turrets and a small chimney that protrude from what looks like the main part of the castle. I can't distinguish the floors, though, because of the haphazard placement of the windows. A high wall surrounds the whole complex. The Scottish flag, with its white X on a blue background, flies proudly above the highest turret.

As we roll up to the entrance, I crane my neck to gaze up at a massive wooden gateway that consists of two halves. Those sections are now open wide for us.

Rory parks in the gravel driveway.

Munro swings the back door open and climbs out, offering me his hand. As I set foot on the gravel, I survey my surroundings and unabashedly let my awe show on my face and creep into my voice. "Holy cow. This really is a castle. I can imagine a regiment of Scottish warriors living here, ready to fight to the death for their people."

"If there were battles here, no one has found any evidence of that. And we have more important matters to deal with today."

"It's time for a war council, hey?"

"Aye, it is."

Chapter Twenty

Munro

I keep hold of Natalie's hand as we follow Rory and Emery into the castle. The main door opens into a vestibule with a big spiral staircase that leads upstairs where three more levels house various rooms including the great hall and the long gallery. I've attended so many events my family has held here that I know the layout by heart.

"This is the ground floor," Rory explains, for Natalie's sake. "Not to be confused with the first floor, which is upstairs. The layout of the castle puzzles most people."

"I'll give her the grand tour later," I say. "Right now, we have urgent matters to talk about."

"Aye, we do. Let's go into my office."

Rory and Emery lead us up to the first floor and through the great hall to a door that stands closed. My cousin keeps his office locked when he isn't here, since he still takes on the occasional client despite being semi-retired. He is only in his forties, after all. Once a solicitor, always a solicitor. I hadn't known Rory had retired until Errol informed me of that fact during our Grand Canyon expedition.

I lead Natalie to the two chairs positioned in front of the large wood desk, where we take our seats.

My cousin sits in the big leather executive chair behind his desk. His wife perches on his lap.

Natalie glances at me, her brows lifting. But I can't explain to her right now why Rory and Emery like to sit that way. Actually, I never could explain it. They are a strange couple, though not as strange as Catriona and her husband, Alex Thorne, the Brit who married my cousin Catriona. I only know about him because Errol told me during one of the many times when he rang to chat to me, which means he did all the talking. Dinnae even get me started on Errol and Ashley, or Magnus and Piper.

Aye, that lot make me seem like the sane, rational person in the family.

Rory locks his arm around his wife's waist. "So, Munro, tell us what trouble you've gotten yourself into this time."

"Why do you make it sound as if I often get myself into trouble?"

"Since none of us knows what you've gotten up to over the past several years, I can neither confirm nor deny whatever you have done."

Natalie is giving me another brows-raised look. I can't clear up what my cousin said because it made no sense. Aye, I'm definitely seeming like the rational one in this room, if not the whole clan.

"If you're referring to the Grand Canyon incident," I say, "that was Errol and Ashley's idea. I went along with it strictly to make sure they didn't get themselves killed. That barmy couple would've rushed headlong into the worst rapids in the canyon and drowned if I hadn't been there."

"You need to describe the current situation. I assume you're wanting our help, and that means we need facts."

"Natalie's husband wants to kill her. I brought the lass here because no place is safer than Dùndubhan."

"True. But—" Rory pauses to listen to whatever his wife is whispering in his ear. Hopefully, it's not a description of how she wants him to shag her tonight. He nods and faces us again. "We are going to help, naturally. But this seems to call for a clan conference."

"What the bloody hell is that? Never heard of a MacTaggart clan conference before."

"It was Emery's idea." His wife whispers in his ear again, and he nods. "But before we convene that meeting, you should give us the basics of the situation. Beyond 'her ex-husband wants her dead,' that is."

Natalie bites her lip and glances at me. I make a go-on gesture.

"I was married to Elliot Rudaski for six years," Natalie says. "He was so nice at first, very loving and attentive. He got laid off from his job, so I worked while he looked for something else. Eventually, he announced he had become an entrepreneur—a dog trainer. Eventually, I found out that was a lie. Elliot had become a smuggler."

"Of what?" Rory asks.

I can see the faint tightening around her eyes that suggests he's worried about sharing the rest with Rory and Emery. So I give her hand a quick squeeze. She aims a grateful smile at me.

Then the lass sits up straighter and tells them the truth. "Elliot had formed a puppy smuggling cartel."

Rory and Emery stay perfectly still for a moment, seeming not even to blink. Then they exchange puzzled looks.

"I know it sounds dumb," Natalie says. "But I swear it's true. Elliot has been smuggling rare and endangered breeds for the past four years. I had no idea. I believed it when he said he'd become a dog trainer. That did explain the hairs on his clothes. What an idiot, right?"

"You are not an idiot," Emery says. "Even the smartest people can get taken in by a skilled con artist."

Rory nods. "Aye, even the magnificent MacTaggarts occasionally fall prey to such schemes."

Natalie seems confused again, probably because she can't tell if my cousin is having her on or if he believes our clan is "magnificent." Well, I suppose we are. Just look at the feats we've accomplished. But I don't have time to explain that to her.

"Perhaps you should tell us the rest," Rory says. "The short version, for now."

"Okay." Natalie sets her hands on her thighs. "I divorced Elliot and moved away, and I thought that was the end of it. But I think he must have been searching for me. Then, he turned up at Munro's cabin, where I was staying, and things spiraled out of control. Munro managed to capture Elliot's three goons. Owen went for help, and Elliot and his men were arrested."

"But then he escaped from the county jail," I say. "That's why I decided to bring her here."

Rory nods again. "That was a sound choice, Munro. Dùndubhan is the safest place to be, and you know the entire clan will stand behind you both."

"Exactly why we came here."

My cousin and his wife whisper a bit more, then both stand up. Rory picks up his desk phone. "Time to convene the conference."

Emery comes around the desk and waves for us to follow her out the door. "Rory will arrange the conference, but you guys have a much more important decision to make right now."

"What's that?" Natalie asks as we exit the office and start across the great hall.

"You need to decide which bedroom you want." Emery halts and studies us both. "Unless you want separate rooms."

I'm about to say no, we don't want that. But Natalie gets there first.

"We'll share," she says. "Thank you for asking, though, Emery."

"Of course."

I stare at Emery's blonde head as we wander to the other end of the great hall and Emery begins to describe all the available bedrooms in the sort of detail only a woman would give a toss about. Whether there's a down comforter or a microfiber blanket hardly matters to me. I don't even know for sure what the difference is. So I pretend to care when the woman I need to shag tonight asks which room I would prefer. And I grunt.

She gives me an exasperated look.

Emery laughs. "You two are so cute. The MacTaggart clan has found another great couple."

Natalie swerves her gaze away from me. Maybe she's embarrassed by what Emery said, but those words didn't fash me at all. I don't care what Emery says. She's a bonnie, sweet lass and one of the cleverest people I know, but she does like to spout barmy nonsense on occasion.

I stay silent, interjecting only the occasional grunt, while the lasses drag me up all four levels of the castle. Natalie wants to explore every room before deciding where we will sleep. When she asks my opinion of each room, I shrug. She punches me in the side, though not hard. Her stern expression makes me want to fuck her right here on the floor of the long gallery.

On the third floor, we visit one bedroom. The other is reserved for Rory and Emery, though they only sleep there once in a while. They have a much smaller home near Ballachulish that's the right size for them and their twin bairns.

Natalie turns in a circle once, then sets her hands on her hips. "No grunting this time, Munro. Which room did you like the best?"

"My answer wouldn't be appropriate to say in front of Emery."

She rushes up to me and stands on her tiptoes to whisper in my ear, "If you want to fuck me tonight, better be more cooperative."

I clear my throat, trying to ignore the fact my trousers have grown tight in the groin. "This room will do."

"Yay!" Emery cries out while clapping. "You guys are going to love staying at Dùndubhan. It's a magical, romantic fortress."

Dinnae think the term fortress is romantic, but then, I'm not a woman.

"Tavish will bring up your bags," Emery tells us. "We'll let you know when the conference is starting."

I lift one brow. "Ye make it sound like that will happen today."

"Because it will." She wags a finger at me. "You're a MacTaggart. How could you not have guessed things would move quickly? Besides, who knows when Natalie's ex might figure out where she went."

"Aye, you're right. Best to take action right away."

Emery leaves and shuts the door.

I have Natalie alone again at last. But she collapses onto the bed and rolls onto her side, punching the pillow to get it positioned just right. And she yawns.

What else can I do? I sit down beside her. "No fucking anytime soon, eh? You look exhausted, lass. Have a wee lie-down."

"Okay," she says while yawning again.

I remove her shoes and crawl onto the bed behind her, tucking my body against hers. Maybe I'm more tired than I realized because even the feel of her supple body and her firm erse pressed against my cock doesn't rouse me to lust. I'd been mildly randy a few minutes ago, but it faded in an instant once I lay down with Natalie.

The next thing I know, someone is pounding on the door.

"Wake up, lovebirds, it's time for the clan conference."

Natalie moans and rolls over but covers her face with her hands. "Who is that? And why is he yelling at us?"

"That's Iain. He's in his fifties and probably has started to lose his hearing already."

"I heard that, Munro," my cousin shouts. "My hearing is fine. And you didn't need to say that so loudly."

"Of course I did. How else would you hear it?"

My cousin issues a long string of Gaelic curses, none of which are flattering to me.

I slap Natalie's erse. "Best get up, *gràidh*. When the clan calls, there's no point in fighting it."

She moans pitifully.

"We'll be right there, Iain," I call out.

"Come to the great hall."

"Aye, we will."

Natalie finally sits up and stretches.

I sit up too. "Feeling better?"

"Yes. Feel like I might be able to handle a clan conference with a bunch of people I've never met."

"Any woman who can handle me can deal with my extended family."

By the time we reach the great hall, everyone is there. Somehow, my cousins and their spouses managed to set up tables and chairs and even a small buffet of snacks while Natalie and I slept. It couldn't have been that long since we went upstairs. I check the time and realize three hours have gone by. We must have been more tired than we thought. Still, three hours must be a record for setting up an event like this, even for my family.

My cousin Evan ushers us to a wee table that seems to have been positioned so that everyone else will see it. We sit down on the two chairs that wait for us. I glance at Natalie, and she seems confused or perhaps amazed by what the MacTaggarts have done. I'm surprised too. I probably shouldn't be, but then, I've stayed away from home for far too long.

Being back here in the Highlands feels like fate.

Just a few days ago, I would've called that idea rubbish. But the events of the past few days have changed my mind about a lot of things.

My cousin Logan rises from his chair, situated directly in front of where Natalie and I sit. "Silence!"

When Logan issues a command, even a single-word one, everyone pays attention. He was an MI6 agent until a few years ago, so aye, he knows how to command attention when he wants to and how to be surreptitious when necessary.

"Listen up," Logan says, his voice echoing off the walls of this cavernous room. "If you haven't met our guest yet, she is Natalie Saari, Munro's lass."

I glance at Natalie again, expecting her to seem annoyed by Logan's proclamation. But she doesn't look irritated. She's almost smiling.

"You should have received your briefing document and read it," Logan continues. "We have all the information we need to reach a decision. So, will we aid and support Natalie in any way that might be necessary?"

A chorus of ayes ripple through the crowd.

"Good. Now it's time to make a battle plan."

Chapter Twenty-One

Natalie

Are we going to war? I suppose we'll have to do that. Elliot won't give up easily, not when he has a hard-on for killing me. I never tattled on the bastard, though I probably should have. I just wanted to get away from him. Elliot wouldn't let me. He hunted me down and left me no choice but to hand him over to the authorities. I couldn't have done that without the help of Munro and Owen.

Is Owen safe now? God, I hope so.

"Who is that man who's talking?" I whisper to Munro.

"Logan. He's my cousin as well as a former MI6 agent and an army veteran."

"Are a lot of your cousins also veterans like you?"

"Magnus is too, but most aren't. They still have skills that could help us, though."

"Who is that man over there?"

Munro peers through the crowd, following the direction of my pointing finger. "Dinnae know. He's with Catriona, so he must be her husband, Alex Thorne. I don't know much about him since I wasn't around when he married Cat."

"You've missed out on a lot, haven't you?"

"Aye. I shouldn't have stayed away so long."

Logan surveys the crowd with the steely gaze and impenetrable composure of a former spy. Not that I've ever met another spy. But I imagine that's how they all must be. No one speaks while Logan simply stands there looking sexy and imposing at the same time. Yeah, Munro's cousin is hot. The MacTaggart clan seems to have an overabundance of attractive men and women. Maybe eating lots of haggis has that effect.

Oh, please. I'm getting way too sentimental about, well, everything.

My gaze wanders to Munro, and I get a strange pang in my chest. He brought me home with him to protect me, though he'd only known me for a few days. He risked his life for me. How far would Munro go to protect me? All the way. I know that with every fiber of my being.

"We need a game plan," Logan announces. "Serena and I have discussed the problem, and we want everyone to split off in groups. Each group will deal with one part of the plan. Then we will convene again in a few hours to bring it all together."

I lean toward Munro and whisper, "Who is Serena?"

"The bonnie woman sitting beside Logan. She's his wife. And the laddie beside Serena is her son, Chase, who is also Logan's teenage stepson."

"How do you know all that when you haven't seen your family in years?"

"Errol insisted on calling and emailing me after our expedition in the Grand Canyon. He was trying to make me 'assimilate' with the clan again."

"But he failed. You stayed locked up in your hermit cabin."

He flashes me a scowl, but it fades away swiftly. "I'm not a hermit. But actually, Errol's bloody annoying tactic worked. I became more interested in the family after I heard about what I'd missed by avoiding them."

I want to ask him why he didn't come home sooner if wanted to see his family again. But Logan starts barking orders, rattling off who will be on each "task force" and in which room in this enormous castle each group will conduct their meeting. Serena then hands out sheets of paper to each "task force."

Maybe that term does sound like overkill. But Logan is a former spy, so I give him the benefit of the doubt. Preparation must be paramount for someone who infiltrates terrorist cells or whatever kinds of covert operations Logan might have implemented.

As the groups split off to find their assigned rooms, Alex Thorne and Logan MacTaggart approach me and Munro. We rise, but I think we mostly do that because it feels weird to have two men towering over us. Or maybe that's just me. Munro probably doesn't care about that.

Logan claps a hand on Alex's shoulder. "I don't think you two have formally met this laddie. Alex Thorne is married to my cousin Catriona, and he has skills no one else in the Highlands can claim to have. Alex has ideas for how you two should participate in the plan. His unique talents could be quite useful."

"How can he help?" Munro asks. "I've heard that he's odd and arrogant, that's all."

Logan turns to Alex. "Why don't you tell them?"

"It's quite simple," the Brit says. "I can teach you how to lie, cheat, and steal."

"We don't want to become criminals," Munro says. "Natalie is trying to get away from that world."

"You misunderstand. I don't want you to steal objects. I want you to use misdirection to steal the wits of anyone who tries to get in your way."

"I'm totally confused," I say. "What exactly are your qualifications?"

Alex folds his arms over his chest and smirks. "I was raised to be a grifter. A con artist, if you prefer that term. For the first eight years of my life I mastered the techniques of pickpocketing, sleight of hand, verbal misdirection, and various other sorts of conning."

"We call him the British Bastard," Logan announces. "Catriona gave him that name, but the reasons why are a long story. Trust me, Alex can con anyone."

"Do we have time to learn all that?"

Alex winks. "With the amazing Alex Thorne on your side, anything is possible. Of course we have time. With me as your teacher, you will master these techniques quicker than you think."

Logan shakes his head. "Don't let Alex's arrogance fool you. He's a good man underneath all that rubbish."

I can't believe this is really happening. I'm going to learn how to con my ex-husband and whatever sleazebags he brings with him. If he finds me here. And if grifting doesn't do the trick, we've got multiple task forces waiting in the wings.

Alex leads us outside and into the courtyard where everyone's cars are parked. He suggests that we should practice our conning skills outdoors because those task forces are taking up the largest rooms in the castle and we need space to practice the new skills he will teach us. It's a beautiful sunny day, which Munro grumpily informs me is not the norm in Scotland.

Our teacher informs us, "The gods of Scotland always smile on a newcomer who is as beautiful as you, Natalie."

I'm starting to understand why Catriona fell for Alex, despite his pretense of being an arrogant ass. He can be quite charming. He's also gorgeous and sexy. Combined with his admittedly amazing talent for trickery, that makes him a dangerous man indeed. Dangerous in a good way.

When I tell Munro that, he doesn't seem surprised. "Every MacTaggart who is in the castle right now brings formidable skills to the table. We are all dangerous when the need arises."

Yeah, I finally understand that. And it makes me feel safer than ever before.

But I suddenly realize something. "What about my parents? Elliot might go after them."

"Relax, lass." Munro pulls me close. "Evan gave us his jet, but as soon as we landed here in Scotland, he told the pilots to fly back to America to retrieve your parents. They should arrive soon."

"Why didn't anybody tell me that?"

"There's been a lot going on. We forgot, that's all. I'm sorry. None of us meant to make you worry." He kisses my forehead. "Your ma and da will go to a safe house in Ballachulish."

"Safe house? Jeez, you guys really are spies, aren't you?"

"No, *gràidh*. Our 'safe house' is the home of Niall and Sorcha, my uncle and aunt. They're the parents of Lachlan and his five siblings." He smirks. "The elder MacTaggarts will keep your ma and da safe. Niall will be joined by Torcall Murdoch, Errol's uncle, and several other men from the Murdoch and Mac-Taggart and clans."

"Holy shit. Are all Scots as amazing as you guys?"

"Of course not." He winks. "Our clan is the best."

I can't refute that claim.

Our training begins with learning about sleight of hand, though I don't see how that will save me from Elliot. Maybe he won't find me here. Maybe he'll give up on punishing me now that he has to evade the authorities. I know that's probably false hope, since Elliot must be even more pissed off at me for getting him arrested. But I need any sliver of hope I can get.

Munro and his family have given me more than a sliver. They've brought a small army.

Once I stop worrying and relax, I pick up Alex's techniques faster than I would have expected. It's kind of fun learning how to con people. I would never do that just to rip people off, but I now understand how these skills can be useful in non-criminal activities. Alex is a great teacher. When I suggest he should start his own school for teaching this stuff, he chuckles.

"I don't think the authorities would approve, pet."

Well, he has a point.

Munro seems to enjoy learning how to con as much as I do. And he's way better at sleight of hand than I am. Alex assures us that our differing levels of aptitude will complement each other, and we could become the best pair of grifters in Scotland. A few days ago, I would never have believed I'd wind up in this situation, learning new and slightly larcenous talents. My entire life has been flipped upside down and inside out.

When we return to the great hall, the rest of our army is already waiting for us. Some of the women have left, the ones who are pregnant or recently had their babies. It's a precautionary measure that seems prudent under the circumstances. Chase, Logan's stepson, has also left. Three new ladies have arrived, though, and Munro introduces me to them.

"Meet my cousins Isla, Elspeth, and Kirsty," he says. "Logan is their brother. These three are known as the Witches of Ballachulish."

"That's cool. I came across Kirsty's metaphysical shop online, but I'd love to visit it sometime."

"Not until after we've dealt with Elliot."

"Yeah, of course." I'd much rather talk about the supernatural than my own problems, so I change the subject. "You girls aren't really witches, right? That's for the tourists."

"Aye, we put on a good show for them," Isla says. "But Kirsty honestly does have *da-shealladh*. Kirsty told you about that, didn't she?"

"Yes. And I'm sorry if I offended you. Sometimes my mouth goes off on its own."

"Oh, you can't offend us. We have elevated our psyches to a higher plane."

Kirsty rolls her eyes. "Isla is full of rubbish, Natalie. She hasn't reached any higher plane or acquired any special knowledge. I do have the second sight, but it isn't infallible."

"Nothing is. But I would love to hear more about you three."

"We are devout Wiccans who occasionally dance naked under the full moon."

"No, we don't," Elspeth says. "Isla is having you on."

"Be that as it may," Isla says, "we came here to help. Our unique talents may prove useful."

"Honestly, I've never believed in magic. But I will accept any help that's offered and be grateful for it."

"We can discuss that later. Logan seems to be getting annoyed with the way we've interrupted his 'conference.' My wee brother is adorably anal sometimes."

Logan is not "wee," but I think Isla means that he's younger than she is. He's certainly not small.

"Go on, Logie," Isla calls out to her brother. "Tell everyone their task force names and call signs."

Did she seriously just call her brother Logie? I can't imagine he appreciates that nickname.

Logan frowns at his sister, but she simply smiles and waves at him. He begins to do exactly what Isla said. Every "task force" does have its own title, and Logan does give everyone a copy of his "call sign manifest." Even Munro and I receive copies. My call sign is "Firecracker" while Munro's is, of course, "Wild Man." I don't see why we need special nicknames. Our actual names would do just as well. But these people are risking their lives for me, a stranger, so I won't complain about anything.

Logan has organized the entire "operation," but one thing remains unknown.

When will Elliot find me again?

Chapter Twenty-Two

Munro

I can tell Natalie is anxious, but that's to be expected under the circumstances. Elliot will search for her. I have no doubts about that. The bastard believes she has information he needs, though Natalie has no idea what that is. My family will remain here at Dùndubhan for the duration, which means until Elliot shows himself and we hand him over to the authorities. His escape from jail will ensure he receives a more severe punishment than he might have otherwise.

But if that bastard comes within a mile of Natalie, I will kill him with my bare hands.

When our conference ends, the sun is sinking below the horizon. We all need to eat, but the whole clan can't fit inside the dining room. So we turn the great hall into a dinner buffet, which Iain informs me is something they've done often over the past several years. Christ, I really have missed too much. I should never have hidden in the Wyoming wilderness. After nearly dying in the Grand Canyon, I'd let myself sink into a hermit's lifestyle and become a great hairy beast. No wonder Natalie was afraid of me when we first met.

Several men and women collaborated to cook a grand feast for everyone. Natalie eats heartily, and I'm glad to see that. She laughs at jokes told by my various cousins too, and that's even better. I'd worried Natalie might become so anxious that she wouldn't think about anything else, even her own health. I should have known better. She is a strong lass who can handle any situation.

Halfway through dinner, I notice two people arguing and gesturing angrily at a table on the other side of the room. The woman is Fiona, but for a moment I'm not certain who the man is. Then I realize it must be Domhnall Sterling. Errol had told me about how Fiona met Domhnall during Alex and Catriona's wedding week at the nudist resort. Their relationship has been stormy ever since.

After dinner, Natalie and I retire to the sitting room with Logan and Serena. We enjoy a bottle of Ben Nevis single malt whisky that Rory gave us, despite the fact his favorite whisky is no longer being produced. He told us to drink the whole bloody bottle if we wanted, but we don't consume that much. Logan and Serena catch me up on what our family has been doing during my absence. I can't believe how much trouble they've gotten into, beginning with how Lachlan met Erica at a night club and seduced her into a one-month fling, then he threw her over and ran back to Scotland. She forgave him after he "groveled like the sorry dog he was," or so Logan claims. I also learn about how Aidan and Rory met their wives in unconventional ways. Rory nearly lost Emery, but Aidan fought hard to convince Calli they belonged together.

Erica and Emery must be extremely tolerant and forgiving lasses. They took those eejits back and married them despite what they'd done. I think my favorite story that Logan shares is the one about Alex and Catriona, though Magnus and Piper have an epic romance that was chronicled in the newspapers. Those two, with the clan's help, captured the bastard who murdered Piper's former boss and framed her for the crime.

No, I don't see any way that Natalie and I can top that story. We aren't a couple, anyway, not like my cousins and their spouses. Could we be like that? Dinnae know. Do I want a serious relationship with her? After my failed marriage, I thought I'd never consider going down that road again. But tonight, I wonder.

After having some whisky in the sitting room, we go to our quarters on the top floor and crawl under the covers. The Scotch has made Natalie so relaxed that she falls asleep as soon as her head meets the pillow. I watch her sleeping for a while, then finally drift off. In the morning, I wake up to find Natalie already dressed and standing by the window that overlooks the courtyard. She seems to be enjoying whatever she sees out there, based on the slight upward curve of her lips and the way she has her head tipped to the side a wee bit.

I amble over there and wrap my arms around her waist from behind. "Good morning, *gràidh*. Sleep well?"

"Mm, very well. I didn't think I would fall asleep so fast, and I definitely thought I'd have nightmares about Elliot. But I didn't."

"You know you're safe at Dùndubhan, that's why." I kiss her neck. "How about a quick morning shag?"

She laughs. "You think everything is cause for a quick shag. Have you seen what your cousins are doing out there?"

I lean around the other side of her head and peer out the window. "Are they playing with swords?"

"Looks like it."

"Not sure that will be useful if Elliot comes to Dùndubhan. He will bring firearms, for dead certain."

"Yeah. But it's fun watching your cousins fooling around with big blades. Do you have any swordsman skills?"

"No." I watch Rory and Aidan jousting with their blades, though neither man comes anywhere close to striking the other. "If ye don't want to shag, at least take a shower with me."

"Already had a shower. While you were asleep."

"How late is it? I thought I'd be up before you."

She slants to the side, squinting at the clock on the nightstand. "It's nine forty-two."

"What?" I step back. "Better have that shower right away."

"Relax, Munro. There's no rush." She grasps my face and kisses me. Then she wrinkles her nose. "Your beard has gotten bushier and raspier. Kind of like kissing sandpaper." I must look fashed because she smiles and pinches my erse. "I fell for a wild man, so I have to live with the rough-and-tumble stuff that comes with that."

She heads for the door.

"Where are ye going, lass?"

"Downstairs. I'll meet you in the dining room when you're done with your shower. Rory made sure to save some food for you."

Natalie leaves, and the door shuts behind her.

Did she say she's fallen for me? Maybe she meant that in some other way, not that she has romantic feelings for me.

I take my shower and do a bit of, ah, personal maintenance. Whether Natalie will approve of the changes I've made, I can't guess. But I will find out as soon as I reach the dining room. It's on the ground floor, so after pulling on some clothes, I trot down three flights of stairs and continue through the vestibule and into the main hallway. The dining room is at the end.

Natalie is already sitting at the table, talking to Emery. The lasses are laughing about who knows what, probably something about how barmy men are. As I enter the room, Emery spots me first. Her brows shoot up, then her lips curve into an appreciative smile.

She nudges Natalie's arm. "Look what the Scottish fairy brought you."

"Huh?" Natalie swivels her head toward the doorway, where I'm standing. Her eyes flare wide. Her jaw falls open. "Munro? What did you do?"

"What do you think? It's dead obvious."

"Don't get grumpy. You can't show up looking like that and expect me not to be shocked. I mean, you were so attached to your scruffy beard and unkempt hair."

Emery pushes her chair back and sashays past me, pausing to pat my arm. "Give her some time to recover from the shock. Trust me, she loves your new look."

All I did was trim my beard so it's more like heavy stubble than a bushy mess. And I also used some hair softening rubbish from a bottle I found in the bathroom. The label claimed it will "tame the toughest tangles and make your hair silky smooth." That sounded like something Natalie might like. But now she's gawping at me as if I've carved satanic symbols on my chest.

I scratch behind my ear and clear my throat. "You don't like it."

"No, I don't like it." She leaps out of her chair, making it tumble over backward, and rushes at me. The lass throws her arms around my neck and kisses me passionately. "I love it, Munro. You were hot as the hairy Wild Man, but the well-groomed version is even sexier. I could fuck you right now on the dining room table."

Am I smirking? Of course I am. "That might scandalize my cousins."

"Since when do you care what anyone thinks of you?"

I link my hands over the small of her back. "Since I met you. Only your opinion matters to me. Everyone else can sod off."

Her laughter, light and sweet, tickles my senses in a way I've never experienced before. I'd love to shag her on the dining room table, but I hear voices out in the hall. That means my cousins are back.

Several of them enter the room just as I sit down and begin to eat the meal Rory had saved for me. It's all designed to be cold, so I don't need to go to the kitchen to heat up any of it. My cousins have already eaten, so they tell jokes and generally act like eejits, though I'm fair certain they're doing that strictly to make Natalie feel better. She seems fine to me, but I appreciate what my cousins are trying to do for her. Once I've finished my meal, the serious conversation begins.

Rory sits at one end of the table with his elbows resting on it and his hands clasped. "Those of us who have connections in American law enforcement have been mining those contacts for information about Elliot Rudaski's whereabouts. And we finally got a hit."

"What is it?" I ask.

"He avoided airports but made the mistake of going to a bus station, apparently thinking there would be no surveillance cameras." Rory sits back in his chair. "He was wrong. We now know Rudaski took a bus from Casper, Wyoming, to Houston, Texas."

"How did he get from Yestermont to Casper? If he'd stolen a car, the authorities would have heard about that. Wouldn't they?"

"Since Rudaski is a fugitive, aye, they should have been notified. How he got to Casper is irrelevant at the moment." Rory steeples his fingers under his chin. "What we should focus on is where he went once he reached Houston."

"Do ye have information on that?"

Rory glances at Logan, who nods and says, "Yes, my contact at Homeland Security told me a man meeting Rudaski's description chartered a small jet at a private airport. It flew out of US jurisdiction and we don't know where it went after that. I'd wager he switched planes somewhere in the Caribbean or possibly Cuba. If he has enough money, he could buy his way to anywhere."

"Elliot must have a lot of money," Natalie says. "He didn't share it with me, but he bought himself a luxury car not long after our divorce. That didn't jibe with how little money he claimed to have when he had to disclose that information during the divorce proceedings."

"Any man who is involved in smuggling, whether it's drugs or puppies, will have a lot of secret income." Logan adopts his deadly calm expression. That's what everyone else calls it. "Dinnae worry, lass. We will catch his scent again as soon as he sets foot on UK soil."

"What if he flies all the way to Scotland?"

"That's part of the UK. You should focus on the training Alex is giving you while the rest of us begin preparations for the invasion."

"Invasion?" Her eyes go wide. "Do you really think Elliot will bring an army?"

"Can't say for sure. Best to be prepared for all eventualities."

I grasp her hand. "Don't let Logan's spy jargon fash you. I will never let your ex-husband get close enough to hurt you. If he tries anything, I'll snap his fucking neck."

My cousins all stare at me as if I've made an outrageous statement. What's daft about vowing to protect Natalie? They're the ones who are off their heads.

Alex ducks into the dining room. "Ready for another round of grifter training?"

"Go on," I tell Natalie. "I want to talk to my cousins a bit more."

"Sure. I'll be with Alex." She kisses my cheek. "Don't get too grumpy."

The lass leaves with Alex, and my cousins keep staring at me. At last, Iain speaks. "You're in love with Natalie, aren't you?"

"No. Why on earth would you say that? I hardly know her."

"But we have irrefutable evidence that you're already in love with the lass. Don't we, Rory?"

"Oh, aye. It's plain for everyone to see."

Magnus nods his agreement. "I did the same thing for Piper, and Errol pointed out what it meant. I wanted to batter the *cacan*, but I knew he was right."

"About what?" I snarl. "Quit your havering and say what you mean."

He chuckles. "You trimmed your beard and combed your hair. That means you are in love with Natalie."

Chapter Twenty-Three

Natalie

After my session with Alex, I feel even more prepared for the part of the big plan that involves me. Maybe I won't ever be as good at conning as the British Bastard is, but I can pull the wool over my ex-husband's eyes for sure. It's all about misdirection. Alex even taught me how to pick someone's pocket. Not sure how that might help me with Elliot, but any skills I can pick up will provide new tools for protecting myself and everyone I love.

Munro tracks me down in the garden, where I've been relaxing after a grueling but fun lesson on chicanery. The concrete bench might not be the most comfortable seat, but I needed fresh air and pretty flowers to distract me from whatever might come next.

The Wild Man sits down beside me. "How are you feeling, *gràidh?*"

"Really good, all things considered."

"Glad to hear it." He picks up my hand, sandwiching it between his palms. "Evan's jet landed at the Inverness airport half an hour ago. Your parents are on their way to Niall and Sorcha's house, which is at the end of a gravel road, away from any village. They used to live in Ballachulish, but after their children all grew up and got married, Niall and Sorcha moved out into the countryside. Your parents will be safe there."

"Thank you for letting me know. I'd love to see Mom and Dad, but I get why that's a bad idea right now."

"You can talk to them on the phone whenever you like."

"I'll do that." I rest my head on his shoulder. "But first, I should give them a little time to acclimate. They've never left the Lower Forty-

Eight before. Plus, they got whisked away on a private jet and flew all night."

"Aye, but I'm sure they slept in the bedroom for at least a wee while."

"Yeah, they probably did." I cuddle closer to Munro, loving the natural scent of him. It's indescribable but perfectly him, like the woods and the sky and the water. "I need you to fuck me, Munro. Right now."

"What?"

"I think you understood my words. Or do I need to learn how to say it in Gaelic for you to grasp my meaning?"

"Stress makes ye *dàrail*, eh?" He hooks a finger under my chin, urging me to meet his gaze. "That means you're randy. So am I, lass. *Is iomadh rud a nì dithis dheònach.*"

"What the heck does that mean?" Based on the sensual tone of his voice, it must be something dirty.

"Two willing people can do many things." He slides his other hand between my thighs, and even through the barrier of my jeans, that sensation makes me tingly down there as if he were rubbing my folds. "I know how ye like it when I touch your *camas* this way. And this time when we fuck, I'll give ye plenty of *coinbheineadh* to get you so randy that you'll be begging me to push my *slat* inside you."

"Please tell me what those words mean in English." But yeah, I can guess that he's talking dirty to me, and I love it.

"I said ye like it when I touch your inner thighs. And when we fuck, I'll give ye plenty of fondling to get you so randy that you'll beg me to push my cock inside you."

"Yes, I want that already."

"Right here? Right now?"

"Anywhere. Just do it, Munro. It's been too damn long since we had sex."

He lifts one hand to cup my cheek, and the roughness of his palm on my skin arouses me even more powerfully. But when he possesses my mouth, the kiss is hot and wild and all-consuming. His tongue tangles with mine, and he teases the roof of my mouth while his other hand slides up to my groin. My clothes are in the way. I need his naked body touching mine.

Munro severs the kiss, but our lips graze each other as he speaks in a rough, hungry voice. "Time to strip, Natalie. Right here in the garden, where anyone might catch us going at it."

"Don't care. I need you to fuck me like crazy, like that night in your cabin."

A low groan resonates in his chest. "Can't deny ye anything ye want."

He starts to unzip my jeans, but I can't wait for him to undress me. I need his skin on mine now. So I jump up and shed my clothes in a rush, not caring where it all ends up, just tossing the clothing away. Munro follows my lead, getting naked in record time. Damn, that body. I'd love to crawl over every inch of his flesh, touching and tasting him like he's a giant sex lollipop.

But Munro has other ideas.

"Kneel in front of the bench," he commands. "Then rest your elbows on it."

Once I've gotten into position, he kneels behind me and pushes my legs apart, opening me for him. He shoves a hand between my thighs to coat his palm with my cream. I gasp from the delicious sensation as the heel of his hand mercilessly rubs my folds and his longest finger torments my clit. Just as I'm on the verge of coming, he yanks his hand away.

"Don't stop, Munro, please."

"Come, *gràidh*, come right now."

His growly tone pushes me over the edge, and I tumble off that cliff straight down into a warm, liquid sea of ecstasy. My body tenses up, waiting for the release I know will come any second. When Munro sinks his teeth into my shoulder, it happens. Pleasure rockets down my every nerve, electric and hot, forcing my inner muscles to bear down despite not having his cock inside me. I make desperate noises, and I don't care how pathetic I sound. My eyes shut of their own volition as I grip the edge of the bench so hard my fingers hurt. By the time the orgasm fades, I'm gasping for breath.

"Not done yet," Munro growls into my ear.

He picks me up to flip me around, though I wind up kneeling again right in front of him. His stiff dick sways between us, the red tip glistening.

Then he lies down on his back. "Fuck me, *gràidh*."

I love that he calls me *gràidh*. It sounds romantic and sweet, not anything I'd expect to hear from a tough guy like Munro.

He slaps my ass. "I said fuck me."

"Yes, sir." I salute him. "Any other orders?"

"Aye, make us both come."

"Bend your knees. That's an order, Mr. MacTaggart."

He smirks and obeys my command.

I kneel over his groin and lower myself onto his cock inch by inch, letting us both revel in the sensations as I take his erection inside me. By the time his cock is seated fully inside my body, we're both struggling for breath. My pulse is racing too, and I'd bet he feels the same way. God, the fullness of him gets me so turned on that I could go off again just from the feel of his cock buried to the hilt. I bend my knees until I'm squatting with my feet on the ground, cradled by his powerful thighs.

Munro slides his hands over my knees and up my thighs.

My gaze gravitates to his palms, then shifts down to my mound and the place where our bodies merge. I begin to rock my hips, feeling him so deeply that the sensation robs me of breath and I can't stop myself from rolling my hips with more vigor, desperate to experience him in a way I haven't before. It feels so fucking good that my lids drift halfway shut and I grasp his hands where they rest on my thighs, pinning them there.

He wriggles his fingers to thread them with mine.

I speed up the pace, rocking faster and faster, but I need more. So I peel our hands off my thighs, keeping our fingers laced, and bounce up and down on his cock while I gasp and he grunts and growls. The wet sound of our bodies colliding fills the air and echoes off the garden walls. Munro snarls something I don't understand. Maybe it's Gaelic, but I don't care. My entire world has telescoped down to our bodies and the impending orgasm I can feel building inside me.

Munro springs into a sitting position, then raises onto his knees and tumbles forward with me in his arms, setting us down on the grass. Now that he's on top, he takes command. The Wild Man grinds his hips into me in a circular motion that drives me so crazy that I babble things even I don't understand. But when he hoists my thighs to set them on his shoulders, I lose the last vestiges of my ability to speak or think. The sizzling pleasure grows stronger and hotter, tingling through my sex and making my nipples ache. I clutch at the grass while he thrusts into me so wildly that my tits bounce and my ass lifts off the ground.

The orgasm slams through me with such power and suddenness that I can't even scream, though my mouth gapes on a silent cry.

Munro pounds into me once more and freezes. A half-strangled roar explodes out of him as he blows apart inside me.

For a moment, neither of us moves. We stare dumbly at each other, frozen in that final moment. He still has my legs on his shoulders, and his dick is still lodged inside me. While we wait for the intensity of what we've done to gradually fade, I lay a hand on my chest. My heart thrashes like it wants to punch a hole through my rib cage. I have never experienced a climax like that. But it figures the guy whose own family calls him Wild Man would show me what real, red-hot pleasure feels like.

He pulls out and lies down beside me, pulling me snugly into him.

I sling an arm across his chest. "Wow, I had no idea sex could be like that. It was even better than our first time together."

"Aye, it was."

A door thunks shut somewhere outside the garden, and I hear the crunching of shoes on gravel. Voices chatter too, but I can't understand the words.

Munro hisses what sounds like a Gaelic curse. "Get dressed, *gràidh*. The family must be plotting something."

As the voices grow nearer, we rush to find and reassemble our clothes. I finish first. But Munro seems to be having trouble with his jeans, which had somehow gotten turned inside out when he tore his clothes off. The crunching footsteps draw nearer and nearer while he finally yanks his jeans on and zips them up. He even manages to hook the top button before the first Mac-Taggarts amble into the garden.

Three men halt just inside the garden entrance when they see us. Evan pushes his glasses up while his brows furrow. Logan shakes his head, though his lips curl up a touch in a smug expression. Jack, who I'd met yesterday, folds his arms over his chest and raises his gaze to the heavens briefly.

Alex Thorne comes up behind them, peering over Jack's shoulder. Then the Brit smirks. "Having a jolly good time in the garden, eh?"

"What do you lot want?" Munro demands.

"I think you forgot something, mate." Alex points at the concrete bench, or rather, what's under it. "Might want your pants later."

"Munro is wearing his pants," I say. His boxer shorts are lying under the bench, not his jeans.

"Alex is British," Jack says. "That means he thinks pants are underwear."

I lift my brows. "Seriously? And I thought Scottish words were confusing."

Munro snatches up his boxer shorts and crumples them in his fist. "Did you lot want something? Or did you get lost on your way to the dining room?"

"We're not lost," Logan says. "We were looking for you two. There's been a new development in the Elliot saga."

My life is now a saga? Well, I guess that term does kind of fit. I had to flee from my ex-husband and then run away to Scotland, after all.

The Wild Man himself strides up beside me and takes hold of my hand. "What now, Logan? Tell us before I batter you for being so bloody cagey."

Jack whispers something to Logan, then the former spy faces us again. "Elliot Rudaski entered the UK earlier today. The jet he chartered in America dropped him off and returned to the US. Security cameras at London Gatwick, an international airport, caught a glimpse of Elliot when he entered the terminal to hire a car."

I grip Munro's hand more tightly. "Do you know where he's going?"

"Yes. I called in a favor with my contact at MI6. I can't give you the full details of how, but he learned that Elliot crossed the border into Scotland twenty minutes ago."

My throat constricts. I feel like a boulder has dropped into my stomach, and I'm waiting for the ground to crumble away beneath my feet. Elliot is in the country. He has a car.

And he's coming for me.

Chapter Twenty-Four

Munro

That bastard will never get anywhere near you," I snarl as I pull Natalie close. "I won't let him. Dùndubhan is a fortress in every way imaginable, and the fortifications go beyond the castle walls. A thick forest and a gate will slow Elliot down. We will have guards on every floor of the house and in every corner of the courtyard and the garden. The green behind Dùndubhan will also be guarded, as will the forest. He will never touch you."

The first hint of tears shimmer in Natalie's eyes. She bites down on both her lips and wraps her arms around my waist. "I know you won't let him hurt me. But I'm worried about you. Please don't take any crazy risks for me."

"I will die for you, *gràidh*."

Jack's brows shoot up so high it almost seems as if they'll peel themselves off his scalp. "I've never heard you call anyone '*gràidh*,' Munro."

Natalie gives me a wee smile. "I love that he uses the Gaelic version of my name."

"The what version?"

Evan chuckles. "I know what's happened. Munro must have accidentally called Natalie '*gràidh*', and he was embarrassed. So he told her '*gràidh*' is the Gaelic version of her name."

Natalie pulls away from me. "That's not what '*gràidh*' means?

I rub my jaw and, for inexplicable reasons, hunch my shoulders. "I might have, ah, skirted the truth when I told you that."

"What does that word really mean?"

Clearing my throat, I grip the back of my neck and wince. "Darling. That's what it means."

She lodges her hands on her hips. "Why wouldn't you want to tell me that? It's a sweet thing to say."

"Aye. And I'm not the sweet sort, am I?"

"Well, no, I guess in general you aren't. But I've seen your softer side."

Laughter splutters out of Logan. "Softer side? Munro? I think you've fallen for a barmy lass. But I suppose that's appropriate for the Wild Man of the MacTaggart clan."

Jack lifts his gaze heavenward as he'd done a few minutes ago. "Could we go back to discussing the dangerous problem that might fall onto our heads at any moment?"

"Not any moment," I say, and I might possibly sound a wee bit grumpier than usual. "Elliot won't be here for at least several hours."

"Unless he violates the speed limit. Murderous criminals aren't famous for obeying the laws."

"Thank you for stating what's dead obvious to even the stupidest person on earth." I bow my head and try to get hold of my emotions. I've never been emotional before, so I have no ruddy clue how to deal with it. Finally, I raise my head and sigh. "I'm sorry, Jack."

"I was not offended. A psychologist deals with all sorts of irrational people."

"But I shouldn't have snarled at you."

My cousin shrugs. "Snarl all you want. The occasion certainly calls for it."

Natalie sidles up to me, and I drape an arm around her shoulders. She gives me a sweet wee smile but it falters quickly. "What do we do now? Elliot will be here within a few hours at most. Can this castle really stop him? He might have some goons with him."

I give her a light squeeze. "And we will be ready for them."

"How can you be so sure?"

Logan approaches us and meets Natalie's worried gaze. "We're sure because we've done this before."

"Done what, exactly?"

"We have defended the castle against murderous criminals." Logan touches her arm in a kind gesture of the sort I've never seen from him before. "Magnus and Piper fled here when Royce Hammond pursued them. Hammond had murdered the curator of a museum and framed Piper for the crime. She and Magnus traveled far and wide to find clues that would exonerate her, but they wound up fleeing to Dùndubhan. We fortified the castle and the entire estate that surrounds it."

Alex walks up beside Logan. "Hammond turned up at Dùndubhan with a band of armed men. But we defeated them."

Natalie almost smiles but can't quite achieve the expression. "I guess you guys do have relevant experience."

I hug her to my side. "Natalie is a strong and formidable woman. She won't shy away from a fight."

"Never thought she would behave otherwise," Logan says. "We all knew that if you ever found your soul mate, she would be as wild and fierce as you."

My soul mate? Dinnae believe in that rubbish. Or at least, I never had before I met Natalie. Do I believe in it now? No time to think about it. We have a battle to prepare for which means we have a lot to do.

I wait until my cousins and Alex leave, then take Natalie inside the house and to the kitchen. Not because I'm hungry. I want a private place. The rest of the clan is out there preparing for whatever might come, whenever it might happen. This is the one room where no one is testing the fortifications or looking for weaknesses in the structure.

"You're wearing your deadly serious face," she says. "Whatever you want to tell me must be bad."

"I didn't bring you in here to deliver bad news." I clasp her hands. "I mean to tell you something else."

"And what is that?"

"No matter what Elliot does, you can handle it. You are the strongest woman I've ever known, and the cleverest too. That bastard thinks you're weak, and that is your most powerful weapon against him."

"I don't understand."

"He will underestimate you, like he did back in Wyoming. I reckon he has always underestimated you, and that will be his undoing."

She threads her fingers with mine and inches closer, tipping her head back to gaze up at me. "He will underestimate you too. Elliot thinks you're a crazy Scottish hick, and he'll probably think the same thing about the rest of the clan. We have a whole shitload of secret weapons that will destroy him."

I can't help chuckling. "You are wonderful, Natalie."

"Thank you." She boosts up onto her tiptoes to peck a kiss on my lips. "And you're pretty damn wonderful too."

"We should go into the command center and see how the plan is shaping up."

"Command center? Didn't realize we had one of those."

I pretend to scoff. "We're Scots. Of course we have a command center."

"Not sure what being Scottish has to do with anything. But yeah, we should check in at the 'command center' to find out the latest news."

We leave the kitchen hand in hand as we make our way up to the first floor and the great hall. The tables that had been set up yesterday have been rearranged and some have been removed completely. Computers and monitors take up one long table that was created using three smaller ones. Evan operates that station with help from Piper and also Luke Turner, Kirsty's husband. Magnus and Lachlan stand in front of an oversize map of Dùndubhan and the surrounding grounds, seemingly deep in discussion though I have no bloody idea what they might be contemplating. Alex and Jack are in the far corner of the great hall, huddled by a window, engaged in a hushed conversation based on the way they lean toward each other. More of my cousins and their significant others roam about the hall, pausing to talk to each other before moving on to another part of the room.

"Wow," Natalie says. "This really is a command center."

Iain marches into the hall carrying a huge widescreen TV under one arm. He glances about but seems to realize no one has noticed him. So he shouts, "Where should I put this?"

Magnus points toward the only vacant table. "Over there, Iain. Do you know how to plug it in?"

Iain, who is considerably older than Magnus, rolls his eyes. "I'm not a Luddite, ye *cacan*. I know how to insert a plug into an outlet. Unless you're implying I'm too old to understand technology."

"Glad you could find your way here from the nursing home."

Iain rolls his eyes again and hauls the television over to the empty table. Lachlan goes over there to help Iain, but the oldest of my cousins refuses the offer. Being Iain, though, he brushes Lachlan off in a calm yet cheerful way. His wife, Rae, calls that expression his Buddha smile. I tell all of this to Natalie, and she laughs. Her smile and sweet laughter affects me much the way a wee nip of whisky might do. If I can keep her spirits up, she'll be much better prepared for whatever Elliot has up his sleeve.

But I meant it when I told her she can handle anything.

I lead Natalie over to the corner where Alex and Jack have been deep in discussion of…whatever they're discussing. "What are you laddies up to?"

"Nothing much," Alex says in his usual breezy manner. "Just 'havering' about blockades and swords and the best method for gutting a '*tollathon*.' Jack thinks a Viking-style blade would work best, but we don't have any of those here."

"Dinnae need that. A claymore will do the trick, and Rory has one of those in his office." I glance in the direction of the door to Rory's private domain and see it's hanging open. "Is the Steely Solicitor in there right now?"

"Yes. He and Errol are poring over a topographic map of the area."

"But Lachlan and Magnus are looking at the map over there."

"A different one." Alex adopts his cocksure air of indifference, which we all know is rubbish. "Apparently, the maps are somewhat different. They insist upon examining both versions in-depth like the stubborn, boorish Scots they are."

"Best watch your mouth, laddie. We Scots are also stubbornly determined to destroy arrogant Brits like you."

"Catriona's brothers have already tried that line a thousand times. Their attempts bounce off my personal force field."

Jack chuckles. "He's been spending too much time with Luke. That laddie loves to haver about technology, especially the fictional kind."

Natalie seems to enjoy listening to all of us harass and insult each other. I haven't known Alex long enough to know whether he means any of what he says—about anything. My cousin Catriona is a clever lass who understands how to handle her husband. Natalie seems to have that in common with Cat. Aye, it's possible I'm a wee bit of a handful.

Alex Thorne sighs with the sort of sarcasm that only a former con artist could muster. "I blame Piper and Magnus for this latest debacle. If they hadn't drawn a murderer to Dùndubhan, we would never have realized this castle is actually a fortress. Now it's become trendy to hide out here and wait for the enemy to assault our bastions."

I cross my arms over my chest and struggle against the desire to toss Alex out the window. "This is only the second time it's happened, ye *cacan*. But if you've gotten bored with the idea of an assault on a medieval fortress, I'm sure you could hide out with Natalie's parents. Niall and Sorcha might even offer you hot cocoa."

"You lot couldn't survive without my amazing skills."

Lachlan turns away from the map he and Magnus had been studying and claps his hands. "Attention, everyone! Quiet, please!"

We all stop talking and face Lachlan.

"Magnus and I have conferred with Rory and Errol," Lachlan says, "and we have an idea about how to defend the forested parts of the estate."

When did they "confer" with Rory and Errol? I hadn't seen them go into the office. I hadn't noticed Rory and Errol coming out of it either. But then, I've been focused on Natalie. I listened to Logan, Jack, and Alex while I kept my focus on the lass. Aye, after forty-three years on earth, I have finally mastered multitasking.

"Are ye planning to clear-cut the trees?" Aidan shouts. "Not sure the government would appreciate that."

"No, he won't do that," Iain says. "Lachlan loves nature, though mostly because he enjoys having a poke with Erica in the outdoors."

"Enough jokes," Lachlan shouts, his voice booming inside the great hall. "This is a serious matter that demands your full attention."

No one laughs or cracks jokes anymore. Every face in this room has become serious. MacTaggarts know when to stop harassing each other and get down to business.

"Thank you," Lachlan says. "Now, here's the plan. We will send our best covert operatives into the trees with Logan leading the brigade. They will be armed with night-vision goggles, thanks to Evan's money and Logan's expertise in selecting the best equipment."

After hearing what he just said, I need to ask a question. "How did Logan and Evan get night-vision equipment so quickly? Natalie and I only arrived yesterday."

"We're MacTaggarts, aren't we?"

I shake my head. "Aye, that explains everything, doesn't it? We're Mac-Taggarts, which means we can conjure high-tech equipment."

Lachlan squints at me. "You know that's not what I meant. Every person in this room has contacts and special skills."

Natalie raises her hand like a wee lassie in a classroom. "Um, I have a question."

"Go on," Lachlan says.

"Do you guys have enough weapons for everyone? Seems like more of you have shown up today. And if we're relying on a few swords…" She hunches her shoulders. "Well, it just seems like maybe we need more than that?"

"We have shedloads of weapons. Don't worry about that."

I sling an arm around Natalie and pull her into my side. "Relax, *gràidh*. We might be an arrogant bunch at times, but we never underestimate our enemies."

She smiles, though it's a halfhearted expression. "I trust you guys. But I can't help feeling anxious."

"We all are, even the arrogant erses like Alex and Luke."

Alex doesn't even scoff at what I said about him. He must be getting anxious too, though the British Bastard would never admit to that.

No more time for havering. The battle will begin at any moment.

Chapter Twenty-Five

Natalie

Why do the commando guys need night-vision goggles? They must assume the "battle" will take place at night, and I assume they know what they're doing. Elliot isn't stupid, so maybe he will wait until nightfall to storm the castle, if he even realizes Dùndubhan is a virtually impenetrable fortress, as Emery told me. I have no choice but to place my trust and faith in the MacTaggart clan, and the only reason I'm not panicking is because Munro has remained calm. His strength bolsters me.

Everyone keeps working on strategies while Munro and I have one final session with Alex. I don't know if grifter skills can help us, but I'll take any assistance I can get. Our teacher gives us both "gold stars that you can never show to anyone" at the end of our final session. He means that we shouldn't brag about having con artist skills, I think. Since I've heard that Alex turned his own parents in to the cops, I imagine he knows the importance of keeping things close to the vest.

The whole gang enjoys a huge feast in the long gallery, which is three times the size of the great hall. Rory explained that to me. So we manage to fit almost everyone in this cavernous room. The few MacTaggarts who couldn't get in here went downstairs to the dining room.

In the afternoon, Munro gives me a lesson in self-defense. First, he teaches me everything I need to know about firing a handgun, despite the fact that he knows I have done that before. Of course, I only fired a gun once—when I shot Elliot. Maybe I should feel weird or guilty or something because I not only aimed a gun at my ex-husband but also pulled the trigger, intending to shoot him in the chest. But I don't regret it. He wants to murder me and had been about to shoot me, so I will do whatever it takes to stop him.

For an hour, I practice with several different models of handgun to figure out which one suits me the best. Munro would prefer I take the semiautomatic .9mm Glock, but it's heavier than the .38 revolver. The .30-06 rifle has quite a kick, just like the .357 Magnum revolver and the Glock, though he thinks it's "moderate" recoil. I get why Munro wants me to choose a heavy-duty weapon, but I finally convince him that what I need the most is something I can easily handle, even if it's not the most powerful option.

"I'd rather you have a weapon that holds more than six rounds," he explains. "But I suppose it's more important that you can easily handle the gun. Take the Smith & Wesson. That's the .38 revolver. I can find you some speed loaders too."

"Speed loaders?"

"They hold extra rounds in a way that makes it easy to dump the spent rounds and quickly insert fresh ones."

"Okay, that does sound useful." I bite my lip. "Is it legal to have all these weapons?"

"Do you care? If Elliot comes with hired soldiers and even bigger weapons—"

"I wasn't chastising you. I don't care about the law right now. Elliot is too damn dangerous for us to follow the rules to the letter."

Can't believe I said that. But I meant it. Have I turned into a mercenary? If I have, it's because Elliot forced me to do it.

Now that I've chosen my preferred handgun, Munro teaches me how to handle a switchblade. Jeez, if I need that, I'm in big trouble. But I follow his instructions and practice until I feel reasonably comfortable with the knife. He informs me that he would have given me a sword, but he decided it would take too long for me to master that weapon. Now armed and ready for action, I experience a tingly excitement that has nothing to do with sex. I can defend myself. No more cowering Natalie. I'm a badass.

Munro chuckles when I say that out loud. "Aye, lass, you are."

I get a warm glow in my chest, all because Munro MacTaggart agreed I'm a badass.

Munro insists that I should relax in the sitting room for a while. I inform him that's unlikely to happen. Relax? With Elliot out there? No way. But the Wild Man will not be deterred. He scoops me up and carries me into the house, through the dining room, and down the hall to the sitting room where he drops me on the sofa.

"Relax," he commands.

Then Munro leaves. A few minutes later, four ladies amble into the room while grinning and laughing. I recognize these women. Erica, Emery, Kirsty, and Serena have arrived—to do what, I have no idea. Erica and Serena take the high-backed chairs near the window while Emery and Kirsty sit at either side of me on the sofa.

"What's going on?" I ask.

Emery pats my knee. "Munro ordered us to help you chill out. He thinks you've gotten 'too bloody anxious' about the whole castle-battle thing."

She makes that sound like it's nothing special, on the same level as golfing or fishing. "Of course I'm anxious. My ex wants to murder me."

"Yeah, we know that. But the looming threat of death shouldn't spoil a beautiful, sunny afternoon."

I gape at Emery.

Kirsty laughs. "Dinnae worry, Natalie. We're here to help, and we aren't as insane as it might seem."

"Uh-huh. I appreciate that you guys want to make me feel better, but nothing short of amnesia could make me stop stressing about Elliot."

"Aye, but a wee bit of conversation can't hurt. Why not let us try to distract you from your worries?"

Sighing, I slump against the sofa's back. "Yeah, sure, go ahead and try."

For the next hour and fifteen minutes, according to the grandfather clock in the corner, these four wonderful women do their damnedest to erase from my mind what's going on everywhere in this castle compound and the surrounding woods. I know, because I heard Logan telling Munro, that the "forest battalion" will be scoping things out in preparation for what everyone assumes will become a real invasion. Yeah, they actually use the term battalion. Maybe if they didn't employ military terms, I might feel better about the whole thing.

Finally, the ladies lead me upstairs to the command center in the great hall and take their places at various tables. Most of them will handle communications. I assumed that would involve walkie-talkies, but I was dead wrong. They have headsets connected to laptop computers that tap into a secure internet connection so the women can talk to the men that way. The MacTaggart army will have cell phones with earpieces. Whatever that means. I don't need to understand everything about this massive and complicated operation. But I'm glad to know that they have a well thought out scheme.

After another big family dinner in the long gallery, it's time for the operation to begin in earnest. Most of the ladies kiss their husbands and fiancés goodbye, but a handful of men stay behind to handle tasks within the house. Munro stays, and so does Alex.

Logan jogs into the command center a few minutes later. "I have news."

Everyone turns to look at him. Ever since the mission officially began, the command center has become a quiet place with only the clicking of computer keys echoing in the room. Logan didn't need to shout.

I spring out of my chair. "You found Elliot?"

"We know his current location, yes." Logan saunters up to me. "He just arrived in Loch Fairbairn."

"How does he know where to go? I met Munro a few days ago and never told Elliot anything about your family."

"But he knows who Munro is. It wouldn't be difficult for Elliot to figure out where my cousin has been staying. And if he stopped at a petrol station and asked about Munro, it's likely someone who works there would know who the Wild Man is."

"Right. Technology is great, but not if you're being stalked by a killer."

Logan grasps my upper arms and bends his head to peer into my eyes. "Elliot will not win this battle. You have my word on that—and the word of everyone here at Dùndubhan tonight."

My throat goes thick, but it's not fear causing that. The way Logan swore we will win this battle made me believe it too, and I'm a little choked up now. I can't even say thank you because my voice won't work. I nod instead, and Logan seems to understand what that gesture means.

Logan gives my arms a gentle squeeze. "We have lookouts posted at strategic points along the driveway that leads to Dùndubhan. Someone will spot Elliot and alert us."

"Can't they just shoot him?"

"It would be preferable to capture him and deliver the bastard to the police. But I understand why you wish we could kill him straightaway, and if it were only me involved, I'd take that shot as soon as possible."

"Yeah, I know. Explaining a dead body would cause more problems."

He nods once, then saunters out of the great hall.

Munro rests a hand on my back. "Is that the only reason you don't want Elliot to die? Or do you also want to watch him squirm and suffer in prison?"

"It might be a bit of both. Why should he get off easy? Elliot deserves to go to the roughest prison on earth."

"Logan and Magnus could probably arrange that for you."

I rest my head on his brawny upper arm. "Sometimes I still can't believe that you're helping me with this insane situation or that your family wants to help too. MacTaggarts really are amazing."

"This will all be over soon. And Logan was right, Elliot will lose this battle."

"What do we do now?"

"Prepare for our part of the festivities."

I glance up at him and scrunch my brows. "Festivities? This is an epic battle. That's what I was led to believe."

"Aye, it can be both. I'll have a bloody great time trouncing Elliot and his men."

"But I thought Logan and his commandos would do that. We're the grifter team that will pitch in as needed—if needed."

Munro chuckles. "Trust me, we will be needed. And those American criminals won't stand a chance."

I wrap my arms around his waist, needing the comfort of his warm, strong, sexy body. "When I was talking to the ladies this afternoon, they said things didn't go quite as planned during the first invasion of Dùn-dubhan. The bad guy had something on his phone that let him disable the power in the castle compound. What if that happens again?"

"Don't worry about that. Errol and Evan instituted stronger security measures after that incident. I can't explain the technical rubbish they used, but believe me, there will not be a repeat of what Royce Hammond managed to do. Besides, Hammond's trick only worked for a few minutes." Munro brushes his fingers through my hair, gazing down at me with unmistakable affection. "No matter how this plays out, I will do whatever is necessary to protect you."

"I know."

He slaps my bottom. "Time to find our posts."

"Uh, where is that?"

"In the courtyard. We will wait in the garden until we're given the go-ahead."

First, we head for the armory—aka the dining room—to grab our chosen weapons. Munro gives me a holster for the .38 revolver as well as the speed loaders he'd promised me. After a quick demonstration of how those work, we both strap on our guns and our blades, then head out into the courtyard. I see men stationed at various points around the walls of the castle compound, and I notice some of them up on the top of the walls too, patrolling what looks like a narrow walkway.

When I close my eyes, I can picture medieval Scottish warriors patrolling the ramparts and a cannon positioned atop the wall. Or maybe they would've put that on the ground in the courtyard. The master of this fortress would stand atop the highest turret on the house, dressed in the clan tartan and wielding a big sword, ready to defeat his enemies. In my mind, the face of that man morphs into Munro. Oh yeah, I can picture him roaring like a demon and running toward the enemy with his sword raised, about to vanquish the villains.

Damn, now I want to have sex with him.

Pushing my lust aside, I follow Munro into the garden. He orders me to sit on the concrete bench and keep my weapons at the ready. He has a sword called a claymore strapped to his hip and the Glock berthed in a shoulder holster. But he doesn't sit down beside me. Instead, Munro saunters over to the doorway that leads out onto the green, though he doesn't open it.

No, the Wild Man leaps up and grabs onto the top of the jamb. Then he hoists himself up until he can set one foot on the upper jamb. I watch in awe as he slings an arm up to grasp the top of the wall, and once he's got a good grip on it, he swings his other leg up and onto the higher jamb. Finally, he takes hold of the top of the wall and raises his head just enough that he must be able to see the green without being seen himself.

Holy shit. I can't believe he did that. A sultry tingle sweeps through my entire body, and my nipples harden while I lick my lips. Yeah, I'd love to devour that man right now. But he's kind of unavailable at the moment.

The instant this ordeal is over, I'm jumping him.

Chapter Twenty-Six

Munro

I swivel my head to survey the green and the surrounding areas that I can see from this vantage point. Not having night-vision goggles doesn't bother me. I've gotten used to relying on my natural vision after dark, though it does take a while to kick in. Technology can fail, but my eyes won't. After a minute or two, I decide the rear of the castle has not been breached. So, I leap off the wall and land flat on my feet. Dusting off my hands and trousers, I walk over to Natalie. "No one out there yet—except for our men."

"Guess that's a good thing. But I kind of wish something would happen so we can get it over with."

I sit down beside the lass and hold her hand. "Don't be in a rush for the assault to begin. It's best if everyone has time to get settled into their roles. That way, they'll know exactly what to do and won't panic."

"Yeah, I might be panicking a teeny bit."

"No, *gràidh*, you are not doing that." I kiss her forehead. "You are a badass, remember?"

"I was surprised when you agreed with me on that. Thought the Wild Man might dispute my claim."

"Not after the way you did everything I asked of you during the assault on my cabin. And you shot Elliot too. No one could deny that you are a force to be reckoned with after all of that."

She rests her cheek on my shoulder. "I became a reckoning force because of what you taught me."

I know she became a stronger, more powerful woman all on her own. But I also know Natalie won't admit to that, not yet. In time, she will realize the truth. I'm glad I was there to watch her blossoming into a strong, confident warrior. Any medieval chieftain would have been proud to take a woman like her for his bride. I would be proud to do that for dead certain.

Being here at Dùndubhan, I can't help wondering about the battles that must have taken place here hundreds of years ago. Yesterday, my cousin Kirsty had told me all about the research she and her husband Luke had done while trying to learn more about our ancestor Kieran. Errol expanded on that research, gathering surprising new facts about him. We didn't have time to discuss those findings in detail, but I would love to delve into the topic after the current battle concludes. I do know that no one has found any evidence of where the castle that Kieran lived in with his three aunts was located.

"What are you thinking?" Natalie asks. "You're wearing a serious-thinking face."

"I was wondering about my ancestor Kieran. His life is a mystery, and his apparent resurrection from death is only one part of that enigma."

"After we take down Elliot, maybe you and I could investigate Kieran together."

"You would want to do that? With me?"

"Sure. It could be fun. Spending time in this castle has made me curious about Scottish history."

Oh, aye. I would definitely be proud to spend the rest of my life with Natalie.

"The quarry is approaching the driveway," Logan says in a hushed tone via the earpieces we all wear. "Forest Battalion, Eastern squadron, watch for them and implement the anti-vehicle security measures."

Anti-vehicle? He should just say "blow out the bloody tires." He's not a spy anymore, so he doesn't need to be cryptic. The women must be doing things behind the scenes to orchestrate our little war.

I hear Magnus respond with "roger" to acknowledge Logan's orders. A moment later, Magnus tells everyone, "Spikes deployed."

Spikes? They must mean to disable the vehicle or vehicles that Elliot and his men acquired. Since Elliot seemed to be alone when he crossed the border into Scotland and still had no one with him when he reached Loch Fairbairn, I assume he hired himself more lackeys who arrived separately. How he did that, I have no clue. Elliot will not arrive alone, of that I'm positive.

"Quarry has entered the driveway," Logan says. "Courtyard Battalion, get into position."

That means us.

I grip Natalie's hand while we exit the garden and approach the massive wooden gateway. We take our position alongside the gates, which are closed and locked, keeping our backs against the cold stone wall. I press my mouth to her ear so only Natalie will hear me. "Relax, we have numbers on our side, and everyone involved has experience with repelling an assault on Dùndubhan."

She nods and gives my hand a quick squeeze. Her determined expression makes me want to shag her right here, right now, damn the rest of the world.

"We're in position," I say to Logan.

"Roger."

I let go of Natalie's hand only so I can step away from the wall to see the walkway on top of it. But I don't see anyone up there. Lachlan and his team must have already crouched to await the arrival of Elliot and his lackeys. I can't see my other cousins who are manning the turrets, but I know they are in position. Other MacTaggart and Murdoch men will have reached their assigned positions at strategic windows up and down the castle's height and breadth.

Logan confirms my assessment. "Wall Walk Battalion, are you ready?" Once he receives an affirmative response, he checks in with the other groups. "Turret Battalion, stand ready. Tower Battalion, take your positions. Green Battalion, keep your eyes open."

I think he has finally checked in with everyone. I return to the wall and pat Natalie's erse to feel the switchblade she has in her back pocket. She lays a hand over her shoulder holster that holds the revolver. I can see the speed loaders hooked onto her belt too.

We are ready.

"Quarry approaching the gravel gate," Aidan says.

Natalie turns her head toward me and mouths, "Gravel gate?"

I plaster my mouth to her ear again. "The metal gate at the halfway point on the driveway."

She nods and mouths "oh."

"Quarry opened the gate," Aidan says. "Moving ahead now. Four vehicles in play."

That means Elliot has indeed brought more lackeys.

"How many in each vehicle?" Logan asks.

"Four."

Static crackles in my ear, then levels out. A voice I hadn't expected to hear announces, "ORVs approaching from the west. Six that I can see."

That's Torcall Murdoch, Errol's great uncle. No one told me he would take part in this battle, but I'm glad he's here. Torcall served in the Royal Air Force as a commando, so he knows how to handle a skirmish. And now we know Elliot has more than four lackeys. Not only did he bring men in cars, but he also brought them on off-road vehicles that can traverse the wooded areas around the castle compound.

Natalie mouths, "Are there too many of them?"

I murmur into her ear, "We can handle it."

Alex ambles out of the house and across the courtyard as if nothing of note is going on outside the walls. When he reaches us, he turns sideways and leans against the wall. His faint smirk doesn't surprise me at all. In the short time I've known the man, I've discovered he is unflappable. So when he hooks a thumb inside the waistband of his trousers, that doesn't fash me. But Alex didn't hook his thumb that way arbitrarily. The action pulled his jacket back slightly, revealing the semiautomatic handgun berthed inside a hip holster.

"Radio silence begins now," Logan declares. "Except in case of emergency."

As I tip my head to the side and let my jaw fall open a wee bit, I detect the faint grumble of car engines. The enemy is approaching.

Pow!

The noise reverberates through the forest. Several more wee explosions follow, but I know those noises aren't caused by bombs. My cousins must have rolled out a long row of spikes in the driveway to slow down the villains, and every *pow* that echoes in the night air represents one tire that's been deflated. Considering the large number of those noises, I suspect all four vehicles have been rendered immobile.

But we still have the ORVs to deal with.

Then I hear screams and roaring engines and crashing sounds. I think the forest battalion just took out those bastards.

"Forest Battalion, Western Squadron, check in," Logan says.

A breathless Iain declares, "ORVs neutralized."

"Bring them in. Forest Battalion, Eastern Squadron, have you neutralized the drivers?"

"Only five," Aidan says. "The rest escaped into the trees."

"What's their heading?"

"Toward the river. They might mean to sneak in that way."

"Bring in the captives," Logan says. "Wild Man, you know what to do."

I straighten and square my shoulders. "Roger. On the way."

Natalie grabs my arm. "What's going on? You're supposed to stay here with me."

"You weren't there for the meeting this afternoon. We all agreed that if it became necessary, I would stop Elliot and his men from using the river to get around our commandos."

She swallows hard enough I can see the movement in her throat. "That time has come."

"Aye." I grasp her face and kiss her hard. "You and Alex will need to handle the grifter battalion alone. I'm sorry, love."

"Go do your thing. We'll be fine."

I kick off my shoes and toss my jacket away, though first I remove a roll of duct tape from the pocket. Natalie gets the sweetest look of bafflement on her face when I do that. Then I race into the garden, through the door and out onto the green. But I don't stop there. I sprint across the grass and straight into the trees, pelting down the trail I know will take me to the river. "Trail" might be a generous way of describing the path. It's very narrow and overgrown on either side. Since we had turned off the courtyard lights before Elliot and his lackeys arrived, my eyes have already adjusted to the darkness. I have no trouble spotting obstacles. A large boulder blocks my way, though the trail veers to the left of it. But I leap up to grasp a large branch, using it to vault myself over the obstacle.

The second my feet hit the ground, I run faster.

"Wild Man," Logan whispers into my earpiece, "the quarry is a hundred feet to your left, heading toward you."

Logan knows I can't respond. That might alert the villains.

A few yards from the stream, I slow down and creep toward the bank without making a sound. I've controlled my breathing too. And of course, I know exactly how to fool any thermal imaging equipment they might have. Wood and water both mask thermal signals such as body heat. So I sit down on the stream's bank and slowly slide into the water. It's bloody cold, but I'm used to bathing in an ice-cold Wyoming river. The water temperature here doesn't fash me at all. I toss my gun onto the ground and kick it under a clump of twigs but keep my claymore. Then I walk toward the middle of the stream, bending my knees until I've sunk in up to my chin, now standing in the center of the waterway. I sink down a wee bit more until only my nose and eyes are above water.

And I wait.

Luckily, our earpieces are waterproof. That means I can hear Logan when he announces, "Quarry within twenty feet, Wild Man."

The crack of a twig snapping echoes through the darkness, and I detect shuffling footfalls too. Whoever Elliot hired to accompany him, they must be as stupid as the laddies he'd brought to my cabin. I sit back on my haunches, ready to submerge my entire head when those bastards get closer. The tactic I'm about to use is hardly new for me. I'd employed a similar technique back in the Grand Canyon, when Errol, Ashley, and I found the hidden cavern that housed an ancient hoard of treasures. Tonight, I will play the Wild Man again for these laddies.

Shadows shift among the trees, and I detect the soft sound of footfalls. They're trying to be stealthier, but it's too late. The first lackey emerges from the trees. He has his knees bent as if he thinks that will help him evade detection. What a bloody stupid *cacan*. I pull in a deep breath and gently lower my head fully beneath the water, exhaling so gradually that even in sunlight no one would notice any bubbles. I can just make out the shapes of more men approaching the first one. So I tip my head back and raise myself enough that my eyes and nose emerge from the water.

Oh aye, these are bloody stupid men.

They huddle on the game trail, no more than a yard from the stream's bank, whispering with so little finesse that I can understand their words.

"I think we should follow this trail," one *cacan* says. "My GPS tells me the compound is over there."

The other scunners nod their agreement. The *cacan* who had spoken sounded Scottish. I must have been right, and Elliot hired local criminals to aid him. I sink under the water again and stealthily roll over onto my back, staying well below the surface. When I come up level with where the lackeys are standing to have their chat, I kneel at the bottom of the streambed again. Now it's time to do my bit.

I crawl to the edge of the bank. Then I surge up out of the water, slap my palms on the ground, and heave myself onto the bank. While the shocked men gawp at me, I grab the nearest lackey and lock my arms around his midsection.

His mates run toward us.

And I plunge backward into the stream with a villain in my arms.

Chapter Twenty-Seven

Natalie

Shouts and gunshots reverberate through the woods from the direction in which Munro had gone. Did those bastards catch him? No, he's amazing at evading the bad guys and tricking them into doing what he wants. My pulse has shifted into high gear, and I feel a little nauseous when I imagine what might be going on out there. How many weapons do those guys have? How much ammunition? Munro has only one gun and a sword. What if that's not enough?

I can't wait here while he gets beaten up or shot or who knows what. Munro might murder me himself for this, but I know what I need to do. So I turn to Alex. "I'll be right back. You'll need to handle the con game for now. Okay?"

"Munro won't be pleased with your plan."

"Screw how he feels about it. I'm going to save his ass whether he likes it or not."

Alex chuckles. "I admire your spirit, but I can't let you go out there alone."

"You need to stay here to mess with the heads of whatever bad guys are being brought in right now."

Though he opens his mouth, to try to talk me out of going after Munro, I hear the Wild Man's voice through my earpiece. "Quarry neutralized. Need help carrying these laddies back to base."

I assume "base" means the castle compound.

"Do you have Elliot?" I ask.

"Sorry, no. He wasn't with these eejits."

Logan speaks again. "Forest Battalion, Eastern Squadron, assist Wild Man."

"Wall Walk leader here," a man says, and I think it's Lachlan. He speaks so softly that I need to concentrate to hear him. "Three figures coming up the driveway."

Alex smiles at me and winks. "We're up next. Are you ready for the grift?"

"Yes. You taught me well."

Naturally, we're still whispering. I listen for the crunching of footfalls on the gravel but don't hear anything. Maybe Elliot and his team veered into the woods in hopes of making a stealthier approach. We've got men out there, though, so I doubt his plan will work.

"Forest Battalion, Western Squadron, calling Team Leader."

Whose voice is that? Must be Iain. I'd spoken to him several times over the past few days and got to know what he sounds like.

"Go ahead," Logan says.

"I have eyes on eight men, armed, fanning out around the compound."

"Roger." Logan pauses, then says, "Eastern Squadron, report."

"Eyes on four Hellhounds heading for the green," Magnus tells Logan. "Just rounded the corner of the wall, may be heading for Green Gate."

"Roger."

The bad guys are surrounding us. That's what I gleaned from those conversations between Logan and his cousins. If Munro captured four of the villains, though, that means they can't sneak up on the eastern side of the compound. That leaves three sides to defend.

"Hellhounds have stopped," Iain says. "Holding position. Must be waiting for orders."

"Aye," Logan says. "Stay on them."

"Roger."

Alex winks at me again, then speaks to someone else. "Team Leader, this is British Bastard. Ready to initiate on your order."

He actually wants to be called that? Well, maybe one of the MacTaggarts decided to give Alex that call sign. From what I've seen of Alex, though, I wouldn't be surprised if he chose that designation himself.

"It's a go," Logan says. "Hellhounds approaching Mount Etna. Court-yard Battalion, implement radio silence."

"Roger," Alex confirms.

A wave of excitement washes over me, though it seems bizarre that I feel anticipation for what might unfold next. But I suppose I feel that way not because I want to see my ex-husband or because I'm hankering to give him a beat-down. Yeah, okay, I would love to force-feed him some come-uppance. But I think the sensation I'm experiencing is part of my psyche preparing for battle. Maybe this is what soldiers feel like right before the enemy attacks. I'll ask Munro about that later.

Right now, Alex and I need to do our part to win the battle.

My partner in crime gestures for me to stand directly in front of the twin gates, keeping far enough back that the big wooden slabs won't bump into me once they're swung them open. The Wall Walk team had attached ropes to the upper sections of the gates, which means they can pull those Goliaths open for me.

Since Logan initiated radio silence, Alex waves to the two men posted atop the wall—Lachlan and Rory. They remain hunched over so that Elliot and his cohorts won't see them, and they slowly haul the gates open. Alex is now hidden behind one of the mammoth wooden slabs.

And I get my first look at Elliot since the day he invaded Munro's homestead. My eyes have adjusted to the moonlight enough that I know it's him.

"May we come in?" he asks. Then he spreads his arms wide, holding his jacket open. "See? I don't have any weapons. I'm as harmless as a puppy."

His lips twitch because he's clearly trying to stop himself from laughing, though he only half accomplishes that. Elliot made a stupid puppy-cartel joke. Seriously? He thinks that's the right move tonight. For all I know, he has a dozen weapons hidden elsewhere on his body or inside his jacket that I can't see.

"Remove your coats," I say. "All of you, not just the puppy-cartel kingpin."

The men strip off their coats.

"May we enter your sanctum now?" Elliot asks. "We're completely helpless."

Yeah, right, I believe that. But I wave for him to come inside the walls. When he gets within ten feet of me, I raise one hand. "That's close enough. What do you want, Elliot?"

He chuckles. "What do you think? The information you stole from me."

"I see." Though I want to peek around the mammoth gate to look at Alex, I can't do that—and I wouldn't even if I could. The expert grifter taught me everything I need to know to pull off what comes next. "Maybe I do have something of yours. Didn't realize that until yesterday. But you were right, and I apologize for not believing you."

"Really." Elliot's gaze narrows, and he tips his head to the side. "Are you also sorry for locking my men in your lunatic boyfriend's booby trap? And what about getting me arrested?"

"No, I'm not sorry about that. I had something I needed to do, and you were in the way. But I'm ready now."

"For what?"

"To make amends." I take one step toward him, resisting an urge to glance at his goons. "Let's go into the garden so we can talk—alone. We need to clear the air between us."

"Uh-huh." He squints at me harder. "Everyone on my team has a thermal imaging device. We know you've got a lot of people here, out in the woods and inside this compound. And we're ready for whatever your new Scottish buddies want to throw at us."

Of course he believes that. Elliot is arrogantly certain that he's smarter than everyone else. But he has never encountered the MacTaggart clan before.

Now it's time to take my biggest risk yet.

I sashay up to Elliot and lay my palms on his chest. "I really am sorry, Elliot, for what I put you through."

"Hmm. You'll have to do a hell of a lot better to convince me to take you back. I assume that's what you're angling for."

"Yes, I would like for us to reconcile."

"What about the Scottish caveman?"

I shrug. "Munro might seem like a tough guy, but he's rather…flaccid in the bedroom."

"Uh-huh." Elliot analyzes me for a moment, probably trying to gauge my truthfulness, which means I'm about to learn how good a grifter I've become. "Are you claiming you prefer fucking me?"

"Yes."

He slings an arm around my upper back and drags me into his body. "All right, cupcake, prove it. Suck me off right here with my men watching."

"Sure, baby. I'd love to." I bite my lip. "But there's one problem."

"I knew it. You are lying."

"No, Elliot, I'm not." Here goes nothing. I snuggle up to him even more and adopt a sultry tone to confuse him while I'm doing what I need to do. "I want you so bad, baby. But the MacTaggarts are out there, and with the gates open, they might rush in to attack you. I couldn't bear to see you hurt."

He still seems not entirely convinced. "Who opened the gates, Natalie?"

I flutter my lashes and do my damnedest to look sincerely clueless. "I opened them. The gates are connected to the electrical system, and I have the remote control for opening and closing them."

"Do you now."

I pull a remote out of my pocket, but it's for the TV in the sitting room, not for the gates. "Would you like me to show you how the remote control works?"

"Sure, why the hell not." Elliot is smirking, a definite sign that he's positive he has control of the situation.

The asshole always underestimated me.

"Okay," I tell him. "I'll show you. But we'll need to back away, otherwise you guys might get knocked down. Those gates are super heavy. Once they start moving, nothing can stop them."

He keeps hold of me as he walks forward to get out of the path of the two mammoth gates. His men tag along, staying close to their boss.

I push a button on the remote.

As the gates begin to move, I have one more task to accomplish. Elliot is focused on me, but his goons are just starting to turn their heads to watch the gates. Nope, can't let them do that.

"Oh, look!" I shout, pointing up at the sky. "Is that a meteor? I think it's coming this way."

Elliot's idiot goons crane their necks and squint at the sky, bobbing their heads side to side as if that will help.

"There is nothing in the sky," Elliot snarls. "Quit staring up at—"

A blazing white object with a comet-like tail streaks across the heavens directly overhead. One goon screams. The other two gape at the sky, eyes wide.

Elliot shoves me away from him. "You fucking bitch."

"Don't you want me to suck you off anymore, Elliot?"

He unleashes a primal roar and hurls himself at me.

I kick his left ankle to the side, knocking him off balance. My ex-husband splats onto the gravel facedown.

Elliot struggles to get to his feet, then spends about thirty seconds picking gravel off his clothes and out of his hair. Then he shoves a hand into his right pants pocket.

I whip the .38 revolver out of my waistband, where it had been tucked up against my lower spine. "Stop right there, or I'll shoot you."

A bitter laugh spills from his lips. "You? Shoot me? Please."

Of course he doesn't believe me. So I demonstrate my determination by firing a round into the earth inches from his right boot.

Elliot leaps backward. "You could've killed me."

"Why would I do that? Knowing you're locked up for eternity will keep me smiling for the rest of my life." I raise the gun to aim it at his groin. "Dump all your weapons, Elliot. Tell your goons to do the same. Otherwise, I'll castrate you."

He reaches into his pants pocket, then pulls the lining out as if he couldn't find what he wanted in there. "What the hell?"

"Looking for this?" I ask, holding up his gun. "I picked your pocket, numbskull. Took your keys while I was in there."

Damn, it feels good to have him cornered.

But my ex-husband isn't done screwing with me yet. He leaps behind his goons.

I hear the crackle of a radio. "Attack now!"

"Team Leader to Firecracker," Logan says, and he means me. Yeah, that's my call sign. "Hellhounds in custody. Bringing them in via Green Gate. Operation Blow Them Away has begun."

Yeah, that might not be the subtlest name for a battle, but it works for me.

An explosion rocks the compound. The flash from the detonation soars high above the castle walls, and within seconds, another explosion goes off, this time from the opposite side of the compound. Errol Murdoch has done his part with spectacular finesse.

Elliot's goons drop to the ground and curl up with their asses in the air, like they think it's a tornado drill.

My ex-husband trains his gun on me and grits his teeth. "Give me the fucking microdot now."

What is a microdot? I have no idea, but it must be the thing he came all this way to get, the thing he claims I have. "Microdot? Sorry, Elliot, I thought you wanted my vibrator."

He roars and leaps at me.

But Alex bolts toward us and seizes the back of Elliot's shirt collar, yanking him off his feet. The Brit flings Elliot onto the ground. Then he casually dusts off his hands. "I do dislike it when I need to get physical with a bloody stupid arsehole. It's tiresome."

Elliot rolls over and glares at the Brit. "You bastard."

Alex leans over my ex-husband. "I'm the *British* Bastard. Please use my nickname correctly, would you? I earned it after years of behaving like a wanker."

"What? You're as crazy as Natalie is."

"Oh, but you haven't met the MacTaggarts yet. They make Natalie and me seem like the sane ones."

Elliot scoffs. "I met that Scottish dickwad. What's his name again? Sissy MacTaggart?"

The bang of a door being thrown open reverberates through the compound, originating from the garden.

Munro jogs into the courtyard and halts beside me. "What did I miss?"

"Elliot thinks your name is Sissy MacTaggart."

"Does he now." Munro grasps Elliot under his arms and hauls the jerk to his feet. Then he hoists my ex-husband off the ground. Munro's fierce expression would make any sniveling creep like Elliot think twice about annoying the Wild Man. He shakes Elliot hard. "I am Munro MacTaggart. And you are a worm I mean to crush under my boot."

I can't resist smirking. Oh yeah, I need to screw Munro right now.

Chapter Twenty-Eight

Munro

Though I would love to make good on my threat, because Elliot Rudaski deserves to be crushed, I won't actually do that. The *bod ceann* needs to go to prison for a very, very long time, and I'm happy to keep hold of him until the authorities arrive. But our plan hasn't concluded quite yet. "I heard something about a microdot."

"Yes," Natalie says. "Elliot claims I have the information he wants and that it's on or inside of the microdot. I don't even know what one of those is."

"It's a wee piece of film that would fit on your fingertip. Aye, Logan?"

"Correct," the former spy says.

"That means he could have hidden it anywhere on your body, Natalie." I give Elliot a rough shake. "Where did ye hide it? Or would ye rather I crush your skull?"

Natalie claps her hands while grinning. "Yes! Crush him."

"Well, whatever the lass wants…" I hurl Elliot onto the ground and raise my boot over his head. "I'll count down from ten. Nine, eight, seven—"

The lass claps again. "Go, Munro!"

"Okay, fine, stop," Elliot almost shouts. "Anything you want, I'll do it. Please don't crush me."

Is it my imagination, or did he whimper a wee bit?

Tears trickle from the bastard's eyes. "Please don't kill me. You can keep the microdot and take over the cartel. I don't care."

I tap my foot on his forehead. "Where is the microdot?"

"Hidden inside Natalie's wedding ring."

Natalie shrugs. "I don't have my wedding ring anymore. I pawned it the day after our divorce was finalized. Who knows where it wound up."

"Doesn't matter." I step away from the *cacan*. "Someone bring the duct tape. We've caught the last Hellhound."

Elliot scrambles to get to his knees. "But you have to find the microdot."

"Why? We don't need the information on it. And everything you've done so far is enough to put you in prison for a good long while."

"No! I can't go to prison." Elliot leaps up and grabs Natalie, whisking a knife out of his back pocket. He holds the blade to her throat. "I will kill her unless you find the goddamn microdot. I *need* it."

My hands ball into fists, and my jaw clenches. "Release her now. I won't ask again. And if you harm her, I will tear your throat out with my teeth."

Natalie slams her boot down on Elliot's foot. He shouts and drops the knife. She spins around and raises the .38 revolver, sighting it in on his chest.

Elliot snatches up the knife. "You can't kill me. You don't have the balls for it, cupcake, and we both know it."

"You don't know me at all, Elliot. But if you tell me why you need that microdot so badly, maybe I won't shoot you."

"What the hell." He stabs a hand through his hair. "I don't own the cartel. My puppy-smuggling operation is kind of a side hustle for the Satanás Rojo cartel that works out of a little town in Mexico called Calixto."

Natalie snorts. "You work for the Red Satan cartel? That figures."

I assume that's what Satanás Rojo means, though I never learned Spanish. What is a red Satan, anyway? Sounds like that cartel is full of eejits just like Elliot and his lackeys.

"Red like blood," Elliot says. "That's what the cartel's name is about. They think it sounds wicked scary."

"Uh-huh." Natalie looks at me. "What do we do with him now? Call the cops?"

"Not yet. I want to have a wee chat with the laddie first. If we can't find that microdot, maybe we can at least rip the truth out of Elliot."

Alex comes up beside me. "Perhaps we can find that microdot. Natalie, do you remember the name of the pawn shop?"

"Sure. It was the Mislaid Treasures Pawn Shop in Hammond, Indiana."

"Well, that shouldn't be difficult to find."

"Okay. But then we have to talk the person who bought the ring into giving it back, at least temporarily."

Alex exhales a melodramatic sigh. "Have you already forgotten everything I taught you? Of course we can get the ring back and find the microdot. The only question is, are you coming with me? Or will I drag Logan along on this mission? His deadly calm stare can be useful, but I think sweet-talking might do the trick with fewer threats of violence."

"I would like to go back to Hammond to pick up the rest of my stuff. Why don't I go with you? Logan can help Munro interrogate Elliot."

"Perfect." Alex glances my way. "Do you mind if I whisk your girl away on Evan's jet?"

"Dinnae seduce her and I won't mind at all."

"Aren't you going to threaten me with violence? That does seem to be the MacTaggart way."

I lift one shoulder. "If you do anything I don't like, I'll drag you to the bottom of the river and keep you down there until you drown. Is that enough of a threat?"

"Yes, that will do."

Elliot sniggers. "I still have a knife, you morons."

"Not for long, laddie." I leap toward him and slam my fist into his gut. While he doubles over, gasping and wheezing, I grab the knife. "Never mess with a MacTaggart—or a feisty American lass."

I wink at Natalie.

She kicks Elliot's shin, then blows me a kiss.

Alex chuckles. "Yes, you'll fit right in round here, Natalie."

Logan and Alex drag Elliot into the castle. Lachlan and Aidan seize the two lackeys and escort them into the castle too, where I'm sure they will receive exactly the treatment they deserve. That means my cousins will not touch the bastards unless they try something. Natalie and I walk into the house hand in hand, heading for the command center in the great hall. The lasses who had operated those stations and kept everything running smoothly are preparing to leave for the night. My cousins who had been outside the compound, corralling the rest of Elliot's chums, are now parading those criminals into the long gallery where they will wait until we're ready to call in the authorities.

Since Logan has contacts in various branches of the government, we won't need to explain why we held these men captive. Besides, we will have all the evidence we need to get all of them arrested and convicted of various crimes.

Once all the prisoners have been contained, I return to the ground floor hall and look for Natalie. I find her in the kitchen, sitting on a stool while devouring a small tub of ice cream.

"Hungry, eh, lass?"

She glances at me and smiles. "There you are. Yeah, I'm starving. I'd kill for a big, thick steak with mashed potatoes and fresh green beans."

I settle onto the stool beside hers. "Happy to cook for you when you come home from America."

"Home?" She sets down her fork, and her expression falls. "I don't know where that is anymore."

"Of course ye do." I lay a hand on her cheek. "It's here with me, *gràidh*."

"Is it? I don't know where I belong anymore. Meeting you, coming here, fighting off my ex-husband… Jeez, it's been an insane week."

"Are you saying you don't want to stay with me?"

"Don't know. Are you asking me to move in with you?"

"Well, ah, I don't actually have a house here in Scotland. Sold it when I decided to live in America."

She stabs her spoon into the ice cream over and over, staring down at it while twisting her mouth from one side to the other. "Honestly? I don't know what I want."

"You've been through a lot. We both have. I suppose we should each take time to sort through it all and figure out what we do want."

"Sounds like a plan."

Her mobile rings. She glances at the screen, then at me. Finally, she swipes to take the call. "Alex, hi. Already? Okay, I'll be there."

Natalie turns her gaze to me and bites her bottom lip.

"You're leaving now," I say. "It's all right. Go with Alex to find the ring and retrieve the microdot. It might be important to building a case against Elliot."

"I know. I should go." She hops off her stool and starts for the door. But she stops there, glancing at me over her shoulder. Then the lass barrels toward me and leaps onto my lap, nearly knocking the stool and us onto the floor. She flings her arms around my neck. "Make love to me before I go. Please."

"Right here?"

"Anywhere you want. Alex said we'll be leaving in twenty minutes, which means we have time." She wraps her arms around me more tightly and crushes her mouth to mine. With our lips still almost touching, she bumps her nose into mine. "I don't care where we do it. I need to feel you inside me one more time."

Why does it sound like she means never to come back? I don't want to ask what she meant because I'm afraid of the answer. Munro the Wild Man is afraid? No one would believe it. But if she decides to stay in America and says she doesn't want me anymore…

"Let's go to the guest wing," I say. "No one is using those bedrooms right now."

"Perfect. Take me there, Munro."

I know she means that in both senses of the word. Aye, I take her to the guest wing where she chooses which room she prefers. Then we undress, and I mean to take her body too. But Natalie's beautiful body now lies spread across the length of the bed, and I need a moment to simply drink in the sight her creamy skin on full display. She is the bonniest lass I have ever seen and the most passionate, fiery, sweet woman in the world. Natalie means more to me than a quick shag or a hard-luck case who needed my help. I don't know what I'll do if she tells me I was nothing more to her than a pleasant distraction.

"Ah, *gràidh*," I murmur as I climb onto the foot of the bed and crawl toward her. "You are more than bonnie, *mo gaoloch*. You are a witch who has enchanted me, and I never want to break the spell."

"You were never this poetic any of the other times that we had sex."

"Are ye disappointed?"

"No. I love it."

My face hovers over hers, and for a moment, we just look into each other's eyes. I swear I can see the love in her gaze, but I'm probably imagining that because I want her to feel that way about me. Aye, I need her to love me. Because I'm in love with her. And it's time I showed her that in the only way I can.

I hover above Natalie and lick my lips. Aye, my hunger for her is intense, but I won't rush, not this time. So I lie down next to her and roll onto my side. My hard cock presses into her. She reaches out to brush her fingers through my hair, then moves as if to roll over toward me. I place a hand on her hip to stop her. She relaxes and waits for whatever I might do. I hadn't given her much foreplay during our previous shags, and I mean to rectify that right now.

Lifting my head, I take her mouth in a slow, sensual kiss while I skate my palm down her throat, beginning a leisurely exploration of her skin. As my hand glides lower, my fingers toy with her nipples, and she moans into my mouth. The soft hiss of her exhalation tickles my skin. I drag my palm down her belly and push my fingers into the curly hairs on her mound, teasing them until she shudders and sucks in a breath. But when I slip my hand between her folds, she arches her back and clutches the sheets. I glide my hand up and down, over and over, as I relinquish her lips to watch the expression on her face.

Eyes half-closed, lips parted, she rocks her hips into the heel of my palm.

Bod an Donais, Natalie is the most beautiful, desirable woman in the universe.

I pull my hand away and roll half on top of her. Then I grasp her knee and skate my palm up so I can grasp her thigh and tug it into me. My thigh lies nestled between hers now, and my erection presses into her folds. I adjust my position to ensure my cock will rub against her clitoris once I begin to move. Her slick heat spreads onto my thigh and my *slat* while the aroma of her cream wafts up to tease my senses. The scent drives me mad, but I won't rush this.

She thrusts her fingers into my hair.

I begin to rock my hips, grazing her cleft with my thigh while my cock rubs into her hard nub. Her breaths quicken. Her eyes darken. Her nipples have turned a bonnie shade of dusky pink, and their tips jut up as if her body is begging me to devour those wee peaks. Instead, I press my chest to hers so that every time I rake my cock over her flesh, my chest rubs against her nipples. She's breathing harder, and when the lass catches her bottom lip between her teeth, I can't wait any longer.

"*Mo leannan*," I growl, "come for me now."

"I want to come with you, please."

"Cannae deny you anything."

Grasping her thigh more firmly, I pull my hips back and plunge into her body. I fight the need to fuck her like mad and thrust in a slow, measured motion. The feel of her wet sheath hugging my cock with every inward lunge makes me struggle for breath, but I keep rocking into her as if I can wait forever for that climax. She plunges her hands into my hair, holding me in that position so we can gaze into each other's eyes. The pressure increases inside me, and heat sizzles down my nerves and straight into my *slat*.

No holding back now.

I thrust faster and harder while still lying half on top of her. Natalie squeezes her eyes shut and holds her breath until the orgasm strikes, then her entire body freezes—except for the muscles inside her that grip me in pulsating spasms. I can't stop the inevitable. Spasms rack my cock, and I punch into her a few more times as I shut my eyes and let the pleasure barrel through me.

She smiles with such sweetness that I get a pang in my chest.

I'm still inside her, and I can't make myself pull away. So I touch her cheek and nuzzle her nose because I seem to have forgotten how to speak.

Aye, I am hopelessly in love with her.

Chapter Twenty-Nine

Natalie

I stand on the tarmac at the Inverness airport, about to step onto Evan MacTaggart's jet for the trip back to America. This isn't the end of my time in Scotland, but it is the culmination of events that started on the day I discovered Elliot's dirty little secret. I don't know how to feel about anything that's happened since the day I met Munro—or how to feel about him. Yeah, my heart has its own opinion. But I'm still confused as hell.

Munro means more to me than I can understand or explain. But do I love him? Do I want to stick around in Scotland to find out the answer to that question? I need a lot more evidence to decide. Hopefully, this time away from Munro will give me those answers. Of course, I might be panicking a little bit since my ex-husband turned out to be such an evil scumbag. Even before he announced he wanted to kill me, Elliot had done everything he could to make me feel worthless and untrustworthy.

I believe Munro would never treat me that way. But am I too emotionally scarred to be any good for him?

"Are you away with the fairies?" Munro asks as he brushes aside hairs that the wind had blown over my eyes. "You're almost frowning, and that's not like you."

"We've known each other for a matter of days. You have no idea what I'm usually like."

"I know you better than anyone else on earth does."

Though I can't deny that, the realization does nothing to allay my anxiety. I know my roller-coaster emotions are tainting my views on everything, especially Munro, but I can't help that. Feelings don't obey my wishes. "Maybe you do know me best, but I need a lot more time to…figure things out, I guess."

"You're worrying about us, aren't you?"

"Of course I am. Neither of us can possibly understand how we feel about each other until after the ruckus dies down."

He bows his head, scratching the back of his neck. "I understand."

This isn't the first time I've seen Munro vulnerable, but it still surprises me. I can't leave him hanging, though I don't want to give him false hope either. All I can do is be honest with him. "I care about you, and I want to be with you. But it's not that simple. I need time, that's all. Can you understand that?"

"Aye." He finally lifts his head to look at me. "I can wait as long as you need me to. Forever, if that's what it takes."

The emotion in his voice makes my throat goes thick. Tears sting my eyes, but they don't roll down my cheeks. I swipe them away. "Thank you, Munro. You are the most understanding man I've ever met."

He chuckles. "Me? No one in my family would claim I'm the most understanding MacTaggart."

"They don't know you the way I do."

Munro reaches for me.

"Are we getting on the plane sometime today?" Alex calls out. He's standing halfway up the stairs that lead into the jet.

"Yes, I'm coming," I holler. Then I smack a quick, firm kiss on Munro's lips. "See you soon."

I jog to the stairs and climb up them while Alex hurries inside. At the top of the stairs, I pause to glance back at Munro. I wave at him. He raises a hand, palm out, as if he can't quite muster the will to wave goodbye. I want to race back down there and kiss him, but instead, I walk into the jet. I have to move aside so the co-pilot can shut the door. But I keep watching Munro until I can no longer see him. Then I rush to the nearest window and watch him again, until the jet begins to roll down the runway.

I slump onto the nearest chair and shut my eyes. God, I'm going to miss him.

"You look like you need a stiff drink."

Peeling my lids apart, I see Alex has sat down on the chair opposite mine. "I'd love to get wasted, but that won't fix my problems."

"I assume you aren't talking about your ex-husband. He is one well and truly cooked goose, and he will be locked in a jail cell as soon as we find the microdot."

Though I get why we need to gather the final evidence before handing Elliot over to the police, I can't help worrying he will find a way to escape. He's done it before. But we didn't have the entire MacTaggart clan on our side back then. Nobody will allow my puppy-smuggling ex to escape from Dùndubhan.

"I wasn't talking about Elliot," I say. "It's, um, something personal."

"Munro."

"Yes. Is it that obvious?"

Alex leans back in his chair and links his hands over his lap. "I married a MacTaggart, so I am fully aware of the clan's irresistible charms. Just don't tell anyone I said that. Most of the MacTaggart men are insufferably cocky as it stands. Can't give them more reasons to believe they are the pinnacle of Scottishness."

"Your secret is safe with me." I tuck my legs under me cross-legged. "Do you think we have any chance of finding my wedding ring and the microdot?"

"I'd wager the odds are in our favor."

"Why?"

"Because the MacTaggarts have taught me the value of believing in fate."

"That's an intriguing claim." I sit up straighter, though I keep my feet under me, suddenly fascinated by whatever he might say next. "You don't seem like the type who would buy into the idea of destiny."

"Oh, no, you've got me wrong, pet. I know fate exists. It's the only explanation for how I survived my childhood as a grifter and found new parents who showed me what love meant. The way I met and lost Catriona, then found her again because of her cousin Logan, who I had never met before... Now that was truly the hand of fate."

I desperately want to ask him to tell me the whole story, but it seems rude to pester him about it. Then my curiosity gets the better of me. "Sorry, but I can't help being curious about what you just said. There must be a great story behind it."

"There is. And perhaps I'll tell it to you one day. Right now, I plan on lying on that sofa over there to have a nice long lie-down."

"I'm too wired to sleep."

Alex rises and stretches. "Feel free to turn the telly on. I can sleep through anything, even an invasion of angry Scots."

"Sometimes I can't tell if you're being serious or making a joke."

He winks. "That's all part of the British Bastard's charm."

"You don't mind being called that, do you? Even though it's not a nice nickname."

"On the contrary. I treasure my title because Catriona gave it to me."

I have no idea how to respond to that statement. Maybe I'll understand one day when Alex shares the whole story with me.

The British Bastard saunters over to the sofa and settles in for a "lie-down." I guess that means a nap. Brits and Scots have their own unique ways of talking, though I have noticed some overlap.

Since I have zero chance of taking a nap, I'd like to get online to waste time and maybe to email Munro. If he ever checks his email. Does the man even have an account? Well, he edits books for Owen, so he must communicate with his clients via email. I doubt he could get away with using snail mail, not these days. But I don't have my computer. I glance at Alex, who lies on the sofa with his eyes closed and his hands clasped over his belly. Should I disturb him to find out if there's a way I can get online?

I wait about ten seconds, then I just go for it. "Alex?"

He doesn't respond.

"Alex," I say with more volume. "Are you awake?"

The Brit cracks one eye open. "What is it, Natalie? Are we about to crash?"

How he manages to sound calm and sarcastic at the same time, I can't fathom.

"It's nothing like that," I say. "Just wondered if there's a way I could get online. I don't have a computer with me."

"What about your mobile?"

"I get a cramp in my neck if I try to stare at my phone screen for too long."

"Hmm. Go ask the pilots. They might be able to help you." Alex settles in again, eyes closed. "May I finish my lie-down?"

"Yes. I'm sorry for bothering you."

"No worries."

I skulk up to the cockpit door like I expect to be tackled to the ground by an air marshal. But this is a private jet, not a commercial airliner. I don't think they have security on these kind of planes. Well, maybe famous people do. I tentatively knock on the cockpit door.

A sweet-faced young man opens the door and smiles. "How may I help you?"

I recognize this guy. He was the co-pilot who shut the jet's door, and he also flew Munro and me to Scotland. He's American, which means I shouldn't have too much trouble understanding him. "Um, I was wondering if there's a way I could get online. I didn't bring my computer."

"Sure. Several of the seats have a built-in computer interface. Let me show you."

"What's your name?" I ask. "I'm Natalie."

"I'm Chad. Just follow me, and I'll show you to one of the chairs that has internet access."

The sweet-faced co-pilot strides down the aisle and stops at a chair that faces another seat. A table lies between them. Chad shows me how to open up the built-in computer screen, which can be operated by touch. I thank him and spend the next two hours playing around online, accomplishing nothing except to distract myself. Finally, I get bored with that and decide to do the unthinkable.

I email Munro.

How long will it take for him to respond? Until the Friday after the end of eternity, I assume. But no, his response arrives three minutes and fourteen seconds after I sent my message. Yeah, okay, I counted the minutes and the seconds on the screen on a world time zone website.

Munro responds with his usual brevity. "Ring me, you daft lass. Use the house number."

Oh yeah, that's definitely Munro talking. Nobody stole his computer. Not even a thief would reply to my email that way. Oddly, though, his grumpy command makes me smile. I feel better having seen his words on the screen. I assume that "house phone" means the landline at Dùndubhan. As far as I know, he's still there with his many cousins.

I dial the number.

"What did you want?" he says in his usual grumpy way.

"To talk to you. Flying is boring without someone to talk to, and Alex is busy having a 'lie-down.' "

"Why don't you watch television? That's what we did on our way to Scotland."

"I know, but…" How can I say this without sounding like a moron? Oh, what the hell. "I miss you already."

He sighs. "I miss you too."

"We're pathetic, aren't we? Can't stand a few hours away from each other."

"That's not pathetic, *mo leannan*. It's—Well, something."

A laugh bubbles out of me. "Something? Gee, your Scottish charm seems to be waning."

"Careful, Natalie. I might spank you when you get back from Indiana."

"Maybe I'd like that." Was that me saying those words? I've never wanted to get even a teeny bit kinky, but with Munro… Yeah, I think I would enjoy that.

"We should try it, then."

For a moment, I become as frozen as an ice sculpture. Then I grin, though Munro can't see that. "Being with you is the most fun I've ever had."

"The same goes for me. Love being with you, *gràidh*."

"I know what that Gaelic word means. But what is '*mo leannan*'?"

He clears his throat. "It, ah, means 'my sweetheart.' That's what you are. Isn't it?"

"Yes. And you are *mo leannan* too."

Munro says nothing for several seconds. "You honestly feel that way about me?"

"Yeah, of course I do." Maybe I hadn't been sure about that a couple hours ago, but hearing his voice erased all those doubts.

"Glad to hear it."

I glance sideways at Alex, who seems to be sleeping. Then I speak in a softer voice. "What are you wearing, Wild Man?"

He laughs. "Are ye trying to seduce me over the phone?"

"Yes, I am. Can't believe I'm doing it because I've never behaved this way before. You make me feel wild."

"All right, then. I'm wearing my kilt."

"Seriously? Or did you make that up to get me horny?"

"Does it matter?"

I sink deeper into my seat as if I'm an escaped fugitive who sneaked onto the plane. "Guess it doesn't matter. So tell me more about what you're wearing and what you're doing right now."

"I'm standing in the garden at Dùndubhan, near the bench where we had a poke the other day. My kilt is hanging low over my hips, almost exposing the hairs above my *bagais*. That's my balls, by the way. They're aching for you, Natalie."

My hand rises to touch my throat, seemingly of its own volition. I begin to pet my skin while I picture what Munro described. "Imagine I'm massaging your balls, and your dick is getting hard. Then I kneel in front of you with my face inches from your erection. My mouth is watering, and I can't wait to taste you."

"Ah, fuck, lass. You're driving me mad."

"I grasp the base of your cock and slide your length between my lips to—"

The phone is snatched away from me. I jump and nearly fly out of my chair, then a second later, my cheeks heat up.

Because Alex is glowering at me.

He still holds my phone. "Would you two cease and desist? I'm trying to sleep, and your antics are having the opposite effect on me. I'm wide awake."

"Sorry. I was bored, so I called Munro."

"That much is obvious." Alex tosses my phone to me. "Please go into the bedroom to do whatever you plan on doing."

"Why don't you call your wife? She might like to—"

"Bloody hell. Just go into the bedroom and shut the door."

Alex stalks back to the sofa and flops onto it. Then he lays a pillow on top of his face.

And I hustle into the bedroom.

Chapter Thirty

Munro

I can hear Natalie's footsteps as she hurries into the bedroom. At least, I assume that's where the lass is going. Alex had sounded furious when he heard Natalie attempting to have phone sex with me. Well, he and Cat did get married at a nudist resort, so they have no right to complain about a wee bit of long-distance mutual masturbation between me and Natalie. He was probably jealous. I would've suggested he should ring Cat, but Natalie beat me to it. And Alex didn't seem to appreciate the suggestion.

"Okay," Natalie says, and I hear the click of a door shutting. "I'm in the bedroom. Now what?"

"Lie on the bed and unzip your trousers."

Rustling indicates she's following my orders. "I did that."

"Slip your hand inside your knickers and describe to me how aroused you are."

Natalie sucks in a sharp breath. "Oh God, I'm so wet for you, Wild Man. My panties are damp, and my clit is stiff."

"Massage that nub, *gràidh*."

She moans and writhes, which I can tell because of the rough sound her jeans make as they scrape over the bedding. "I wish you were inside me right now."

"So do I. Now slide your fingers down to your opening and push two of them inside you. Pump those fingers to fuck yourself."

Her breathing grows harsher and faster. "I'm so close, Munro, keep talking dirty to me, and make it growly, please."

I close my eyes and envision Natalie spread out on the grass in the garden, naked and touching herself. I'm not in the garden, of course. I'm reclining on the sofa in the sitting room. But I swear I can smell the scent of her desire and taste her cream. "Imagine me devouring you, lass. That's what I'm picturing while I unzip my trousers and stroke my cock."

"Yes, Munro, yes, keep talking. I love it, and I'm so close to coming."

The sitting room door bursts open. "Bloody hell, Munro. What are you doing? You've got a room upstairs where you can wank off in private."

I jerk upright, breathing hard, and glare at Errol. "*Falbh a ghabhail do ghnùis airson cac*, Errol, before I strangle you."

"Away and take my face for a shit?" Errol laughs. "You are the most bizarre MacTaggart of all."

My cousin grins.

"Are you still there, Munro?" Natalie asks. I can barely hear her since I'm holding the phone to my chest. The sitting room has a landline phone, like most rooms in the castle.

I raise the phone to my ear while still glaring at my cousin. "I'm here. But Errol interrupted, and ahmno pleased with the way he barged in."

"Chill out, Munro. He must have a reason for bothering you."

"Aye, and it had better be a good one. I'll call you back later."

"Sure. But I'll need to finish myself off."

My cock jerks, because I want to listen to her coming while I do the same. But I can't. Errol wants something. "Goodbye, Natalie."

"Talk to you later, Wild Man."

I toss the phone onto the coffee table. "What do you want, Errol?"

"Are you at all interested in Kieran MacTaggart?"

"Our ancestor? I might be interested, but that depends on what you want me to do."

"Ashley thinks we need fresh eyes on the mystery of Kieran, and she seems to think you're the one for the job. She ordered me to ask for your help."

"Your fiancée orders you about? Grow some *bagais*, laddie."

Errol sits down on the coffee table facing me. "Please, Munro. It would make Ashley happy, and I know you don't want her to be disappointed."

The bloody *cacan*. Using a lass to get me to go along with whatever mad scheme he's concocted this time is a dirty trick. But he's right. I can't disappoint the lass. "Fine, I'll help you. But not until after Natalie and Alex come back and we hand Elliot over to the authorities."

"Brilliant! I'll tell Ashley. She'll be very excited."

The lass herself bursts into the room, grinning as she drops onto the sofa beside me. Ashley kisses my cheek and hugs me. "Thank you, Munro."

"You two are insane. Do ye know that? And you must have been eaves-dropping to know what I told Errol."

"I was. But only because this project is so important."

"Learning more about a man who died hundreds of years ago can't be that important."

She kisses my cheek again. "It is to me and Errol. Kirsty and Luke will be thrilled too."

"If you four couldn't figure out what happened to Kieran, I don't see how you think I can. I'm not a historian or an archaeologist—or a time traveler."

"But you are very smart. Your brain is all we need."

I still think these two are off their heads, but I can't deny that the mystery of Kieran MacTaggart does intrigue me. Ever since Errol told me about it, I've wondered why our ancestor left such cryptic clues for his descendants to follow. Kirsty and Luke began the quest for answers. Then Errol and Ashley continued the search. Now I'm volunteering to participate in the barmy quest.

After Errol and Ashley finally leave the sitting room, I recline on the sofa again with my hands clasped behind my head as I gaze up at the ceiling. I mean to fantasize about Natalie and all the ways I could make her come once she returns from America. Instead, I wind up contemplating the Kieran conundrum. I know he had been banished from his clan after Simidh Gunn accused him of stealing from his fellow MacTaggarts. Kieran had nowhere to go except for an abandoned castle, where he lived with his three aunts for years after his banishment. He was later accused of witchcraft and convicted, then executed.

But Kieran did not die. Except he did. Only he didn't. The evidence is sparse and bloody confusing. The annals state that he was indeed executed. Yet his grave in the MacTaggart cemetery is empty, and the inscription on it states that he lived on.

Nothing about the man makes any sense.

All right, maybe I am intrigued. Maybe I do want to search for answers in the hopes that I might uncover something everyone else had overlooked. I've never been anything but a hiking guide in Scotland and a river guide in America. What can I bring to the search for Kieran?

Since I have no clue, I give up ruminating on the mystery and head upstairs to find out what my cousins have done with Elliot and his mates. I'd been too consumed by thoughts of Natalie leaving to think about the logistics of housing and containing all of Elliot's men. Fortunately, Dùndubhan is large and has many bedrooms as well as a wine cellar. I'm interested to see exactly how those men have been housed, restrained, and interrogated.

I meet Rory in the vestibule. He's just come down the stairs from an upper floor and seems quite pleased with himself.

"Did you skelp those scunners?" I ask. "You look like a man who had a good time up there."

"We've all been flexing our muscles and brains to convince those men to tell us everything they know. Didn't take long."

"I hope you left at least one for me. Terrifying criminal bastards is sort of my specialty."

Rory chuckles. "I've heard that. You took on the persona of a selkie in the Grand Canyon, didn't you?"

"Aye. You should've seen those laddies gawping at me like I was a supernatural creature sent to devour them."

"Wish I'd been there." He moves closer to clap a hand on my shoulder. "Glad you're home again, Munro. You shouldn't have stayed away for as long as you did, and I hope one day you'll tell me why you shut the family out."

"Aye, one day I will. After this little escapade is over."

Rory squeezes my shoulder. "We saved Elliot Rudaski for you. Thought you'd want to be the one to have a wee chat with him before Natalie comes back and wants to skelp him herself."

"Thank you for saving that *tolla-thon* for me." I crack my knuckles. "I would love to have a wee *chat* with Elliot. He might not look as pretty afterward, though."

"Don't worry about that. The entire clan will corroborate the fact that he assaulted you."

Whether it's true or not, that's what he means. Elliot deserves to get smacked about, but I have no plans to leave him bloodied and bruised. He needs to look presentable when the police arrive to take him away. But I can still scare the living daylights out of the *bod ceann* without laying a hand on him.

"Let us know if you need any backup," Rory says. "None of us are leaving the compound until everything is settled."

"How are Elliot's mates holding up?"

My cousin smiles like a wolf who just ate a bear. "They won't be a problem. Logan and Magnus worked their magic on those laddies."

"Good. Where can I find Elliot?"

"In the tower bedroom. Luke offered to lend you his lie-detecting gear, but I assured him you don't need high-tech equipment to figure out if Elliot is being truthful."

My cousin is right about that. Sometimes the old-school methods work best. I know nothing about lie-detection equipment, so my ways are the only ones I need.

Rory heads toward the guest wing to find his "blethering, wayward wife"—his words, not mine—and I jog up two flights of stairs to reach the tower bedroom. We call it that because it lies within a cylindrical turret that had once been used for battles, presumably. The tower would have protected bowmen while they fired arrows at the enemy. These days, it's a place to sleep, or on occasion, a place to interrogate a villain. I cross through the long gallery and march up the steps that lead to the bedroom. Errol's great uncle, Torcall Murdoch, stands guard at the door.

"I need to speak to Elliot," I say. "Alone."

Torcall steps aside. "Be my guest, laddie. I'll go down to the kitchen to have a piece. Aidan and Lachlan are guarding him."

While Torcall trots down the stairs, as spry as any man half his age, I open the door and walk into the tower bedroom. Lachlan and Aidan had been sitting on chairs at either end of a long table, but now they rise.

"Elliot and I need to have a chat," I say. "Give us a wee while, eh?"

"Of course," Lachlan says. "I'd say ring us on your mobile if you need us, but I know you aren't up to speed on technology."

"I know how to use a computer, don't I?"

Aidan punches my shoulder as he walks past. "Give him hell, mate."

He and Lachlan leave, and the door clicks shut behind them.

Elliot and I are alone.

I had shared my plan with my cousins earlier today, so they will be prepared to do their bit when the time comes. I will rely heavily on the facts Natalie gave me back in my cabin—namely, that Elliot is claustrophobic and will panic under the right circumstances. Aye, the scunner is a coward too.

Natalie's conniving, slimy ex-husband sits on the bed, leaning against the headboard. He lifts his chin and folds his arms over his chest. "You can't hurt me. Assault is illegal."

"Aye, but I don't mean to assault you. Torture is more my style."

"That's illegal too."

I roll up my sleeves and crack my knuckles. "The way I do it, no one will ever be able to prove I tortured you. Won't be a scratch on you."

He rolls his eyes. The laddie might not believe me yet, but he's about to learn the truth.

"Why do ye think my cousins didn't restrain you?" I ask. "It's because they know you can't escape. The tower bedroom was once a torture chamber where the lord of this castle used whatever methods were necessary to wring information out of his enemies." I glance around, taking in everything between the floor and the ceiling. "This room used to be soaked in blood. Must be more than a few spirits trapped in here, where they died, desperate to enact vengeance."

"You're full of shit, Scotty."

"My name is Munro. Call me the wrong name again, and I'll invite those phantoms to molest you."

He rolls his eyes again. "You and your cockamamie ghost story don't scare me."

"Don't they? Maybe I should start with practical methods before invoking the spirits."

Elliot scoffs. "Give it your best shot, jackass."

I saunter up to the side of the bed, rest one hand on the headboard, and slant toward the laddie. Then I adopt my growliest, nastiest voice. "I've lived in the wilderness alone for six years, and I know how to skin a bear while it's still alive. Ripping the flesh off the bones with my teeth is my favorite way to eat wild game. You are nothing but another animal to me." I gnash my teeth. "My canines are sharp enough to shred you to bits."

"Oh, please. Your Hannibal Lecter routine is lame."

"Back in medieval times, when food was scarce the clan that lived here would kill their enemies and make stew with the remains." I step away from the bed and scan the room. "Who knows how many people died in this room? Their spirits inhabit the castle, just waiting for one of their descendants to invoke the right magics and set them free."

Elliot makes a petulant face, but he's begun to wring his hands.

I pull a roll of duct tape out of my back pocket.

He leaps off the bed and runs for the nearest door, cranking the handle. But it's locked. I let him scurry to the other door, strictly so he can fail to open that one too. Breathing hard, his eyes wild, Elliot rushes at me.

I seize him mid-stride and lash my arms tightly around his midsection. He can't move his arms, and his pathetic attempts to kick me and bite my nose fail. So I toss him onto the bed, on his belly, and bind his hands and feet with the tape.

"Thought you weren't going to hurt me," he says. "Scotty is a big fat liar, huh?"

"Said I wouldn't leave a mark on you." I flip him over and drag him to the headboard so he can sit back against it. "This tape will come away cleanly."

Elliot scowls at me.

"Let's find out if you're a die-hard skeptic after all." I spread my arms wide and tip my head back. "Laird of Dùndubhan, unleash the enemy spirits."

"Oh, brother. That's the lamest attempt to—"

The walls rumble, and the bed shivers.

Elliot squirms but maintains his mulish expression. "You probably had one of your buddies get out his tuba and blow a long note. Still not buying your bullshit, Scotty."

"My name is Munro." I take two strides toward the bed, edging past the long table. "Guess I need to give you more proof."

He crosses his arms over his chest again and smirks. "Give it a try, moron."

"My name is pronounced Mun-roh. Do ye have a hearing problem? No, I reckon you just aren't that intelligent." I move to the foot of the bed, spread my arms again, and throw my head back to shout, "Laird of Dùndubhan, *feasgar math. 'S e Albannaich a th' annainn.* Show this wayward soul how to *fannadh,* for his *bigealais* is wee and shriveled. *Cho cinnteach is a tha bod 's an each,* his *acainn cungaidh* will be *breallach,* if it isn't already."

A deep, loud roar echoes through the walls, accompanied by a shrieking racket.

Elliot stiffens, and his eyes go wide. "This is bullshit."

The elevated pitch of his voice belies his words. The bastard is afraid now, and I'm only getting started.

"*Ith do chac,* Elliot Rudaski!" I shout, my voice echoing in the room. "And pray the ancient, vengeful gods will spare your soul."

Pounding erupts, rattling the door fiercely, even as the roaring and shrieking continues. Then the lights go out.

And Elliot screams.

The tower bedroom has two doors on opposite sides of the space. But now, inhuman voices bellow wordlessly. The voices aren't inhuman at all, and I know that, but Elliot won't have a sodding clue that Lachlan and Aidan are making those noises.

"I don't believe you," Elliot shouts, his voice higher pitched and shaky. "This is total bullshit. You and y-your friends won't trick me. I'm not that stupid, you lying piece of—"

A light comes on outside the window, thought it seemingly originates from nowhere. The glow coruscates in what seems like an unnatural manner, moving back and forth in front of the window, its light shimmering through the room. Then the howling begins.

"You aren't fooling me!" Elliot all but shrieks. "This is crap!"

My eyes have adjusted to the dark well enough that I can make out the shapes of the bed, the table and chairs, and Elliot. The bed shakes. The roaring and bellowing grows louder. The glow outside intensifies.

A witch rises into view outside the window, cackling and scratching at the glass.

"You—can't—fool—me!" Elliot screams.

"Laird of Dùndubhan," I shout. "Will you spare this sorry soul? Or will you send him down into the depths of Hell?"

"He…must…die…"
The roaring voice echoes from seemingly nowhere and everywhere.
Elliot passes out.

Chapter Thirty-One

Natalie

Alex and I walk into the Mislaid Treasures Pawn Shop in Hammond, Indiana, at eight nineteen on the morning after I left Munro and Scotland. We got to America much faster than most people could, thanks to Evan's top-of-the-line jet that can reach speeds approaching mach one, though it can't break the sound barrier. Since we arrived in Hammond too late to visit the pawn shop, Alex and I checked into a motel—with separate rooms, of course—and tried to get some rest. Neither of us got much sleep. Alex admitted he wants to get this over with so he can go home to his wife and their new baby.

I can't wait to return to the Highlands and Munro. It's five hours later there, which means he's probably having lunch right now. I miss him so much that it's almost embarrassing.

Alex pushes the shop's door open, which makes the bells above it tinkle, and he holds the door for me so I can enter first. Despite his reputation as the British Bastard, Alex is a genuinely nice guy. We approach the counter, which is a glass enclosure full of pawned items, mostly jewelry. I don't see my ring in there. Well, it couldn't possibly be that easy to find what we need.

A gray-haired man walks up to the counter across from us. "Good morning. How may I help you today?"

"We're looking for a wedding ring," I say. "I pawned it here a while ago, and I was hoping it's still available. I'd like to buy it back."

"Do you have the pawn ticket?"

"No, sorry."

My partner in crime drapes an around across my shoulders and smiles with what seems for all the world to be genuine sweetness. "I'm Alex, and this is my fiancée, Natalie."

"I'm Chuck."

"How lovely it is to meet you, Chuck. Your shop is impressive. We will be sure to mention it to our friends."

"That's very kind of you."

"Not at all." Alex gives me a quick squeeze. "We're terribly sorry to inconvenience you, but we desperately hope we can find that ring again. My wife and I went through a rough patch and ended up divorcing. But we've reconciled and plan to remarry. That ring means a great deal to us both. Can't you take a look in your back room? Perhaps the ring is there."

"We don't get a lot of wedding bands," the shop owner says. "Most people don't want to wear somebody else's ring. I suppose I could check in the back where I keep the stuff that's harder to sell. Can you describe the ring?"

"I can do better than that," I tell him. "I have a picture of it on my phone."

"Yes, I remember that picture," Alex declares with perfect sincerity.

Digging my phone out, I open the camera roll and find the photo of me in my wedding dress, holding a bouquet. I zoom in to show the shopkeeper the ring.

He studies it for a moment. "What a lovely ring. I do recall something like this, now that I've seen the picture."

I had scrolled through gobs and gobs of photos on my camera roll until I finally found the right one. Yeah, I need to weed out a lot of them, especially the ones with Elliot in them.

Alex kisses my cheek. "See, darling? All is not lost yet."

Damn, he's one smooth operator. I almost believe he's in love with me.

"Take a look around," the shopkeeper says, "while I look for the ring. You might find another one you like even better."

Chuck disappears into the back room.

Alex keeps his arm around me and maintains his "I'm just a guy who's in love with a girl" persona even when no one else is around to see it. I do my best to play the same role, but I have no clue if I'm totally blowing it or genuinely rocking the con.

It's kind of fun to play this game.

The shopkeeper returns as we're pretending to browse various types of rings housed within a glass case near the door. We wander back to the main counter.

"I couldn't find the ring in my stock," he says. "Wish I still had it, but I searched all my records of wedding ring sales. I don't have the one you want, but I did find the receipt for it." He waves the slip of paper. "It has the customer's name and phone number on it. I could give her a call right now on the off chance she might want to pawn it."

I don't need to fake my relief. "That would great, Chuck. Thank you."

He picks up the phone and dials. After several seconds, he says. "Good morning. This is Chuck from the Mislaid Treasures Pawn Shop. Are you the one who bought a fancy wedding ring here?" He listens intently for a moment. "Well, I've got a couple here who were the original owners. They wondered if you'd like to sell the ring to them."

Could it really be this easy? I gnaw on the inside of my lip as I wait for Chuck to share the woman's response with us.

"I understand, of course," he says. "Had to give it a try." He hangs up. "She doesn't want to sell."

Alex hugs me firmly to his side. "We really are desperate to reacquire the ring. Do you think you could give us the new owner's phone number? We would be ever so grateful."

"Sorry, I can't give out that information. Gotta protect the customer's privacy."

"Of course. You've been wonderful. Thank you, Chuck." Alex seems like he's about to leave. But then he pauses as if he's just remembered something. "Oh, there was another item we would love to find. I never gave my darling Natalie an engagement ring. Perhaps you have one in stock?"

"Sure thing," Chuck says. "Let me show you what I've got."

Alex nuzzles my hair, but he's really doing that so he can whisper in my ear. "You need to use the restroom."

I feign being lovey-dovey, strictly so I have an excuse to turn my head toward him. "What should I do in there?"

"Let me distract him while you sneak behind the counter to find that receipt."

"Gotcha."

Alex releases me and starts walking toward the glass case near the door. "Chuck, I'd love to explore the ring options you have here. Perhaps you could explain the differences?"

"Sure thing."

Ever the consummate grifter, Alex leans over the glass case and points at various items, which ensures that Chuck leans over too. They both peer down into the case.

I head toward the restroom but veer behind the main counter once I see Alex has the shopkeeper fully engaged. Chuck won't notice what I'm doing. So, I carefully poke around until I find the receipt we need. It does indeed have the buyer's name and address. I stuff it into my pocket and return to the restroom door, pretending that I've just exited, and hurry over to where Alex stands.

"Oh, that's a pretty one," I say as I gaze at one of the rings in the case with an appropriate amount of excitement, no more, no less. "What do you think, honey?"

Alex slings his arm around me. "Yes, it is quite nice. But I can't decide it embodies your spirit and the strength of our renewed connection."

I pretend to study the ring again. "Maybe you're right. We should think about it some more before we decide."

"Yes, darling, I always trust your judgment."

Chuck glances at Alex and then me. "So, you don't see anything you like."

I squint at the ring, then shake my head. "No, this isn't the perfect one. But we'll probably come back in a few days, once we've settled on the type of ring I really want. Thank you so much for helping us, Chuck."

"My pleasure. Congrats on the engagement. You two belong together, I can tell."

Alex and I leave the shop while holding hands and smiling at each other. But once we've moved out of sight of the shop, we drop the act. Alex winces. I shove my hands into my jeans pockets. We both seem uncomfortable now, and it's no surprise to me why that is. He loves Cat. I love Munro. Of course we don't like pretending to be a lovey-dovey couple when we'd rather rush home to them.

I thought the words "I love Munro." And I meant it. Holy shit, I do love that scruffy, grumpy Scot. He looks less unkempt these days, ever since he trimmed his beard to make me happy. I would've still loved him with the wild, disheveled hair and beard, but he looks even hotter these days.

"Want to run to the airport and leap onto that jet?" I ask Alex. "We could be back in Scotland before dinnertime."

"Yes, let's do that."

"Oh, I almost forgot. I need to go to my apartment to pick up my belongings and cancel my lease."

"That shouldn't take long." His lips kink up at one corner. "I can talk anyone into doing anything, which means your landlord won't get the chance to argue about terminating the lease. He will do it happily."

"I will never again question your grifter skills."

Alex does sweet-talk my landlord into breaking the lease with no penalty fees. While I'm quickly stuffing all my belongings into whatever boxes I can find, Alex tells me he has an errand to run and he'll be back in fifteen minutes. After exactly that length of time, he returns—with four brawny men.

"These blokes will finish packing for you," he says. "They're professionals and will take excellent care of your things. By the time we reach the airport, they will have transported the lot to the jet."

"But the airport is only ten minutes away."

"You've already forgotten, haven't you? I did too." He offers me his hand, helping get up off the floor. "We need to visit Annabeth Carver."

"What if she won't sell us the ring?"

"Honestly, have you learned nothing from me? 'No' is never the last word for an experienced grifter."

I use the maps feature on my phone to chart a route to Annabeth Carver's house, and the drive takes only five minutes. We park along the curb in front of a cute little house that has beautiful flowering shrubs in front. Alex and I hold hands again, resuming our little con, and trot up the steps. I ring the bell.

The door swings open, and a pretty gray-haired woman greets us with a casual smile. "May I help you?"

"Yes, Mrs. Carver," I say, "I hope you can help. I'm Natalie, and this is my fiancé, Alex. We would like to talk to you about the wedding ring you bought at the Mislaid Treasures Pawn Shop."

She lays a hand on her chest. "Oh, dear, did I buy a stolen ring?"

"No, no, it's nothing like that. Alex bought that ring for me, but after we got divorced, I pawned it. Then Alex and I realized we'd made a huge mistake by splitting up. We're getting married again, and it would be so romantic to have that ring again. We'll pay any price."

My pseudo-fiancé tugs me against him. "We know it's a big ask, but if we could at least see the ring..."

"I don't know." Annabeth studies us for a moment with her brows wrinkled. Then she smiles and pulls the door open all the way. "You two seem like such a sweet couple, and you're clearly so in love. Please come in. I'll show you the ring, but I don't know if you could offer me enough to make me want to sell it."

"Just a glimpse will do," Alex says. "That ring has sentimental value for us. Thank you, Mrs. Carver."

"Call me Annabeth."

She leads us into the living room and invites us to sit on the sofa. We wait while she goes into another room to retrieve the ring. I feel a little bit anxious, but mostly, I'm excited to find the ring and hopefully retrieve the microdot. Then we can go home. And yeah, I've started to think of Scotland as home, not Indiana. Will I move to the Highlands to be with Munro? That's a question we need to discuss together.

Annabeth emerges carrying a small velvet box. She settles onto a high-backed chair and holds the item out to me. "Here, sweet child."

I accept the box. "Thank you, Annabeth. You have no idea how much this means to us."

My pulse revs up as I flip the lid open. A shiver of excitement rushes through me. It's *the* ring. The one Elliot had given me. I recognize the gold band itself, with its delicate, elegantly curving lines that had been my idea to have engraved in the metal. I carefully lift the ring out of its velvet cushion, and Alex takes the box. I tip the ring this way and that, examining every inch, but I can't see any microdot. Well, if it's "micro," doesn't that mean microscopic? No, it must be visible to the naked eye or else no one would be able to find it once it was placed on the ring.

I get out my phone and use the camera app as a magnifier, zooming in so I can scrutinize the inside of the gold band. But it's hard to hold the phone steady while doing that.

"Let me take that for you," Alex offers. "I'll hold the camera steady."

He figured out what I was trying to do without asking. He knows I'm looking for a microdot, but still, he's a smart man to realize my intent.

Alex takes the phone, holding it with both hands, and moves it back into position. I resume analyzing the inner band, turning it side to side until something catches my eye. At first, it seems like a smudge of dirt. But something niggles at me...

"What are you looking for?" Annabeth asks. "Does the ring have a flaw?"

"No, it's flawless and genuine," Alex tells her. "But Natalie seems to be fascinated by the inscription."

I'm not, and he knows it. But Alex is trying not to give away our true motives. The inscription reads, "To Annabeth, with all my love." That's very sweet, but hardly fascinating. Elliot hadn't included an inscription when he gave me the ring. Big surprise.

I focus on the smudge again. "Can you zoom in any closer, Alex?"

He increases the zoom to maximum.

And I see it. A miniature black circle that can't measure much more than one millimeter. That must be the microdot. I cautiously pick at the edges of the itty-bitty circle until it peels up the tiniest bit, then I slowly slide my fingernail under it to peel the rest of the dot away from the gold band. The thing is so tiny that I could easily lose it.

"What is it?" Annabeth asks, now leaning forward to peer at the ring.

"I found a flea squashed into the gold, but I removed it." I hold out my finger to Alex. "Can you get rid of this?"

"Of course."

Annabeth wrinkles her brows again. "You can just throw it out. There's a trash can in the kitchen."

"Oh, of course," I say. "You stay here, Alex. I can toss this tiny piece of gunk on my own."

While Alex chats with Annabeth, handily distracting her, I go into the kitchen and hunt around for some clear tape. I can't be too vigorous in my hunt for that, though, or I might accidentally drop the microdot. At last, I find a roll of clear packaging tape and carefully transfer the microdot onto that. Then I fold the tape over to seal it. Slipping the taped microdot into my jeans pocket, I return to the living room.

Annabeth is laughing boisterously at something Alex said.

I lay a hand on his shoulder. "Let's go, honey. We've taken up enough of Annabeth's time." I smile at our hostess. "Thank you so much for inviting us into your home. It's beautiful, and you are such a wonderful woman."

She beams.

And we hurry out the door, zooming to the airport.

I can't wait to see Munro again.

The journey back to Scotland seems to take forever, but I'm sure that's only because I miss Munro so badly. Something about seeing my wedding ring again made me think about the hot Scottish bear and wonder what life with a MacTaggart man might be like. Thanks to Munro, I've learned things about myself that I never could have imagined would be true. I'm a badass and a con artist. Whatever comes my way, I can handle it. And I never would have learned that about myself if it weren't for Munro.

I call the landline at Dùndubhan, hoping to reach Munro, but I wind up talking to Mrs. Brody instead. She's the housekeeper at the castle, and her husband Tavish is the groundskeeper. I'd met them briefly during my stay at Dùndubhan. She informes me that all the MacTaggart men are there, including Munro, but that my Wild Man is busy helping his cousins round up Elliot's men in the courtyard so they can "enjoy some fresh air." Once Alex and I get there, we will all examine the microdot. Only after we know what's on it will we call the police to retrieve the bastards. The biggest a-hole of all, my ex-husband, will remain in Munro's custody until he's arrested. Mrs. Brody also tells me that Munro "had a bloody good time today in the tower bedroom" and that convinced Elliot to tell the truth.

He did what? My ex would never cave. But he is a coward, so maybe Munro snarled and glared at him until he gave up.

The pilot announces we are about to land at Inverness.

I'm coming home.

Chapter Thirty-Two

Munro

Natalie is coming home today. Whether she thinks of Scotland as home, I can't say. But I hope she will come to love the Highlands as much as I do because I never want to leave here again. Logan had informed me a few hours ago that Natalie and Alex would arrive soon, and I became unusually restless after receiving that news. All right, I'm excited to see the lass again. I love her, and I need to tell her that.

We've just herded Elliot's lackeys into the wine cellar again, and I'm heading back to the vestibule, when Jack races up to me.

"You'll want to go out into the courtyard," he says. "The car is coming up the drive."

"What car?"

"Rory's Mercedes. He drove Natalie and Alex from the Inverness airport."

"Oh, aye, of course." I hadn't forgotten about that, but my mind had been on other things. So, that means I did forget. No, I was distracted. "Thank you for letting me know, Jack."

I jog out into the courtyard and wait. Nothing happens. I wait and wait and wait…

The crunching of tires on gravel draws my attention to the open gates, and Rory's Mercedes pulls into the courtyard. He parks near the vestibule door.

Before either Rory or Alex get out of the car, Natalie throws her door open and sprints toward me. She flings her arms around my neck, her feet lifting off the ground, and kisses me with so much passion and enthusiasm that I should probably feel a wee bit embarrassed. But I'm not the sort who experiences embarrassment. I bathe in the nude outdoors, after all. We consume each other like the world might disintegrate at any moment, tongues tangling, teeth bumping, while my *slat* begins to rouse.

Finally, I force myself to end the kiss and set her down, though I keep my hands on her hips. "Happy to see me, eh?"

"Yes, yes, I'm ecstatic." She plants a firm, hard kiss on my mouth. "I love you, Munro."

"I love you too, *gràidh*." Ever since Natalie left yesterday, I've wondered how difficult it would be to tell her how I feel. But it came easily.

She glances around. "Where are the bad guys now?"

"All but one of them are in the wine cellar, where the worst they can do is get drunk. Elliot is in the tower bedroom."

"How much trouble did he give you?"

"Not as much as you might expect." I shift my hands down to her erse. "Shortly after you left, I came up with a plan. My cousins helped. Believe me, that ersehole will never bother you again. In fact, he's very keen to confess everything to the police."

Her brows knit together over her nose, where the sweetest dimple has formed. "I don't understand. Elliot would never confess, unless you..." Her brows hike up. "Did you torture the truth out of him?"

"In a manner of speaking."

"You don't need to be cagey about it. If you tortured him, I'm cool with that. I mean, Elliot emotionally tortured me for years, though I couldn't admit that even to myself until I discovered his criminal enterprise."

"Not being cagey, *mo leannan*. But we should talk about this alone, in the sitting room."

"Okay."

Alex and Rory watch as I lead Natalie into the house. We pass through the vestibule and the ground-floor hallway, then cross through the dining room to reach the guest wing. I open the sitting room door for her.

She pats my cheek and smiles. "Who knew the Wild Man would turn out to be such a sweetheart? Not many guys these days hold doors open for women."

"All those other blokes are erseholes."

"Yeah, they are."

I shut the door behind us and gesture for her to sit on the sofa. I sit right next to her, one arm draped across the sofa's back. "I played a wee trick on Elliot to convince him to tell me everything. I wanted to know what he knew before we hand him over to the police."

"Makes sense. But what kind of trick did you play on him?"

Cannae help smirking. "I summoned the spirit of the laird of Dùndubhan and asked him to awaken his entire clan to punish Elliot."

"I see." Her lips twitch as if she's amused by my statement. "My ex-husband doesn't believe in the supernatural. He would've laughed at you."

"Aye, he did scoff. But only until the show started. My cousins helped me put on a great spectacle for Elliot, and he literally pissed his pants. The Witches of Ballachulish made an appearance too. Lachlan and Aidan, with Luke's help, used electronics and brute force to create an unholy racket. Once the lights went out, Elliot went completely off his head." I lean back and clasp my hands behind my head. "He won't trouble you ever again."

"Munro, that's amazing. I wish I could have seen it." She wriggles around to face me. "What exactly did you say that scared Elliot so much?"

"Care to hear my speech right now?"

"Absolutely."

"I said most of it in Gaelic, but I'll give you the English version." I straighten and clear my throat. "Laird of Dùndubhan, good afternoon. We are Scots. Show this wayward soul how to masturbate, for his cock is wee and shriveled. As sure as a horse has a penis, his healing tool will soon be impotent, if it isn't already. Eat your own shit, Elliot Rudaski, and pray the ancient, vengeful gods will spare your soul."

"What's a healing tool?"

"Another term for a man's cock."

She bites down on both her lips while her shoulders quiver with what is surely contained laughter. "And you said all of that in Gaelic so Elliot wouldn't know you were insulting him."

"That's right. It was half English, half Gaelic."

"I know this might sound like a strange request, coming from me. But could I see Elliot? Just for a few minutes. I gave Evan the microdot, so he and some of the others will be examining its contents."

"You can see him whenever you like." I get up and offer her my hands. "We can do that right now. Or if you'd rather wait a while, I can cook us dinner."

She accepts my hands and lets me help her up. "I'd rather confront Elliot one last time first. When will the cops come to get him and his cohorts?"

"After my cousins have finished studying the microdot."

"Let's go see Elliot now."

We leave the sitting room and make our way through the dining room. But as we're about to mount the vestibule stairs, Natalie's mobile rings.

She glances at the caller ID, then answers. "What's up, Evan?"

I watch her facial expressions while she listens to whatever my cousin has to say. At first, she seems intensely focused. Then her brows crinkle. She bites her lip and glances at me briefly. "Yeah, I understand. We should talk to you guys first, before we confront Elliot. Uh-huh. Right."

She ends the call.

"What did Evan say?" I ask.

"I'll let him explain since I'm not entirely sure I get it. Sounds like very technical stuff."

"Computer rubbish, I imagine."

"No, microdot rubbish."

"Cheeky lass." I sweep her up in my arms. "Just for that, I will insist on carrying you to the great hall."

"I thought it was renamed the command center."

Shaking my head, I cluck my tongue. "That's what happens when you leave the country for nearly two days. Life moved on without you."

"Did it really? Not for me. I couldn't stop thinking about you."

"I was being facetious. Of course I didn't move on without you."

She kisses my cheek. "I know you wouldn't do that. So, what is the great hall called today?"

"Most of the equipment has been taken away, so now it's just the great hall again."

The lass tries to convince me to release her by wriggling in my arms, but I don't let go. "I can walk, Munro. You don't need to carry me."

A grunt is my only response. But that doesn't fash her anymore. I think she likes my wordless responses now.

I ascend the stairs with Natalie in my arms, taking the steps two at a time. In the great hall, I set her down. She swivels her head this way and that to take in the dramatically altered room—which means it's empty. She never saw what it was like before the siege since the command center had already been set up when she arrived. The waning light of the sun casts a gentle glow on the entire room and creates golden highlights on her red hair. For a moment, I stand here admiring her profile and the way her amber eyes turn luminous in this lighting, bringing out the darker rims around the irises.

My chest aches, but in a good way. This beautiful lass loves me.

I don't see anyone else here, not my cousins, not their spouses, no one. So naturally, I shout, "Where are you, Evan?"

He pokes his head out of the office doorway and pushes his glasses up. "In here, Munro. No need to bellow like an angry bear. You could have simply walked in."

"It's more fun to bellow. Then I get to hear my voice echoing in the great hall."

My cousin sighs and shakes his head, though he smiles a wee bit too. "Get your erse in here, Munro. We have news about the microdot."

He disappears into the office.

Natalie and I traipse across the big, empty hall and enter Rory's office. The man himself sits behind the desk while Evan and Logan hover behind him. Rory waves for us to take the two chairs across the desk from him.

He rests his elbows on the desktop and steeples his fingers under his chin. "We had all assumed the microdot contained only information about Elliot's puppy-smuggling activities. But it includes much more than that."

I drum my fingers on my chair's arms. "More? Such as what?"

"Everything. It seems that Elliot was in charge of the puppy smuggling, but he had grander plans for himself." Rory hands me a sheaf of papers. "This is a printout of about twenty-five percent of the information on the microdot. What we have so far proves that Elliot wanted to siphon off money and assets that belong to the Satanás Rojo cartel."

"For what purpose?"

"To create his own international cartel for more than smuggling animals. He wanted to take over Satanás Rojo gradually in the hopes they wouldn't notice what he'd done."

I finally look at the papers Rory had given me, and Natalie leans toward my chair so she can look too. I can't believe what I'm seeing. Elliot isn't that clever. But as I turn to the second page, suddenly it makes sense. "Elliot has been cooking the cartel's books, right? I'm no accounting expert, but it looks that way to me."

"That's exactly what he's done," Evan says. "Hidden amongst the financial data on the microdot, I also found secret bank accounts Elliot had created. He believed he'd fireproofed himself with aliases and offshore accounts, but he left enough holes that Satanás Rojo could surely figure it out. They won't go after Natalie, though, because Elliot kept those accounts anonymous."

"What does all of that mean for us?"

Logan rests his erse on the desk's edge. "It means the cartel will discover what Elliot has been doing, and they won't be happy. Munro's performance last night, coupled with the special effects provided by several members of the family, ensured that Elliot has become quite amenable. He has already offered to confess to every single one of his crimes. Even if he gets out of prison eventually, he will never go after Natalie again. He has devils of his own to contend with."

"And that means…"

My cousin looks straight at Natalie. "It's over. Your ex-husband will never bother you again."

Chapter Thirty-Three

Natalie

The Wild Man orchestrated the downfall of my ex-husband, bringing in his entourage of cousins to get the job done. I have no idea how to respond to that. Munro did that for *me*. Sure, we both said the L-word, but I never could have imagined he would go to extreme lengths to make sure I'm safe and to reduce my anxiety about Elliot. That might be the most romantic thing any man has ever done for me. I want to kiss him, but we are not alone. We need privacy for the way I want to kiss Munro to show my appreciation.

I can express my appreciation to the group, and I need to do that. "I didn't quite believe it when Munro described how the MacTaggarts will do anything for each other. Now I've seen it's true, and I've seen that you guys will do the same thing for a stranger. This family is amazing. No words could ever be enough to express how grateful I am, but this is all I can say. Thank you."

"No need to thank us," Logan says. "Munro vouched for you, and that's all the evidence we need. Besides, MacTaggarts help strangers too."

"But now she's part of the family," Evan says. "That means you don't need to ask, Natalie. If you need something, we will do whatever is necessary to help you."

My throat has tightened up a little because I'm overwhelmed by the generosity of Munro and his family. "You guys waged a battle for me. If I can ever do anything for you or anyone else in your family, just ask."

Munro and his cousins exchange glances and seem to reach some kind of decision. I have no idea what it is, but suddenly, they all turn to me.

"Uh, what's up?" I ask.

"You and I had talked about investigating Kieran," Munro says. "I mentioned that to Logan yesterday, and he blethered about it to everyone else in the clan. Kirsty and Luke found a wee bit of evidence, and so did Errol and Ashley. Now it's our turn. Wouldn't you say, Natalie?"

"Absolutely. I meant it when I said I wanted to research Kieran with you."

Logan and Evan seem very pleased by that statement.

"Neither of us knows a dang thing about this kind of research," I tell them. "So don't get too excited."

Munro slings an arm around my waist. "We are two clever, resourceful people. Our brains are the most important tool available to us."

"You're right about that. Our little gray cells got us through the siege at your cabin."

"And your mental acuity helped us capture Elliot here at Dùndubhan."

Logan lifts his gaze to the ceiling. "Are you two done giving each other verbal massages? Might as well shag right here on the floor."

Shouting reverberates through the castle, though I can't understand the words. It sounds like a male voice. But then a woman's voice echoes into the great hall too.

"What's going on?" I ask. "Sounds like there's a skirmish going on downstairs."

The three Scotsmen shrug.

"Bloody hell, Fiona," a man shouts. "What do you want me to do?"

I can't make out Fiona's response.

"That's Domhnall and our cousin Fiona," Evan says. "We best get down there and make sure they don't break any priceless antiques."

Logan and Evan rush downstairs. Munro and I follow at a slower pace.

"What's going on?" I ask. "Your cousins don't seem surprised to hear a ruckus going on down there."

"No, they wouldn't be surprised. My cousin Fiona got involved with Domhnall Sterling a few years ago, but their romance has been a rocky one. I know this based on the stories Errol told me."

"Do they get violent with each other?"

"No. Lachlan, Aidan, and Rory would have skelped Domhnall a long time ago if he did anything like that. They argue, that's all."

As we reach the first-floor landing, the voices below us in the vestibule have died down.

"Evan was worried Domhnall and Fiona might break priceless antiques," I say. "So they must have a history of throwing things."

"Not that I'm aware of."

As we come around the final section of the spiral staircase, the vestibule comes into view. Domhnall has his head bowed, hands on his hips, while Fiona stands tall with her arms crossed and her chin lifted.

"What's the bother?" Munro asks. "Sounded like a right rammy."

"Nothing like that," Fiona says. "I should have known better than to get involved with a man who behaved like a *tolla-thon* during Cat and Alex's wedding week."

"She called him an ersehole," Munro tells me.

Fiona puckers her lips. "Aye, because he is an ersehole."

Domhnall raises his head. "Could we discuss this in private? Dinnae need your family interfering."

She seems like she might have steam erupting from her ears any second, but before she can speak, Lachlan steps out of the ground-floor hallway and into the vestibule.

"One of you had better tell me what the bloody hell is going on," Lachlan demands. "Or I might batter Domhnall preemptively and figure out what happened later."

"It's between me and Domhnall," Fiona says. "That means it's none of your concern, Lachie."

"Fine, I'll let you two batter each other." He turns to me. "Your ex-husband is about to be escorted away from Dùndubhan. I thought you might want to witness that."

"Thank you, Lachlan, I would like to see that."

"Come out to the courtyard whenever you're ready."

Lachlan walks out the vestibule door.

Fiona seizes Domhnall's massive bicep and drags him down the hall and out of sight.

"Should we keep an eye on them?" Evan asks.

Logan sighs. "Let's leave them be for now. Those two have been arguing for weeks now."

I can't contain my curiosity, which has become a chronic condition for me lately. "Did Domhnall and Fiona get along better before the past few weeks?"

"Not sure," Logan says. "They kept their private lives to themselves and nobody heard or saw them arguing. But their relationship has been a roller-coaster ride. Fiona met Domhnall when he was trying to steal Jessica O'Connor away from Grey Dixon. That's Alex's half-brother. Seems like an inauspicious start to me."

Munro lays a hand on my back. "We should head out to the courtyard."

I let him guide me out the vestibule door, and as soon as we veer toward the area in front of the big wooden gates, I spot Elliot standing in the middle of the gravel area with his shoulders slumped and his head slightly bowed.

"The others have been taken away already," Munro tells me. "And we learned earlier today that the three laddies Elliot had with him in Wyoming have grown a backbone and decided to testify against their former boss. That and the microdot will seal his fate."

"I've never seen Elliot looking so…ashamed."

Munro chuckles. "Aye, we showed him the way to redemption."

"You mean you scared the shit out of him until he cracked."

"Same thing."

Munro stops us a good twenty feet from my ex-husband. "Do you want to speak to him? No one expects you to do that, and I wouldn't blame you for not wanting to."

"I need to put the last nail in that coffin."

He nods. No more words are necessary because he understands me like nobody else ever could.

Rolling my shoulders back, I march up to Elliot.

My ex-husband flinches, his head still down, and eyes me sideways as if he thinks I might pull out a gun and shoot him in the head.

"This is the last time you will ever see me," I tell him. "Don't you have anything you'd like to say?"

He swallows hard, and his Adam's apple jumps. His eyes have widened. "I'm sorry, Natalie. What I did to you was unforgivable, and I can't ever make up for it."

"No, you really can't. But I appreciate the apology."

Elliot hunches his shoulders and winces. "I, uh, want to give you something that you should have received as a divorce settlement."

"It's a little late for that."

"Yeah, but Rory worked it out with the authorities. I want to give you the money I cheated you out of during the divorce proceedings. It's a hundred and fifty thousand dollars."

Could I use the money? Of course I could. But taking it from him feels like accepting dirty money from a drug cartel.

Munro walks up beside me and clasps my hand. "You earned that money, *gràidh*. Being married to this *bod ceann* must've been the hardest job of all."

"I don't know…"

Elliot clears his throat and can't quite look at me. "It's not cartel money, if that's what you're worried about. I, uh, kind of embezzled it from your landscape design company. I needed start-up cash for my puppy-smuggling business, and I wasn't in with the Satanás Rojo cartel yet at that point."

It's clean money? Well, sort of. He stole it from me, but I earned that cash from honest hard work.

"Take the money," Munro murmurs to me. "You deserve it."

I hesitate for only a second. "Okay, Elliot, I'll take the money you embezzled from me."

My ex-husband's shoulders slump. "Thank you, Natalie."

A police car is coming up the driveway. We all watch as the vehicle crosses through the gates and halts just inside the courtyard. Two young men in uniform get out and approach our little group.

"Thank you for coming so quickly, Constable MacBay," Magnus says. He had been in charge of the prisoner when Munro and I entered the courtyard. "This is Elliot Rudaski, who is wanted in America too."

"We'll take it from here, Magnus," Constable MacBay says. "Thank you for taking care of the fugitive for us."

The two constables slap cuffs on Elliot and escort him to their car. They stow him in the backseat, then climb in up front. As the car rolls through the open gates, Elliot glances back at me.

I turn and walk away.

Munro stays by my side as we go back into the house, but I halt us in the vestibule.

He claims my hands, facing me. "You're free now, love. What would you like to do next? You must be exhausted from the stress of all that Elliot rubbish and two trips on Evan's jet this week."

"Actually, I feel fantastic. Awake, alive, and ready for anything." I step closer and tip my head back to gaze into his eyes. "Are you wiped out? Because I have an idea for what I'd like to do now."

"Not sleepy at all. Tell me your idea."

"Let's investigate Kieran MacTaggart."

Munro's lips curve into a wicked smile that makes my pulse speed up. "I was hoping you'd say that. With you beside me, I know we can uncover the truth about Kieran at last."

"Can we get started right away?"

"Of course we can. We should begin by talking to the two couples who initiated the search for answers. That would be Kirsty and Luke, and Ashley and Errol." He keeps hold of one of my hands as he leads me down the ground-floor hall and through the dining room into the guest wing. Munro veers into the sitting room. "Sit down, lass. I need to make a call."

We both sit down on the sofa, then Munro picks up the landline phone that rests on the end table.

"Are you ever going to give in and buy a cell phone?" I ask. "Or should I buy a megaphone so I can get your attention when you're out and about?"

"Cheeky lass." He rests the phone on his thigh and whispers in his deepest, sexiest tone, "Maybe I should buy a mobile. Then I could ring you so we can finish our interrupted phone-sex session."

"See? Cell phones do have worthwhile uses."

"Let me make this call, then we can drive into Loch Fairbairn. There's a wee shop in the village that sell mobiles."

"Perfect." I kiss his cheek. "Welcome to the twenty-first century, Wild Man."

Munro dials a number on the landline.

How much will we uncover about Kieran? I can't wait to find out.

Chapter Thirty-Four

Munro

We agree to meet my cousins and their significant others at Kirsty's metaphysical shop in Loch Fairbairn. I've been there before, but Natalie gets more excited than seems reasonable when she hears that's where we're going. I suppose I should make allowances for her. She had never visited Scotland until this week, so everything will seem exciting and wonderful to her. Natalie's enthusiasm does infect me a wee bit, though mostly because the lass enchants me.

I expected to see Kirsty and Luke when we arrived. But Ashley and Errol are already here too. Both couples seem as excited as Natalie, and they spend an inordinate amount of time havering about how romantic it is that she and I have become a couple too.

Finally, we get down to business.

Kirsty had shut her shop for the lunch hour. That means we won't have tourists wandering in to pester us about crystals or tarot cards. We sit around a circular table that Kirsty often uses when she offers tarot readings once a week. Fitting six people around that table is no small feat. But Errol insists on having Ashley sit on his lap, then Luke does the same with Kirsty. What barmy people. But at least that does solve the space issue.

I lean back in my chair. "All right, tell me what you've learned so far about Kieran."

Kirsty and Luke exchange glances, then she speaks. "Old family stories tell us that Kieran MacTaggart was banished from his clan after Simidh Gunn spread lies about Kieran being a thief. We have corroboration of that story thanks to the diary of Efrica MacTaggart, one of Kieran's three aunts. It turns out those tales are all derived from the diary."

"I've heard about that from Errol."

"Gunn also conspired to have Kieran arrested for witchcraft, tried, and convicted. He should have been executed, and what little history we have from that time says that did happen."

"Aye, I know that part too."

Kirsty gives me an exasperated look. "Ashley, why don't you try to tell my cousin the facts. He has a soft spot for you."

"Sure thing." Ashley sits forward and gazes straight into my eyes. "Efrica wrote in her diary that Kieran was executed. She kept writing after that and marked the day when Kieran's daughter was born six months later."

Errol wraps an arm around his wife's waist, tugging her close. "But ground-penetrating radar confirmed that Kieran's grave is empty. Ashley and I found text in the diary that had been concealed with an encryption that could only be solved by holding a diary page up to Kieran's gravestone."

Just as I'm about to open my mouth and point out I know that bit too, Natalie beats me to it.

"Munro, you might already know this stuff," she says, "but I think it's fascinating. And besides, you might have forgotten some of what your cousins told you. It's been a while, right?"

"Since they told me? Yes, but I have a good memory."

Natalie slides a hand onto my thigh under the table. "I'd like to hear everything. Okay?"

"Go on, then."

Errol grins. "Natalie, you are a miracle worker. Or maybe you're a witch like Kirsty. I see no other way that you could talk Munro into doing something he doesn't want to do."

I glower at him. "Haud yer wheesht, ye *cacan*."

Ashley slings an arm around Errol's shoulders. "The last and possibly most important thing we've learned is this. Kieran's grave is empty, but the headstone provides a cryptic clue. Using the encryption Errol found, we discovered an inscription that says 'Death shall not destroy my spirit. I live on. We live on. Do not grieve for that which is not lost. Seek us out when the time has come.' "

Natalie's brows furrow. She must be considering the information my cousins have provided. "It's written in the first person which suggests Kieran wrote the secret inscription himself. What also seems telling is that he said he lived on but then added 'we live on.' That sounds like a reference to his wife and daughter."

"Possibly his aunts too," Kirsty says.

"Could be. Sounds an awful lot like Kieran somehow faked his death."

Ashley nods. "Yeah, I've thought that too. But we can't figure out the last line—'Seek us out when the time has come.' What does it mean?"

Natalie shakes her head slowly. The other four seem equally confused.

I cross my arms and tap one finger on my chin, trying to puzzle out the meaning of the cryptic message. "Has anyone scoured the witchfinder records?"

Four heads shake.

Natalie looks at me. "You have an idea, don't you?"

"Not sure. But it wouldn't hurt to dig into the witchfinder records."

"How do we find those?"

I shrug.

"Try the Loch Fairbairn Historical Society," Kirsty says. "Luke and I found things there, but we never got round to searching the entire storehouse. Diarmid Fraser is in charge of the historical records. I'm sure he would help you."

"It's a place to start."

"Be warned, though. The archives are not digitized, and there's only a card catalog that isn't well maintained. Diarmid tries, but he's only one man."

Before I can respond, Natalie does. "Munro won't get grumpy with Diarmid. We'll both be patient. Won't we, honey?"

For a moment, I don't realize she was referring to me when she said "honey." Then I notice the lass is watching me, clearly waiting for my response.

I shift uncomfortably in my chair. "Ah, yes, we will be patient."

Natalie kisses my cheek.

Why? I have no bloody idea. But she seems pleased with whatever she thinks I did or said. I give up on trying to understand.

Pushing my chair back, I rise. "We will let you all know what we find, if anything."

Natalie rises too and hooks her arm around mine. "We won't stop until we find something."

"Don't get their hopes up, *mo leannan*."

"Why not? Hope is a powerful force."

"We can't 'hope' our way into finding information about Kieran."

Kirsty leaps off Luke's lap. "Maybe we can. I have a tool that might give you the upper hand."

My cousin races down one of the aisles that hold various types of metaphysical knickknacks. She roots about until she finds the item she wants. Then Kirsty trots back to the rest of us, halting beside me and Natalie.

"Take this," she says, handing me a small item. "I know you don't believe in the supernatural, but at least give it a chance."

I accept the small, oval, golden-colored stone and turn it over several times in my hand. "This is a fine rock, but what is it meant to do for us?"

"Citrine has many metaphysical properties that could be helpful to you and Natalie." Kirsty closes my fingers around the stone, caging my hand with hers. "Citrine can open your mind and balance your psyche to give you more patience and optimism. It also promotes perseverance and focus."

My first instinct is to say something grumpy, but I can't do that to Kirsty. She honestly believes this stone might help me. And Kirsty is one of the kindest people I've ever known. I kiss the lass's cheek. "Thank you, Kirsty."

"You aren't going to tell me it's 'rubbish' or 'bollocks'?"

"No. I might not be a hundred percent convinced, but I can't swear that the metaphysical doesn't exist. Maybe it does. For all I know, this stone might actually promote optimism and focus. I'll give it a go, at least."

Kirsty grins and releases my hand. "That's all I ask, Munro."

I hold the stone between my thumb and forefinger. "How does it work? Do I need to chant or dance naked under the moon?"

"No, of course not. Just keep it close to you and treat it as if it were a treasure."

"Well, in that case..." I grasp Natalie's hand and place the stone in her palm, closing her fingers around it. "You should hold on to it, *gràidh*. I will always have you close to me, and you are my treasure."

All the women say "awww" at the same time and aim sappy looks at me. I will never understand women. Luke and Errol seem amused by the lasses' reactions to what I said.

Natalie and I offer our goodbyes and leave the shop. Rory and Emery let us borrow their Jaguar F-Type convertible for the duration of our mission to uncover the mysteries of Kieran MacTaggart, and they delivered the car while we were in the metaphysical shop. I had asked Emery and Rory to make it a surprise for Natalie. And I let the lass drive first. She got very excited when she saw the car, with its top down. She settles into the driver's seat, grinning and running her hands over the soft leather.

"How fast can this car go?" she asks, as she buckles up her seatbelt.

"Too fast. Stick to the speed limit, will you?"

"If that will make you feel better." She starts up the engine. "We're only going to the other side of Loch Fairbairn, anyway."

"Aye. But please drive reasonably even for a short trip."

"Okay. I have the citrine stone. It will keep me focused on the road."

I groan and do up my seatbelt. While Natalie keeps her eyes on the road, I give her directions for finding the Loch Fairbairn Historical Society. Luke had drawn a crude map to help us get there. But as we drive through downtown, I spot something that I know will make Natalie happy.

"Pull over," I say. "Got an errand to run."

She parks along the side of the street and turns off the engine. "What is it?"

I jump out and rush around to the driver's door. "Come with me and you'll see."

Before she can open her door, I pick the lass up and set her down on the asphalt.

"Thank you, Munro."

"You aren't going to remind me that you could have gotten out on your own?"

"Nope. I've adjusted to the Wild Man style of doing things."

We hurry across the street and go into a shop.

Natalie stares at me. "You must have walked into the wrong place. This is a mobile phone store."

"I know."

A young woman approaches us. "My name is Jane. How may I help you today?"

I waggle my brows at Natalie. Then I tell Jane, "I need to buy a mobile. Never had one before, so I'll let my girlfriend decide which one is best for me."

Natalie doesn't seem at all surprised that I referred to her as my girlfriend—or that I want her to choose a mobile for me.

Half an hour later, I walk out of the store with my brand-new device. For my first call, I ring my cousin Errol.

"Hello," he says. "This is Errol Murdoch."

"I know who you are, ye *cacan*."

A brief silence follows. "Munro? You must have borrowed Natalie's mobile, eh?"

"No, I did not. I bought my own."

"That's brilliant! Congratulations, Munro. You finally stepped into the modern era."

I rattle off my new phone number. "Share that with the family. Natalie and I have work to do."

Errol says goodbye, and we get back on the road. Ten minutes later, Natalie and I stroll into the old building that houses the Loch Fairbairn Historical Society. We meet Diarmid Fraser, who encourages us to call him Dee. The elderly gent leads us into the bowels of the building where shelves and boxes full of historical documents fill the space. We have quite the task ahead of us. I know Kirsty and Luke had scoured this room, so before Natalie and I have a go at it, I need to make sure of something.

I catch Dee's arm as he's about to walk out the door. "Are there any other rooms? Or storage closets? We'd like to be thorough."

He studies me for a moment, then digs a keyring out of his pocket. "There is one more room, but it's a bloody mess. No one has cataloged it or even tried to organize the contents."

"Could we see that room?"

"Aye. Follow me."

Chapter Thirty-Five

Natalie

Dee takes us down a long, dark stairwell into the depths of the building. Only the occasional bare bulb lights the way. Munro insists on following me instead of leading the way, and though I catch him ogling my ass, I don't think that's the main reason he wanted me to be ahead of him. The walls consist of stones that look as old as Scotland itself. If we're ever going to uncover new evidence about Kieran, this seems like the best place to search.

At the bottom of the stairs, Dee reaches above his head to yank the delicate chain attached to another bare bulb. "There are more lights you can turn on if ye like. Please remember to turn them all off when you leave. As I mentioned, nothing down here is organized in any way, shape, or form. Good luck to you both."

Our host shuffles up the staircase and out of sight.

Munro wanders among the boxes and shelves, switching on every bulb he sees. The lights provide more illumination, though the space is still far from well-lit. We'll make do. We agree to split up so we can, hopefully, speed up our search. Munro takes the boxes while I head into the stacks where books are haphazardly shelved. Dee did not lie. I see no evidence of any sort of cataloging scheme, not even a list of items. Holy heaven, this could take months.

I choose a row and start flipping through the books one by one. Some are histories written by nineteenth-century scholars while others are bound diaries like Efrica's, composed by men and women who lived in this part of

Scotland at various times in the past. Some of the diaries include the dates when each entry was written, but others offer no clues to the time period. Why couldn't medieval Scots be more meticulous? Hearing what Luke and Kirsty went through while trying to find information about Kieran does not give me much hope for the search Munro and I have undertaken.

As I crouch to study the volumes on a lower shelf, something tumbles out of my pocket. I glance down at the citrine stone. How did I drop it? I'd stuffed it deep into my pocket so it wouldn't fall out. Guess I didn't push it in there good enough. I snatch up the stone and stash it in my bra this time. It won't fall out now unless I do a headstand.

Oddly, this neglected old room doesn't smell musty. It smells like books instead, an indefinable aroma that always makes me feel at home. Maybe that's weird, but I don't care. I love books almost as much as I love landscaping.

I've carefully pulled out a sheaf of papers bound only by a leather folder and the string tied around it. The leather has no markings on it. I squat on the floor and carefully untie the string, opening the folder with as much care as possible. Inside, I find five sheets of what seems to my amateur eye to be very old paper. I move into a cross-legged position and lay the open folder on my lap, then cautiously lift the top sheet so I can examine it. Nothing on the front side. I turn the sheet over and raise it to my face, squinting at what might be faded words. Could that be… No, it's nothing. I dig my phone out and use the camera to zoom in as close as possible.

No, still nothing. I guess this is just a sheaf of unused antique paper.

The citrine stone begins to feel pleasantly warm, thanks to my body heat, I'm sure. Maybe I should give the stone to Munro. I mean, he's a descendant of Kieran MacTaggart. Not sure why exactly I feel like I should give him the citrine, but what the heck, it can't hurt.

I hunt down Munro, where he's been rifling through boxes while sitting on the floor with his legs spreads and his knees bent. He frowns at the document he'd been examining, then sets it down on a pile of similar-size pages.

"How's it going?" I ask. "My search has been less than fruitful."

Munro groans and rubs his back. "Same for me."

I kneel beside him and pull the citrine stone out of my bra. "Here, take this. It might help."

He eyes the stone askance. "It's a rock."

"Just take the damn thing and see what happens." I grab his hand, then slap the stone onto his palm. "Can't hurt, right? Since you are Kieran's descendant, maybe the citrine will help you balance your mind so you can uncover a vital clue."

Munro holds the stone between his thumb and forefinger, gazing at it with curiosity. Then he shoves the rock into his hip pocket. "All right, I'll keep it with me. But I think my greatest asset in this search is you." He pats the floor beside him. "Sit down, *gràidh*."

"I am sitting."

"No, you are kneeling. Rest your bonnie erse on the floor right beside me."

"Okay." I obey his command, wriggling to get closer to him. "What now?"

"Let's test Kirsty's theory, which you have latched on to. The citrine should help, if she's right." He takes hold of my hand, lacing our fingers. "We will close our eyes and both reach out at the same time to pick up something from the box in front of us."

Munro shuts his eyes first, then I do the same. The warmth of his rough palm gradually seeps into my hand, which had grown cold while I hung out in the stacks. This room doesn't seem to have a furnace or any other kind of heating equipment. I let all thoughts drift away, focusing on the feel of his palm, the scent of him, the sensation of a slight draft tickling my skin.

"Time for the test," Munro says. "I will count down from three. Then we both reach out to grab something. Three, two, one."

I thrust my free hand out and take hold of what feels like a sheet of paper.

"Open your eyes, Natalie."

My lids open, and I blink rapidly as I try to comprehend what I see. "What is this? It looks like it's folded up. Does that mean there's more to it on the other side of the paper?"

"Yes, I believe so." Munro gently unfolds the paper, revealing a two-foot-square sheet that seems to represent a line drawing. "This looks like the floor plan of a large, multi-story building."

"The lines are kind of faded but still legible."

"Aye, they are." He skims his fingertips over the line drawings as if he's trying to deduce their meaning. "I think it's a castle."

"Maybe it's the place where Kieran and his aunts lived after his banishment."

"I think there's a date in the lower left corner, but it's hard to read."

I lay a hand on his shoulder. "Use the camera on your new smartphone. You can zoom in to see more details."

"Good idea. I've seen Errol do that." He pulls his new cell phone out of his pocket and opens the camera app, then zooms in until we can read the numbers on the paper. "Fifteen ninety-five. That's the date."

"Does it match up with the dates related to Kieran?"

"His gravestone gives fifteen ninety-eight as the year of his death. We know his aunts lived in an abandoned castle for ten years, and Kieran moved in with them a few years before his supposed death. When he moved in with them, he might have added that date to the plans."

"Maybe he made changes to the castle, and that's why he marked the date." I lean forward to peer down at the medieval floor plans. "That would mean the castle was built earlier than the fifteen nineties."

Munro stabs his finger onto the paper. Then he zooms in on that spot with his phone. "Look. This inscription in the far-right corner has a different date. It says the castle was erected in fifteen seventy-two."

"So this might be the place where Kieran and his aunts lived."

"It's possible." He spins the paper this way and that, squinting and screwing up his mouth. Then Munro freezes. "No. It can't be…"

"What did you find?"

He scrubs a hand over his mouth. "It's impossible. But I'd swear… I need to double check."

"Please finish a sentence, Munro. You look stunned, and I'm getting worried."

"Can you help me take pictures of this document? We can't take it with us, but I need to verify this."

"Sure, I can do that." I snap photos of the castle floor plan from various angles and at various zoom levels until Munro seems satisfied. "Okay, now you need to tell me what has you so weirded out."

"Wait until we're in the car."

He must not want Dee to overhear our discussion, but I can't figure out why. Still, I do what he said. I wait until we've climbed into the car before I ask the question. We say goodbye to Dee on our way out of the building, thanking him for his help.

"What's the big secret?" I ask, once we've both climbed into the convertible.

"It's impossible."

"You said that already."

He jams the key in the ignition and cranks it. As the engine rumbles to life, he smacks his palms on the steering wheel. "The coincidence is too much. It can't be, but it is." He shuts his eyes for a moment, then stares straight at me. "The document we found has all the same features. It looks like Dùndubhan."

"Why is that a shock? Your family lives there."

"No, you don't understand. Rory bought Dùndubhan less than a decade ago. Before that, it had been in various hands over the centuries."

I still can't grasp the depth of his discomfort, but I need to understand. "Maybe Rory bought the castle because it had once belonged to Kieran."

"No one knew where Kieran's castle was. That information died with him. For Kieran to have lived at Dùndubhan… There's only one explanation that fits."

"What is the explanation?"

"Fate."

Chapter Thirty-Six

Munro

We don't speak again until we reach Dùndubhan and park in the courtyard near the vestibule door. Natalie stays in her seat while I shuffle around to the passenger side and open the door for her. She takes the hand I offer. Then we trudge into the castle, halting in the vestibule. I gaze up at the spiral staircase. "The stairs must have been different back then, but the rest of the layout has remained essentially unchanged. This is the castle where Kieran lived."

"That's incredible. Your cousin Rory has lived here for years without ever knowing the significance of Dùndubhan."

"We need proof. No one will believe us otherwise."

"Is that why you didn't want to talk about it until we were in the car?"

"Yes." I hold her hand more tightly, unwilling to let go. The magnitude of what we may have discovered has rocked me to the core. "How can we prove the document at the historical society is genuine?"

"Lab testing, I guess. Didn't you say your ground-penetrating radar proved Kieran's grave was empty?"

"How does that help us?"

"Well, during the time I've been here, I heard a lot of things—like that you have cousins who are archaeologists, and so is Alex Thorne. Surely they could help us verify the find."

I rub my neck, staring down at the floor. "Let's go outside and just…have a wee look around."

Natalie wraps her arms around me. "Relax, Munro. We'll figure it all out. But some fresh air does sound like a good idea."

We go out into the courtyard and wander into the garden to admire the flowers and the trees. Natalie admires those things. I study her face, her smile, her bonnie red hair, those entrancing amber eyes. I could see myself marrying her and having children as beautiful and sweet as she is.

The sound of gravel crunching draws our attention to the bit of the driveway we can see through the garden doorway. I don't recognize the vehicle that's just pulled into the courtyard. Natalie and I amble out there to greet the visitor.

Domhnall Sterling is shutting his car door. When he notices us, his expression becomes pinched.

"What are you doing here, Domhnall?" I ask. "We weren't expecting you. Where's Fiona?"

"I was hoping to find her here. We had a row, and she stormed out of the house."

"We haven't seen her, but we only arrived a moment ago."

Something chimes in his trousers. Domhnall pulls out his mobile and answers. "Fiona? Where the bloody hell are you? I was worried, of course."

Natalie and I exchange glances, though neither of us seems to know what etiquette requires in a situation like this.

"Yes, we can talk later," Domhnall says. "I understand. Goodbye, Fiona."

He shoves the mobile back into his pocket, still seeming uncomfortable.

"Relationship troubles, huh?" Natalie says. "I'm sure you guys will work it out. You clearly love each other."

"But I keep cocking things up. Fiona has a right to be angry with me. I've let my past get in the way and refused to make a real commitment to her. My first marriage wrecked me, then I behaved like a sodding ersehole after Jessica threw me over. Maybe I'm not suitable for any woman."

"Of course you are." Natalie glances at me as if she wants me to agree.

But I can't do that. "I don't know Domhnall well enough to comment on his relationship with Fiona."

"Fair enough," Domhnall says. "I wish I could find a way to distract myself for a while."

Natalie raises onto her tiptoes to whisper to me, "Why don't we ask him to help us find evidence that Kieran lived here?"

I stifle a groan. "Aye, fine, let's do it."

The lass grins.

What else can I do? I turn to Domhnall. "Would you like to help us with a historical search? We're trying to find proof that my ancestor Kieran lived at Dùndubhan hundreds of years ago. No one else knows about our search yet."

"You want to work with me?"

"Why shouldn't I?'

"Because your cousins Lachlan, Rory, and Aidan despise me."

I shrug. "Never cared what anybody thought of me. And I'm sure they'll come round eventually. You never know, finding proof Kieran was here might make Fiona see you in a different light."

My suggestion makes Domhnall straighten his posture, and his lips curl into a slight smile. "I'm happy to help."

I scan the courtyard. "We were thinking of using ground-penetrating radar to search for signs that a MacTaggart lived here long ago. But we would need to contact my cousin Iain or Alex Thorne since we know nothing about how to use GPR."

Domhnall smirks. "Alex has never threatened to murder me, so I would suggest asking him."

"That does sound like a better idea. A murder in the courtyard would slow down our secret archaeological expedition." I get out my new mobile but realize I don't have anyone's number programmed into it yet except for Natalie's. "Ah, Domhnall, do you have Alex's number?"

He taps his phone screen several times, then tips it toward me. "Here it is. Alex always talks to me at family events, even when Fiona is upset with me. He gave me his number too."

"No need to explain." I type in the digits on my mobile, and soon it's ringing at the other end. "Alex, it's Munro MacTaggart. We need a wee favor."

"You know I'm always happy to help."

"This will need to be a secret for now."

"Wonderful. I do love intrigue. Tell me more."

I explain the situation to Alex, including Domhnall's participation in our plans. He agrees to help. Alex knows a bloke at a university here in the Highlands, and he tells me he can bring the GPR equipment to us within the hour. "Don't you need to ask your friend first?"

"Yes, but that won't be a problem. He lives in Loch Fairbairn. Hold tight, and the Amazing Alex Thorne shall ride to your rescue."

A few minutes later, the three of us go into the house to grab a piece in the kitchen. We get to talking to Domhnall, and I realize he isn't the flaming ersehole Fiona's brothers had made him out to be. He shares humorous tales about his clients at the gym he co-owns, and we learn that he lived in America for years—until he met Fiona. Then he and his business partner expanded into Scotland with a gym in Inverness. Earlier this year, they had expanded again by joining forces with Kate, my cousin Callum's wife, to merge her physical therapy business with their chain of gyms. Domhnall is an intelligent man, and charming too in his own way. Whatever mistakes he'd made in the past, he clearly wants to make it work with Fiona.

Finally, Alex arrives with the GPR equipment. He gives us the instruction manual and briefly explains how it works, but then he leaves. He won't admit it, but I can tell his trip to America made him want to spend more time with his wife and wee bairn, and I don't blame him for that. I missed Natalie deeply while she was away—as much as Alex missed Cat, I'm sure.

We manage to get the GPR working.

Domhnall gets comfortable with the technology before Natalie or I do, so we let him operate the machine. He slowly walks back and forth in the courtyard, moving further away with each pass to ensure he doesn't scan the same areas over and over. After a while, I suggest he should take a break. But Domhnall doesn't want to do that. So Natalie and I let him keep going. Maybe it's therapy for him since he does seem almost serene while scanning the grounds.

In the garden, he stops.

Natalie and I have been hovering just outside the doorway that separates the garden from the courtyard.

Domhnall's head pops up. "I found something. A long, thin metal object."

We trot over to him and both stare at the screen attached to the GPR unit, but I can't make any sense of it. "Do you understand what this image is telling us, Domhnall?"

"I read the manual from cover to cover. That means yes, I do understand most of it." He points at the screen. "Something is buried right below us."

"Time to get a shovel."

We find two of those in the carriage house, so Domhnall and I both carefully begin to dig at opposite ends of the area where the GPR had detected something. After I've excavated down to six feet below the surface, my shovel finally hits a solid object. I climb into the hole and use my fingers to wipe the dirt away until I catch a glimpse of tarnished metal. Natalie jumps into the hole with me. Soon, we're able to gently lift the long, narrow object. Domhnall takes it from us and sets it on the ground while we climb out of the trench.

"It's a sword," Natalie says, her voice filled with awe.

"It does look like that." I kneel and brush away more of the dirt that had encrusted the object. "Get some water. We need to clean it."

Domhnall rushes off, returning moments later with a bucket of water and a sponge. We cautiously clean the grime off the object. And aye, now we can tell for sure what is. Natalie was right. It is a sword. Designs near the hilt draw my attention, and I wipe away more dirt from that part of the weapon.

"It has an inscription," I say. Then I pull out my mobile and use the camera to zoom in on the words. I swear my heart literally skips a beat. "Ciaran mac in tSagairt."

"What does that mean?" Natalie asks, kneeling beside me.

"It's the Gaelic version of a name—Kieran MacTaggart. This was his sword."

Natalie's eyes flare wide. "Holy shit, Munro, we found it. The proof that Kieran was here."

All three of us leap up and dance about, whooping and shouting. Once we've calmed down, we call in the experts—Iain, Alex, and Catriona. She brings her bairn. It is a momentous occasion, after all. The MacTaggart archaeologists begin scouring the entire compound, finding more medieval artifacts. Is it a coincidence that Rory and Emery turned Dùndubhan into a museum? I don't know. But something incredible has happened, something none of us can explain. Maybe we don't need to understand everything. Kirsty might have been right all along.

It's magic.

Chapter Thirty-Seven

Natalie

For the past five weeks, Dùndubhan has experienced a different kind of siege—the sort that involves archaeologists, historians, journalists, TV reporters, and so much more. The discoveries at Kieran's castle have caused a sensation worldwide, not only because it's a previously unknown chapter in Scottish history, but also because of the witchcraft angle. Kieran became the victim of a genuine witch hunt and lost his life because of that. Yeah, we decided to keep the "not dead" aspect of the story to ourselves. Who would believe that, anyway? If we ever find proof that Kieran lived on after his supposed execution, then we will share that information.

The engraved sword now resides in the Dùndubhan museum, where it belongs.

News stories portray the discovery of Kieran's sword at a castle owned by his descendant as a fantastic coincidence. But all the MacTaggarts, including the most diehard skeptics, now admit that something magical did indeed occur here. We keep that belief under wraps.

We haven't forgotten about Owen, but he's been so busy working on a new book that we don't hear from him that often. The day after Elliot got whisked away to jail, Munro and I used his new phone to have a video chat with Owen. He felt bad about not coming with us to take part in the battle, but we assured him we had plenty of help.

"You work too hard," Munro told him. "Take a holiday. The UK is nice."

"I'll think about it."

I hope Owen will find his soul mate soon. He's such a great guy.

One day, Munro and I decide to visit the empty grave that belonged to Kieran MacTaggart. Munro tells me that he wants to pay his respects to his ancestor, and since he doesn't know where Kieran's body was actually buried, he'll settle for the vacant grave. But as we approach that spot in the clan cemetery, we see a woman standing there, facing the headstone.

"Good morning," Munro says.

The woman jerks as if we'd surprised her and swerves her attention to us. "Oh. I didn't know anyone else was here."

"Aye, that was clear." He offers his hand to the woman. "I'm Munro MacTaggart. The man whose grave you're studying was my ancestor."

She steps away from the headstone. "I should go. This was a bad idea."

"What was?" I ask. "You seemed fascinated by the inscription."

"No, I—" She hugs herself. "I have no idea why I came here. Had this crazy impulse to come to Scotland, and I dropped everything to do it. When I saw the sign that said this is the MacTaggart family cemetery, I couldn't stop myself from having a look."

"You must have seen every headstone in this cemetery. This one is in the oldest section which is furthest from the entrance."

"I walked straight to this spot." She eyes the headstone, biting her lip. "I think I've lost my mind."

Munro lifts his brows. "Why would you say that, lass?"

"Because I can't explain anything I've done lately. I felt...drawn here." She shakes her head once as if she's casting off a fevered dream. "Sorry. I should go."

The woman jogs away, out of our sight.

Well, that was bizarre.

Munro and I brush off the strange incident and head back to the house we bought last week. Since his many cousins helped us furnish and decorate our new digs, it didn't take long to make it feel like a true home. I found my home the day I met Munro, and now that my parents are moving to Loch Fairbairn too, I finally have everything I've ever wanted or needed.

Once we're sitting on the sofa in our living room, Munro starts rooting around in his pants pocket. He brings out a small box. Munro MacTaggart, tough-guy Wild Man, drops to one knee in front of me with his eyes glistening as if he might cry.

"Natalie, I love you," he says, his voice hitching a tiny bit. "Will you marry me?"

"Yes, Munro, I will."

He wipes his eyes and grins. "You know what that means."

"A big party at Dùndubhan?"

"That too. But first..." He drags me down onto the floor, on our plush new rug. "We need to have an epic shag."

"Yes, we do."

Three days later, we announce our engagement. A week after that, we hold a Scottish party called a ceilidh to celebrate our upcoming nuptials. Domhnall and Fiona attend the event, together, but I sense there's still tension between them. Since I've been granted provisional membership in the American Wives Club, I suggest to Munro that maybe our group should give Domhnall and Fiona a gentle push in the right direction.

The Wild Man groans. "I knew I couldn't stop you from meddling with the other lasses."

"So, that means you're okay with it. Right?"

"As long as it doesn't interfere with us having a poke."

I decide to interpret that as "yes, my darling love, please meddle."

While I dance with Munro in the great hall, my thoughts keep returning to his ancestor who once lived here. Maybe the mystery of Kieran hasn't been fully solved, but I believe that one day we will know exactly what happened to him, his wife and daughter, and his aunts. The MacTaggarts truly are an amazing clan with an incredible and mysterious history. But for now, I'll be happy to make some history with my fiancé.

While we're naked, naturally.

As the party winds down, I see Domhnall and Fiona on the other side of the room. She throws her hands up and races downstairs. He bows his head and leans against the sill of one of the huge windows. I drag Munro over there, of course.

Munro slaps Domhnall's arm. "Don't worry, mate. You and Fiona will work it out."

"I don't see how."

"The way to a woman's heart is simple." Munro slants closer and lowers his voice to a whisper. "Be unstoppable."

"What does that mean?'

"She wants a commitment. Prove you can give her that by never backing down and being willing to humiliate yourself."

When did Munro become a relationship expert? But I agree with most of what he told Domhnall. If he wants Fiona back, he can't give up so easily.

Domhnall nods slowly, and his lips curl up at the corners. "Be unstoppable. Aye, I can do that. Thank you, Munro."

Oh boy, I sense disaster on the way.

Experience Domhnall and Fiona's story in
***Unstoppable in a Kilt* (Hot Scots, Book Fourteen).**
Solve the mystery of Kieran MacTaggart in
***Banished in the Highlands* (A Hot Scots time travel prequel).**
Owen Metzger returns in *A Novel Secret*
(A Hot Brits/Hot Scots/Au Naturel Crossover).

Love the

Hot Scots

series?

Visit
AnnaDurand.com

to subscribe to her newsletter
for updates on forthcoming books in the series
&
to receive free gifts for signing up!

Anna Durand is a bestselling, multi-award-winning author of contemporary and paranormal romance. Her books have earned bestseller status on every major retailer and wonderful reviews from readers around the world. But that's the boring spiel. Here are the really cool things you want to know about Anna!

Born on Lackland Air Force Base in Texas, Anna grew up moving here, there, and everywhere thanks to her dad's job as an instructor pilot. She's lived in Texas (twice), Mississippi, California (twice), Michigan (twice), and Alaska—and now Ohio.

As for her writing, Anna has always made up stories in her head, but she didn't write them down until her teen years. Those first awful books went into the trash can a few years later, though she learned a lot from those stories. Eventually, she would pen her first romance novel, the paranormal romance *Willpower*, and she's never looked back since.

Want even more details about Anna? Get access to her extended bio when you subscribe to her newsletter and download the free bonus ebook, *Hot Scots Confidential*. You'll also get hot deleted scenes, character interviews, fun facts, and more! Plus you'll receive audio bonus content narrated by Shane East, Vanessa Edwin, and Ava Lucas.

Visit AnnaDurand.com to sign up.

www.ingramcontent.com/pod-product-compliance
Lightning Source LLC
Chambersburg PA
CBHW061257210726
48293CB00003B/1009